GALLEON POINT

W9-AAB-802

NORTH

LEHDER'S HOUSE
"VOLCANO"

HALF
MOON
BAY

COMPASS
POINT

NORTH
HARBOUR

PIRATE'S
WELL

DOLPHIN HEAD

NASSAU
50 MI.

MIAMI
210 MI.

CONCH
BAY

SILVER
BANKS

PIECES
OF
EIGHT

SKIPJACK
POINT

DOUBLOON
BAY

HOTEL/DIVESHOP

SOUTH
HARBOUR

MY HOUSE

SMUGGLER'S
COVE

AIRPORT

MARINA

BATTERY
POINT

Bordon '90

TURNING
THE TIDE

TURNING THE TIDE

ONE MAN AGAINST THE MEDELLIN CARTEL

Sidney D. Kirkpatrick

with Peter Abrahams

A DUTTON BOOK

DUTTON
Published by the Penguin Group
Penguin Books USA Inc., 375 Hudson Street,
New York, New York 10014, U.S.A.
Penguin Books Ltd, 27 Wrights Lane,
London W8 5TZ, England
Penguin Books Australia Ltd, Ringwood,
Victoria, Australia
Penguin Books Canada Ltd, 2801 John Street,
Markham, Ontario, Canada L3R 1B4
Penguin Books (N.Z.) Ltd, 182-190 Wairau Road,
Auckland 10, New Zealand

Penguin Books Ltd, Registered Offices:
Harmondsworth, Middlesex, England

First published by Dutton, an imprint of New American Library,
a division of Penguin Books USA Inc.
Distributed in Canada by McClelland & Stewart Inc.

First Printing, June, 1991
10 9 8 7 6 5 4 3 2 1

 REGISTERED TRADEMARK—MARCA REGISTRADA

Library of Congress Cataloging in Publication Data:

Kirkpatrick, Sidney.
    Turning the tide : one man against the Medellin Cartel / by Sidney
Kirkpatrick and Peter Abrahams.
        p. cm.
    ISBN 0-525-24998-2
    1. Drug traffic—Bahamas. 2. Medellin Cartel—Bahamas. 3. Novak,
Richard, 1930–   . 4. Crime prevention—Bahamas—Citizen
participation. I. Abrahams, Peter, 1947–
HV5840.B2K57   1991
363.4′5′092—dc20
    (B)   90-23025
                                                              CIP

PRINTED IN THE UNITED STATES OF AMERICA

Set in Primer
Designed by Leonard Telesca

This is a true story, based entirely on interviews with the participants, court transcripts,
and court testimony. Dialogue has been re-created based on these documented sources.
Many of the criminals depicted in these pages are still at large and have threatened
the lives of those who have sought to expose the truth. In consequence, the names
and identities of the following people have been changed for their protection: Lawrence
Ferguson, Gus Holeran, Andy Havens, Dougie Hollins, Josh Berger, Bobby Eliot, and
Elvis Welles.

To my father, Dale Kirkpatrick
—S.K.

PROLOGUE

~~~~~~
~~~~~~

Like fighters at a weigh-in, the two men were granted a look at each other before their struggle. Unlike fighters, neither knew what lay ahead, but both might have been mistaken for boxers, lightweights specifically: each was about five and a half feet tall, trim and well muscled. The Colombian was twenty-eight years old; the American, strong and fit but in reality too old for the ring, was forty-seven.

It was the spring of 1978. The Colombian, Carlos Enrique Lehder-Rivas, made his entrance like a titleholder, followed by an entourage. He strode to the reception desk of the Treasure Cay Hotel on Abaco Island in the Bahamas, pulled out a thick roll of United States currency, and booked an entire floor. The American, Richard Novak, who had arrived as a hitchhiker on an acquaintance's charter fishing boat a little while before, watched from a chair in the lobby. He was alone.

By inclination and training, Novak was an observant man. He counted the men in Lehder's party—there were ten; noted that none of them looked at all like tourists or vacationers, but more like businessmen from some sort of business where a way with people was not a requirement; and paid a little more attention when the money was produced. At that moment, Lehder glanced up and saw Novak watching him. Perhaps he thought that Novak himself was a charter boat captain, smelling the possibility of some business. It would not have been a wild mental leap—Novak had the look of one who had spent years at sea in the tropics, as indeed he had. Perhaps it was that simple—Lehder imagined the sight of his bankroll had excited a Pavlovian reaction in a small-time fishing guide, and this thought had amused him. For whatever reason, Lehder smiled at Novak. He had a big, loose smile.

"Hello," Novak said.

Lehder nodded, then stopped smiling, put his money away and walked off down the hall, trailed by his companions.

Novak left Treasure Cay soon after, but he remembered that smile. Novak led a simple life and had time to dwell on such things. Carlos Lehder's life was much more complicated. He quickly forgot all about Richard Novak.

1

The Bahamas are hot in August. The thermometer hits ninety degrees by midmorning and days pass without a decent breeze before three in the afternoon. Tempers can get short, especially when two cultures collide, as they often do when one culture is impatient and paying the bills and the other is more cautiously accepting of the virtues of the work ethic but needs the money.

So, given August, and a place that encourages cultural friction, Nassau International Airport, for example, the probability is high that people will soon be snapping at each other. And, on a day in late August 1978 as Richard Novak stood in a long line at the Bahamasair ticket counter, they were.

As he moved slowly forward, one place at a time, Novak made an effort to shut out the sounds of tempers rising, and to control his own impatience. Avoid stress, his cardiologist had told him. The advice itself was stressful; just thinking about the doctors, the hospital, the so-called heart attack, annoyed Novak. And who could fail to feel stress in his situation, standing in the same line in the same hot, inefficient airport for the eleventh time in the past two weeks? Under the circumstances, he felt fine—better than ever, he said to himself as he advanced, forehead creasing with irritation, to the head of the line.

The agent regarded him without interest. Novak laid

his ticket on the counter, as he had ten times previously, and said, "Norman's Cay."

And for the eleventh time he was told, "That flight is cancelled."

"If the flight's going to be cancelled every day, why do you bother listing it?" Novak asked, pointing to the board showing scheduled flights. The agent looked past Novak to the next customer. That made Novak mad, and his temper started to get the best of him. "What's today's excuse?" he said. "Mechanical failure? Weather conditions? Pilot hangover? Norman's Cay is only forty-five miles from here. Why can't you people ever seem to get there?" He came close to pounding his fist on the counter.

The agent looked at him blankly. Novak felt the explosion building inside him and was trying to defuse it when a voice said, "Norman's? I can take you there."

Novak turned and saw a tall, tanned man in a tropical suit and a silk shirt. At first, still struggling with his emotions, Novak didn't recognize him. Then he took a closer look at his sharp features and saw that his benefactor was Lawrence Ferguson, a pilot he had met once or twice at the bar of the South Ocean Beach Hotel, where Novak had been staying.

"You can?" Novak said.

"No problem."

"Wonderful."

Ten minutes later, Novak was in front of a hangar, loading his gear—a duffel bag and two scuba tanks—onto Ferguson's Cessna 210. Not long after that, they were rolling down the runway. As Ferguson opened the throttle and lifted the plane off the asphalt, Novak watched closely. He knew something about flying, having flown often with his son Chris, a promising young pilot. Satisfied that he was in capable hands, Novak began to relax a little and gaze though the window as the tops of the jack pines, then a white beach, and finally the sea, first translucent green and quite suddenly deep blue, swept by below. Before the little plane rose too high, Novak scanned the waters for any dark torpedo shapes lurking just beneath the surface. This time he spotted none, but he had often seen sharks from airplane windows in the past.

They reached cruising altitude and leveled off, flying southeast. Novak stared out at the shining blue sea, a sea like some magical cloth studded here and there with little green gems, until he grew aware that Ferguson was speaking to him.

"Why do you want to go to Norman's so badly?"

Novak was silent for a moment. He hadn't really been aware that he had wanted to go *badly*, but of course it was true. Why else would he have persisted so long at the airport? Ferguson's question was a good one.

"I'm looking for somewhere to set up a dive facility," Novak said. "For research, primarily."

"Why Norman's?"

That was a good question too. The true answer was that he had run out of places to look. He had closed Poseidon's Locker, his dive shop in Key Largo, months before, fed up with Florida and the continuing degradation of her reefs and marine life. He remembered a time when his dive flag had been the only one between Key Largo and Marathon. Now the reefs were swarming with humanity and he'd come to blows with poachers and souvenir hunters three times. Once he'd even rammed his dive boat, the *Reef Queen*, into the craft of one of the worst poachers. He couldn't put himself into situations like that anymore, not after the heart attack. So-called. Florida was finished, as far as diving was concerned. And in other ways? In other ways, he wasn't sure. Other ways meant Dorothy. Dorothy was his wife. He had been in love with her since college on Staten Island, in New York. She'd stuck with him through everything—his hitch in the Marines, his climb up the academic ladder at Concordia College, near New York City, the move to Florida and the establishment of Poseidon's Locker. She'd borne him five children. He loved her and loved the children. The problem was they weren't his first love. His first love was the sea.

Richard Novak grew up on Long Island Sound. His earliest memory was of fishing from a small boat with his father. In high school, he studied marine science and conducted the first of many research projects, an investigation into the mating patterns of horseshoe crabs on Calf Island in the Sound. He became the youngest person to captain the Greenwich ferry, and while still a teenager was certified to pilot one-hundred-gross tons. He donned scuba tanks for the first time at age sixteen, strapping on a friend's gear and plunging into the sea without a lesson or a second thought. He was hooked on diving from that moment, and in the Marines learned everything there was to know about it. The sea drew him like nothing else. For one thing, it had convinced him of the existence of God. He didn't understand how anyone who has sailed in an open boat on the open ocean could fail to believe in God. His belief had led him to Lutheranism, and he had approached that as he approached everything that interested him: fully. He had studied in Munich, learning German, and at Columbia. Now he was a professor of German, a husband and father of five, a success in almost anyone's eyes. But the sea still drew him, and he dreamed of some pristine bay where he could devote himself to it. He was forty-seven, not much younger than his father had been when he had died of a heart attack while rowing out to his favorite fishing spot on Long Island Sound. Although he would never have used the expression himself, he felt unfulfilled.

So he took a sabbatical, left Dorothy and the five kids, three grown up, and began searching the Bahamas for the pristine ocean stretch of his dreams. Maybe, if Dorothy hadn't had her accident, she'd have come too in the end, but the accident had happened. Not long before his heart attack, she'd been leading a dive trip off Key Largo when she suddenly began swimming straight down into the depths. Novak quickly realized she had succumbed to nitrogen narcosis, losing all judgment and sense of direction, and he'd shot down after her, grabbed her and swum her by force to the surface. Dorothy hadn't been in the water since. In fact, she seldom came down to Florida after that, preferring to remain at Concordia, where she worked as an administrator. Novak had kept Poseidon's Locker going, but after the heart attack came problems with his partner and financial difficulties. Novak had sold out, bought the *Reef Witch*, a twenty-four-foot Proline he was still paying off, and begun looking for a harbor to put her. Maybe if he found the right place, got properly established with a nice house and the right setup, Dorothy and the kids would join him. Was that asking too much, asking to have the best of everything? Novak didn't know. He wasn't comfortable with questions like that. He wasn't comfortable articulating his dreams, even to himself. All he knew was that he had tried Treasure Cay on Abaco and eight other locations in the Bahamas. He was still looking. Norman's Cay was the last on his list.

That was the long answer to Lawrence Ferguson's question. Novak gave him the short one: "I've heard that Norman's is a breeding ground for hammerhead sharks. I'd like see if it's true."

Ferguson showed no interest in hammerheads. He asked Novak who he knew on the island.

"No one."

"No? Norman's isn't the kind of island to land on unless there's someone to meet you. It's not really a tourist spot."

Novak didn't consider himself a tourist, so he didn't take Ferguson's remark personally. "That's what I hear," he said. "The hotel and marina are a well-kept secret."

Novak noticed Ferguson smiling. "I suppose Gus Holleran told you that," Ferguson said.

Holleran, a customs inspector at the airport, had indeed told Novak about Norman's. He had also introduced Novak to Ferguson.

"That's right," Novak said.

"What else did he tell you about Norman's?"

"Not much." Novak began describing Holleran's account of the island: the tales of hammerhead shark migrations, his special interest; the eleven miles of virgin reef; the pretty ten-room hotel; the three-thousand-foot strip and natural harbor. Holleran had said that Norman's was a perfect size, small enough to be walked from one end to the other, big enough to support a modest number of permanent residents, a nice restaurant, a market. The island was known for its pond, a saltwater lagoon enclosed on three sides and one of the safest refuges from storms in the Bahamas. It had a colorful history, according to Holleran. Once it had been headquarters for an English pirate who had given Norman's its name; during Prohibition bootleggers had run booze from the island into Florida. Now it was a haven for sailors and beachcombers, who found it unspoiled and peaceful.

Ferguson showed little interest in Novak's recital of Holleran's account, except for a quick smile at the mention of the bootleggers. He was silent for a minute or two. Then he said, "Norman's isn't run like the other islands."

"What do you mean?"

"It's private, for one thing. Private and exclusive. It's almost impossible to buy a house, and the cost of renting—a boat, a room, anything—is astronomical."

Novak didn't care about that. He knew how to live rough. He could spear all he needed to eat, and sleep on the beach. He'd done it before.

"It's not just that," Ferguson said. "The people down there don't take much to strangers."

"I'm not going to bother anybody," Novak told him. "I'm interested in the reef and the lagoon. Period." If the water was right he could work out the rest of it—setting up a shop, finding a place to live, bringing down the *Reef Witch*—later.

"Good," said Ferguson. "Because there's no one to help if anything goes wrong. The residents look after themselves."

"Fine." Novak had always looked after himself. He turned back to the window.

Ferguson banked between two clouds, cut back on the

throttle, and came down over the Exumas, the island chain of which Norman's is a part. The Exumas are the kind of islands northerners have reveries about in winter. Small and green, with long sand beaches white enough to hurt the eyes with their glare, they are set in turquoise water so clear the bottom can easily be seen from a plane; and the whole—green of the islands, white of the beaches, turquoise of the shallows—is surrounded by deep water that shades from blue to violet. Novak had never seen the islands before. He reacted as everyone reacts, and immediately forgot all the other sites he had visited. The Bahamas are one of the most beautiful island groups in the world; the Exumas are the quintessence of the Bahamas.

Ferguson descended over a few small cays and one larger one—Highbourne Cay—and then headed for the next major link in the chain. "Norman's Cay," he said. Novak leaned forward. The island resembled a fish-hook—a narrow dark-green fishhook with its barb pointed south. Norman's Cay was almost entirely banded with long white beaches, and enclosed a lagoon of a green much lighter than its vegetation. "That's the pond," Ferguson said, as the Cessna followed its shadow across the water. Even from the air, Novak could see how shallow it was; and more: silhouetted against the milky sand bottom lay a school of big sharks. The water was so transparent that he could easily make out their hammer-shaped heads. Now Novak's face was pressed to the window. Greedily, he drank in everything he could see.

At the end of the longer, western arm of the hook, Novak saw the hotel, set on a little rise overlooking the marina. Nearby were a pair of tennis courts, waiting empty in the shade of tall palms, and a few small houses by the shore. The airstrip had been sliced diagonally across the broadest section of the southern tip of the island. From it, a single paved road cut northward through trees so dense they looked like jungle, past a string of bigger houses, finally becoming invisible under the green canopy.

As Ferguson tuned his radio and called in his tail numbers, Novak noticed a number of tall antennae on the island, and a few large cisterns, one or two still under construction. Then the radio crackled, and an American voice, flat and terse, gave them clearance to land. Ferguson made his approach, flying in between two rows of pines and setting the plane down in a perfect three-point landing on the concrete. He ran the length of the strip, a very long one for the out islands, then turned and taxied slowly back, stopping beside a small, boarded-up customs house.

There was no one in sight. Ferguson switched off his engine. It was very quiet. So was Ferguson when he spoke. "There've been some changes on Norman's," he said.

Novak had already unbuckled, and was turned around, pulling his scuba tanks out from behind the seat. "Yeah?"

"Yeah. There are some new residents. They're kind of a closed group."

"I'm not here to socialize," Novak said. "I just want a look at that pond, and the reefs outside."

"Sure," said Ferguson. "But if there's trouble, talk to Phil Kniskern or Chuck Kehm. Kniskern's the builder. Kehm's the island manager."

"Don't worry. I'll be back in Nassau on the next flight."

"The next flight?" Ferguson said. Novak thought of the eleven straight cancellations at Bahamasair. "There are a lot of private planes on Norman's," Ferguson said. "That's your best bet."

"Thanks," Novak said. "And thanks for the ride. Can I buy you lunch?"

Ferguson shook his head. Novak gathered his gear and stepped down from the plane. Ferguson remained where he was. It had begun to occur to Novak for the first time that Ferguson might not be getting off the plane at all when a big man in a business suit stepped out of the trees and came forward. With a glance at Novak but without a word, he slung two heavy canvas sacks into the plane, then climbed in after them and sat in the seat just vacated by Novak. Ferguson switched on his power, gunned the engine, and over its noise called out, "Good luck." Then the Cessna taxied down the strip, rose in the air, and soon shrank to a speck in the northern sky.

Novak stood in the silence and the heat beside the boarded-up customs house. Now he remembered bits from a conversation with Gus Holleran. Had Holleran said something about Ferguson flying frequently between Nassau and the Exumas? And had he mentioned the reason? Novak realized he hadn't asked Ferguson why he was flying to Norman's that day, and that Ferguson hadn't volunteered the information. Surely Ferguson hadn't made the flight just for him. Of course not: the big man in the suit had been waiting. And who exactly had given landing clearance on the radio? Novak looked around. The island seemed deserted. He tried to recall what Ferguson had been telling him about Norman's. In truth, he hadn't been listening closely. He had been too busy thinking about those hammerheads in the lagoon. Perhaps there were a few questions he might want to ask Ferguson now, but the Cessna was out of sight, and Novak's mind was returning to thoughts of the lagoon. As he hefted the tanks on his shoulders and started toward the hotel, he wondered whether he'd be able to get settled in time to make a dive before nightfall.

2

Novak, carrying his tanks and his suitcase, walked along the road from the airstrip on Norman's Cay. He moved right down the middle of it; there was no reason not to, without a car or a person in sight. Palms lined the road, but provided no shade from the overhead sun. By the time Novak had passed the tennis courts—clay courts that looked well constructed and maintained, although the lines needed brushing—then rounded the marina and mounted the steps to the hotel, he was sweating.

Norman's Cay Club read a sign over the entrance. Novak pushed open the door with his foot and entered the lobby. It was a small square lobby with a glassed-in bar and dining room to the left and a reception counter on the right. Novak moved to the reception counter, set his gear on the floor, and looked around. There was no one in the bar, no one in the lobby, no one behind the counter. Novak knocked on its wooden top. He was about to knock again, a little harder, when the door behind the counter opened and a tall, handsome Bahamian woman came out. Her eyes seemed to search his face for something familiar, and when they didn't find it, assumed a guarded look.

"Yes?" she said.

"I've just come from Nassau," Novak told her. "I'd like a room."

"Have you got a reservation?"

"I tried calling from Nassau," Novak replied. "But they

said the telephone and telegraph lines have been down for the past month."

"So you don't have a reservation?"

"I told you. The lines were—"

"There's always ship-to-shore," the woman said.

Novak gestured toward the marina, perhaps more vigorously than he should have. "There doesn't seem to be a lot of boat traffic coming this way," he pointed out. He took a deep breath. "My name's Richard Novak. I'm sorry I don't have a reservation. But I would like a room."

The woman tapped a pencil on the counter. "For how long?" she asked.

"Just a night. I've come to take a look at the reef."

The woman peered over the counter at his duffel bag and his tanks lying on the floor. Then she looked at him closely for the second time. He remembered Ferguson's comment about the exclusivity of Norman's and it crossed his mind that his appearance might be causing the problem. Dressed in shorts and a T-shirt, with his sun-bleached hair clipped short and his tan deep and rough from the sun and wind, except for the thin pale scars on his jaw and the bigger, uglier one where a shark had taken a bite out of his leg, Novak realized he looked much more like a crewman on someone's yacht than its owner. But there was nothing he could do about that, so he just returned the woman's gaze. She said, "I'll see what I can do," then looked away and, taking the reservation book, disappeared through the door, closing it behind her.

She was gone a long time. When she came back, she was shaking her head. "All the rooms have been booked already," she said. "Months ago."

"Months ago?"

"I'm sorry. I tried raising Mr. Kniskern, but he's not around. There might have been room in one of his houses."

Novak tried to recall the other name Ferguson had given him. "What about the island manager? Kehm?"

There was a silence. "Mr. Kehm is no longer island manager," the woman said.

"Maybe you could get in touch with the new manager," Novak suggested.

The woman's eyes lost a little of their wariness. "I am the new manager," she said, with some pride. "Paulette Jones."

They shook hands. "Is there anything to stop me from sitting by the marina till Kniskern shows up?" Novak asked.

Paulette Jones thought for a moment and then smiled. "No," she answered.

Novak left his gear in the lobby and walked down to the marina where he sat on a bench. He looked out over a glare of salt flats, across the pond glittering under the sun, toward some small cays in the distance. A few boats were tied up to the dock, but no one was on them. After a while a plane appeared and began circling the island. It was a private plane, bigger than Ferguson's. Novak soon tired of watching it. He got up and started walking along a narrow dirt path that circled the hotel. It led to a low cement building that had been divided into two stores. One was the Exuma Trading Company, the market. It was closed. The other was a dive shop. It was open. Novak walked in.

The dive shop was hot, cramped, and poorly lit. Novak quickly took in the heaps of unsorted gear, the rusting compressor, the smell of sea-rot. In one corner a big man with muscles and a tan was packing a crate. He glanced up.

"Closed for renovations," he said. "There's gear for rent on Highbourne Cay."

Novak had his own gear, in a much better state than anything he could see around him now. "I'd like to take a trip to the reef," he said.

"It's not possible."

Norman's, as Ferguson had foretold, was different. Novak asked, "Does that mean it's not possible or it's just not convenient right now?"

This brought a little smile. "It's not possible and it's not convenient."

Novak fought a brief battle with his temper and said, "I see," although he didn't.

The other man tossed a weight belt into the crate, sighed, and introduced himself. "Dave Woodward's my name," he said. "It's nothing personal. I've got a bent shaft and I'm waiting on a part out of Miami. I can't risk taking the boat out to the reef." He regarded Novak for a moment. Maybe he thought Novak looked like a diver. He sighed again and added, "Forbes might take you out. He'll be at the tennis courts."

"Thanks."

Novak left the dive shop, with its odor of decay and failure, and returned to the hotel. Overhead, the plane still circled. Novak wondered for a moment whether the terse, flat voice had refused its pilot clearance to land. Then he went inside, hoping that Paulette Jones had heard from Kniskern, but no one was there and this time his knocking on the counter went unanswered. He went back outside and onto the empty road, which he followed past the hotel cottages lining the marina until he reached the tennis courts.

It was much too hot for tennis, and no one was playing. There was a man on the court, but not, as Novak had pictured, a white man in whites with a gin-and-tonic waiting nearby. This was a young black man in ragged shorts and a T-shirt. He was small and thin, although he had big hands and muscular shoulders. The man was brushing the taped lines on the court and didn't glance up until Novak said: "I'm looking for Forbes."

"I am Forbes," said the man. "Victor Forbes."

Novak walked forward and introduced himself. Forbes watched the tracks Novak made in the soft clay. "I'm told you might take me out to the reef," Novak said.

Forbes moved around Novak and brushed away the footprints he had made. "Who be tellin' you that?" he asked.

"Dave Woodward."

Forbes nodded. He studied his bare feet for a few moments and then named a price. It was double the going rate in Nassau, but it was the first positive answer Novak had received since landing on Norman's and he agreed immediately, skipping the haggling session Forbes undoubtedly expected. "When can we get started?"

"Get started?"

"Yes," Novak said. "I can be ready in ten minutes."

Forbes giggled. "Oh, not today, man. Tomorrow. Tomorrow morning. Nine sharp. Ten at the latest." It developed that Forbes was taking some friends of an island resident out to the reef anyway and he had room for Novak. When Novak heard that, he wished he had haggled, but it was too late. He agreed to meet Forbes at the dock next morning and left. Forbes followed him to the edge of the court, brushing his tracks away.

Novak walked back onto the road and was halfway to the hotel when a little shuttle bus appeared, moving toward him. When it was quite close it swerved to a sudden stop directly in his path. A Bahamian in a beige uniform jumped out and came toward him, clipboard in his hand. "Papers," he said, as though this were Nazi Germany instead of a tiny backwater in a small, undeveloped island nation.

"Papers?"

"Your papers, man. This is a private island. You think you can come and go as you please?"

"I didn't know," Novak said, realizing that his passport was with the rest of his gear in the hotel lobby.

"Papers," insisted the uniformed man, holding out his hand.

"They're at the hotel."

The uniformed man pointed with his chin. Novak walked the short remaining distance to the hotel. The uniformed man followed in the shuttle.

Paulette Jones was back behind the counter when they came in. She understood the situation at a glance. "It's all right, Sleepy," she said to the uniformed man. "Mr. Novak is a guest of the club."

The man nodded and left. *Sleepy?* Novak thought, as

he listened to the shuttle's motor fade away. "Have you reached Kniskern?" he asked.

"No," replied Paulette Jones. "But I've got a room for you."

"You have?" Novak said, and almost asked sarcastically if there had been a sudden cancellation.

Paulette Jones said, "It's one of our nicest," making him glad he hadn't. She led him down to the cottages, and he soon found himself in a large, airy room with a ceiling fan and sliding glass doors opening onto a beach by the marina. It had a teak bed, bureau, and table, and two slingback chairs. Fresh hibiscus blossoms floated in a bowl on the table, and their smell filled the room.

"Sorry for the confusion," the woman said. "We haven't had a lot of tourists this summer."

"No problem," Novak said. "This is perfect." He opened his suitcase and took out his passport. On top of his clothes lay a worn copy of Faust in German, a Bible, also in German, and his .357 Magnum. If the sight struck Paulette Jones as odd, she gave no sign of it. Novak thought that she was either very polite and well trained or accustomed to armed guests. Because she didn't ask, he didn't explain that he carried the pistol in case of shark emergencies. He handed her his passport; she glanced through it and gave it back.

"Is there anything else you need?" she asked, turning to leave.

"Just the room key."

Paulette Jones smiled. "There are no keys on Norman's," she replied. "They're not necessary in a place like this, Mr. Novak. Enjoy your stay."

Paulette Jones left. Novak finished unpacking, then opened his sliding glass doors and looked outside. He was thinking to himself how much he liked everything he saw, when he noticed that the airplane was still circling the island. As he watched, it dipped low across the lagoon. Novak could clearly see a man in the passenger seat. He had a long-lensed camera in his hands. He leaned out and pointed it in Novak's direction as the plane flew by.

3

Novak slept with the sliding glass doors open to the sea. During the night he heard the sound of a fast boat coming close, then fading away. Later he thought he heard distant music; it might have been the Beatles. Then a soft breeze rose and lulled him back to sleep. He slept more deeply than he had in a long time.

Novak awoke at first light, full of energy. The sea was calm, the sky clear: a perfect day for diving. He threw on shorts and sneakers and went for a run on the beach. His route took him past a few houses under construction, then back by the hotel and marina. There he saw a man taking pictures. He couldn't tell whether he was the same photographer who had leaned out of the airplane the day before.

"A photographer?" Paulette Jones asked when he went into breakfast. "It must be for a brochure." She explained that real estate prices on Norman's were rising sharply. She quoted a few numbers, numbers beyond his reach. Novak tried not to worry about that as he sipped his coffee.

At a quarter to nine he was at the marina dock with all his gear. A few minutes later an American couple arrived. Novak remembered that he would be diving with friends of one of the island's residents. He hoped they wouldn't get in his way; the woman looked fit and reliable, but he would probably have to keep his eye on the man. That was often the case in his experience.

Before ten, but not long before, an old and battered Boston Whaler came around a point to the south with Forbes at the wheel. He called out a hearty "Good morning" as he tied up, and no one said anything about the long wait. They were on island time now.

Norman's Cay is almost entirely surrounded by coral reefs. Passage through them is tricky because of numerous shallows and isolated coral heads. Novak quickly saw that Forbes knew how to read the depth from the changing colors on the surface, and although Forbes didn't always pick exactly the same channel he himself would have, he kept his mouth shut.

As the Whaler rounded one of the tiny eastern cays, called Pieces of Eight by the locals, Novak spotted a tramp steamer heading toward the northern part of Norman's. The steamer, which had a white superstructure and a reddish hull, interested Novak for several reasons: it was miles from the nearest shipping lanes, and much too big, almost two hundred feet long, he estimated, to be safe in these waters; it was also loaded high with what looked like construction supplies.

"What's that doing here?" he called to Forbes over the engine noise.

"Maybe one of the owners be putting up a new pier," Forbes replied without much interest.

"No one seems to use the pier they've already got," Novak said.

Forbes shrugged.

A few minutes later, they were gliding along a narrow green channel flanked on either side by shimmering yellows and red-browns: coral reef. Forbes backed the throttle into neutral, then went to the bow, picked up the anchor, and raised it high.

"Hold it right there," Novak said, maybe more loudly than he intended. Forbes froze, and the American couple stared at him in puzzlement. "Look," Novak said, "every time you toss that hook into the reef you kill a part of it.

Just drop it down in the sand. I'll make sure it's secure when I get down."

"Okay, man," Forbes said. "Okay." And he dropped the anchor with a delicate motion, as though it were made of glass. Novak was aware of the American couple watching him, but he made no more effort to explain himself. The chucking of anchors onto the reef was one of his bêtes noires; he had almost come to blows over it in Key Largo, more than once.

The divers suited up and plunged backward over the side, one hand on their masks, the other on their regulators. Novak went last. His body relaxed as soon as it felt the water. The sea was warm and soothing. He had been away from it too long. Novak checked the other divers, and when he saw them swimming slowly toward the reef with at least moderate competence, drifted down to check the anchor. He stuck it deeply into the sand and joined the others.

They swam along the edge of the underwater forest. Novak finned past tall stands of elkhorn coral, huge round brain corals, radiant gorgonians. As they went deeper, he grew aware that the reef was teeming with life: he saw tiny tropical fish, such as sergeant majors and blue tangs, and bigger ones—French angels and parrot fish, pursing and unpursing their luridly colored lips; at sixty feet a school of barracuda flashed by like a patch of an Impressionist painting on the move.

They angled toward the edge of the reef. Novak's depth gauge read seventy-five feet, and the bottom, though it seemed only a kick or two away, was much farther than that. He realized with a thrill how clear the water was: the clearest water he had ever seen. Checking the American couple once more—they were staring at a big spiny lobster in a hole partly hidden by pink sea fans—he dove down.

He descended to 125 feet, farther than he should have given that he had no extra tank for decompression. He stayed there for only a few seconds, time enough to see a big feathery bush of black coral, and an enormous manta ray winging by. He forgot everything: his financial difficulties, the heart attack, all the trouble he had encountered in trying to get to Norman's, Ferguson's odd behavior, the strange atmosphere on the island, Dorothy. He luxuriated in the sea.

And then, on the way up, came the capper. Three hammerheads glided by, not twenty feet from his face. The first was ten feet long, the others slightly shorter. One had its mouth open, revealing the rows of sharp teeth. Novak went very still, not out of fear, but to drink in the sight fully. The sharks's little eyes, torpedo-shaped bodies, and deadly maws might have induced fear or disgust in most people, but not in Novak. He knew the hammerheads were killing machines, but they were wonderful and sleek killing machines, and the most worthy objects of study that he knew. The hammerheads swam away, turning into shadows and then dissolving to nothing. Novak ascended, but his mind absorbed no details of the ascent, climbing into the boat, doffing his gear. He was euphoric.

All the way back to the harbor, he grilled Forbes. Forbes seemed to know something about the local waters, and what was more he showed an interest in them. Novak decided he liked Forbes after all.

Forbes told him that hammerhead sightings were not at all uncommon around Norman's. Schools of hammerheads had been migrating to the island to mate in the pond as far back as the oldest Bahamian on Norman's could remember.

"Have you seen them yourself?" Novak asked.

"Sure, man. So thick they make the waters black."

"When do they come?" Novak asked.

"When?"

"What time of year?"

Forbes shrugged.

"Is it seasonal?"

"I don't know, man."

Novak wondered about the credibility of Forbes's account; still, it made his pulse race. He had heard stories of hammerhead mating grounds, but never anything precise or documented, and he had never located one, despite years of trying. Neither had any other marine researcher. And now it was in his reach, a hugely fertile area of the kind of study he loved, and more than that: a life work.

Forbes's Whaler cut through the glassy green sea. Novak heard the idle chat on board, but he wasn't listening. His mind was full of jumbled images of what lay ahead: raising capital, negotiating leases, finding a house on the island, telling Dorothy. Would it be better to let her know right from the start or wait until he could present her with a fait accompli? He wasn't sure. He would have to think about that. There would be a lot of decisions to make. But he had already made the most important one: Richard Novak would make a life on Norman's Cay.

4

Carlos Lehder rose early. It was a beautiful morning in August 1978. He got out of his bed, a big bed, but empty now, since his Cuban wife, Jemel Nacel, was back in Florida and his German mistress, Margit Meie-Lennekogel, was in Nassau. He thought about them both for a moment—Jamel, short, dark, with a finely sculpted face; Margit—tall, blonde, big-boned, and buxom. If his thought aroused any desire, that need could soon be met: Chocolata, a pretty Bahamian prostitute with a slim, boyish body, was nearby. Lehder was a fortunate man; he had a complaisant wife and all the women he wanted. And sometimes he wanted them badly. He had spent too long in places where there were no women at all. It's true that not every man would have been happy with Jemel. For one thing, she liked to spend money—on a recent afternoon she had parted with twenty thousand dollars at Bloomingdale's—but that kind of money meant nothing to Carlos Lehder.

He switched on his sound system, put on the White Album, filling the house with the sound of "Back in the U.S.S.R.," "Glass Onion," "Helter Skelter." The White Album was Lehder's favorite. Did he know it had also been number one on Charles Manson's hit parade?

He moved to the porch. He liked his new house. Lehder had named it Volcano because of the conical shape of its central section. He had purchased it a few weeks before from Charlie Beckwith, a part-owner of Sea World in Fort Lauderdale, for $190,000. Cash. That kind of money meant nothing to Carlos Lehder. He had made the payment in small bills. Perhaps it hadn't been exactly·190,000. Lehder couldn't have sworn to that because·he had not bothered to count the money, but had weighed it instead. The vendor had not complained.

Volcano was a big house. It had been built by a rich minister who had hoped to use it as a retreat for religious scholars. That's why there were seven bedrooms. Lehder didn't need seven bedrooms, but he liked having them. He liked his new house, his new sound system, the big ski-chalet-style fireplace in the living room, the ocean view from his porch. He liked everything about Norman's Cay.

Carlos Lehder picked up his barbells and began pumping them. He wasn't a big man, but he had muscles. He worked on making them bigger for a while. He was good at pumping weights, and had spent a lot of time doing it. There are two places in America where pumping weights is the main pastime. One is the gym. The other is prison. Carlos Lehder worked up a good sweat before he went inside and got to work.

The first thing he had to do was count out eighty-eight thousand dollars; his scale was in Florida. Eighty-eight thousand dollars was his monthly membership in the Square Deal Club, a group of businessmen headed by Nigel Bowe, a well-known Bahamian lawyer who was personal attorney for Prime Minister Lynden O. Pindling. Nigel Bowe flew into Norman's on the twenty-second of every month to collect. Lehder knew that eighty-eight thousand per month was not the normal membership fee for the Square Deal Club, but his own specially adjusted rate. He didn't mind. That kind of money meant nothing to Carlos Lehder.

He was a businessman, and doing business in the Bahamas cost money. Lehder knew that. It was why he kept an entertainment suite at the Playboy Club on Paradise Island in Nassau. The suite was an ideal place for receiving guests like Everette Bannister, prominent businessman and financial adviser to Prime Minister Lynden O. Pindling, or George Smith, cabinet minister in the government of Lynden O. Pindling, or officials of the Bank of Nova Scotia. Spend money to make money: his donation to the George Town Regatta on Great Exuma, for example. Why not? It was the favorite boat race of Prime Minister Lynden O. Pindling.

Carlos Lehder was a businessman, a legitimate businessman. His first legitimate business was Autos Lehder, a Chevrolet dealership in Medellín, Colombia, his native land. His second legitimate business was Titanic Air, an airplane brokerage that bought big, used passenger craft and converted them to cargo planes. If that business often required the acquisition of lots of planes, boats, and radar and communications equipment, well, why not? They were legitimate business expenses. Then there was Air Montes Limited, a charter service in the Bahamas that also involved a lot of buying and selling of aircraft; and Air Montes Corporation; and Chelique IV Limited; and Fernandez Limited; and International Dutch Resources Limited; and three houses in Medellín and in his little hometown of Armenia, Colombia, an enclave of settlers from Germany; and soon there would be a hotel, and a ranch that he would stock with exotic animals.

All legitimate.

And that was nothing. Nothing compared with what he had in mind. Carlos Lehder was a creative man. He dreamed big dreams. Norman's Cay was part of his dream. He had big plans for Norman's Cay. When he had finished counting out the eighty-eight thousand dollars, he reached for one of the spiral notebooks he liked to outline his plans in and began making sketches of what Norman's Cay might look like in the not-too-distant future. With his pencil, he lengthened the runway, broadened the entrance to the harbor, erected tall antennae, built luxurious new houses. But he wanted more than that—he wanted a little class. He was proud of the half of himself that was German: European, cultivated, civilized. He was fluent in German, having learned it from his father and the German expatriates who came to his parents' small hotel, the Pension Alamena, in Armenia. In fact, he spoke it with a touch of elegance, as he did Spanish, too. His English, learned on the streets in U.S. inner cities, was coarser, although just as fluent. No, it was true, he himself had not been educated beyond seventh grade, having been expelled for his behavior, but he was a lover of books. His bedroom at Volcano was full of books. He had a few special favorites, which he read over and over. *Demian* by Herman Hesse was one. *The Archetypes of the Collective Unconscious* by Carl Jung was another. And *The Prince* by Machiavelli. And *Mein Kampf.* Lehder wanted Norman's Cay, the future Norman's Cay that existed now mostly in his mind, to reflect the civilized side of him. He would be open to any suitable ideas. Something cultural, or scientific perhaps. He had a vision of an island nation reflecting the personality of its ruler, the way a feudal society was the face of the king, or the way that the Reich had been the face of Hitler.

Norman's Cay was perfect. He liked its long landing strip, its marina and safe anchorage. Most of all he liked its location, near enough to both Colombia and Florida to permit nonstop flights by small planes. Sole, undisputed possession of Norman's Cay was indispensable to his plans. That would take money, of course. Money wasn't a problem. But there was always the possibility that some property owners might not be willing to sell. Carlos Lehder was prepared for that. He wasn't alone. He had competent employees: Jack Reed, a former test pilot and race car driver and now one of his best pilots, who captained the Aero Commander 450 Kilo Charlie and had a fifteen-year-old girlfriend and always carried a leather satchel with a pistol inside; Humberto Hoyos, who liked to wear flashy clothes and jewelry and was the brother-in-law of the wife of one of his Colombian partners; Larry

Greenberger, a whiz with numbers, and Lehder had big numbers to deal with; Stringbean Robinson and Chuck Moyer, pilots; Manfred and Heinrich, recruited at a school for bodyguards in Stuttgart; and Stephen Francis, a Bahamian from the Exumas who was Lehder's eyes and ears on Norman's. Now he wondered whether Francis was capable of performing that duty by himself. He made a note to have a discussion with Victor Forbes.

Then there was the problem of the Fat Man. Lehder had been on to the Fat Man from his first day on the island, from the moment, in fact, when he had seen the Fat Man's house and its huge antenna. His suspicions had been confirmed the day he learned that the Fat Man owned two identical twin-engine Beach Bonanzas, each white with brown trim. It would be an easy matter some night to paint identical numbers on the tails, too. Lehder admired the Fat Man's ingenuity, but Norman's wasn't big enough for the two of them, if they remained competitors. Lehder was sure, however, that he could convince the Fat Man of the wisdom of pooling their resources.

Lehder closed his notebook. There was much to be done. He had radar and communications equipment to buy. He had to have his boats brought to Norman's—his favorite possession, a thirty-seven-foot red racing Scarab called *Fire Fall*, after the term the Vietnam grunts had used to describe their ordeals by fire; his sixty-seven-foot steamer, the *Margaret Lee*, and his ninety-foot steamer, the *Gentleman Jim*; his fifty-eight-foot cabin cruiser, the *Chelique IV*. But first there was one more trip to be made to Medellín. There he would meet with a few men, businessmen like himself, but more conservative. His task, and it was probably the most important one of his life, would be to convince them of the wisdom of his plans. That is, he had to show them that if they did what he said they would make more money than the uncountable amounts they were already making. He knew they wanted more; that wasn't the problem. The problem was that these men didn't like to take risks. They were producers, close to farmers, really, and to be honest, almost bump-kins in a way, with limited knowledge of how the world worked outside their mountain citadels. He, Lehder, was a middleman, and middlemen had to take risks. They were also more worldly. Carlos Lehder had learned the hard way how the world outside little Third World towns like Armenia, Colombia, works. He had learned as a teen-age gang member in the slums of Detroit and New York; he had learned at the federal correction institution in Dan-bury, Connecticut, and at the cruelly named Bella Vista prison in Medellín; he had learned from his mother, who had carried one of his very first shipments on her own body. He had also learned to fly a plane, learned how to hire pilots at remoter airstrips all across the United States (he preferred Vietnam veterans because they knew how to keep their cool while flying at low altitudes under pres-sure), and learned to perform every job in his operation himself. Now it was time for the payoff. He got dressed and headed for the airstrip.

On August 16, 1978, Carlos Lehder returned to Nor-man's Cay from Colombia in the company of Jorge Ochoa, one of Medellín's leading conservative businessmen, in the latter's Mitsubishi twin-engine turboprop. Señor Ochoa brought with him sixteen suitcases. Their contents weighed 314 kilos. Carlos Lehder promised Senor Ochoa that he would be fully reimbursed for the loss of any part of his goods, from a single kilo to the entire amount. Lehder's employees then divided the 314 kilos into small lots. Lehder's pilots then flew Senor Ochoa's goods in dif-ferent planes, at different times, by different routes, into Florida, without the loss of a gram. For this service, Lehder was paid one quarter of the value of the shipment. The shipment was worth fifteen million dollars.

Senor Ochoa returned to Medellín to report to his asso-ciates. It didn't take them long to accept Lehder's terms. He was put in charge of all their transportation. Were the businessmen of Medellín too insular to understand the consequences of their decision? Did they not see that in making Carlos Lehder their delivery boy they were putting him in the same position vis-à-vis the U.S. cocaine market that A.T.&T. had enjoyed in telephone communication before the breakup?

5

Richard Novak's hair was still not quite dry from his dive off Norman's Cay when he landed in Nassau, flown there by the American couple who had accompanied him on Victor Forbes's Whaler. So Norman's was still with him physically, in a small way, and mentally in a much larger one. He couldn't stop thinking about it. He was sure Norman's was perfect. What he wasn't sure of was how to make it happen. From that standpoint, his trip had not been a success. He had left his phone number with Paulette Jones, and had given some indication of his thoughts to her and to Forbes, but neither had shown much reaction.

Now he stood at the window of the South Ocean Beach Hotel, seeing not what was outside, but the internal images he had carried back from Norman's. The phone rang.

"Richard Novak?" said a voice. "My name's Phil Kniskern."

The builder, Lawrence Ferguson had told him: the man to get in touch with on Norman's. "Yes?" Novak replied.

"I'm sorry I missed you on Norman's. I think we should meet."

Novak and Kniskern met at Novak's hotel later that same day. There was nothing of the slick real estate huckster about Kniskern, and Novak liked that from the beginning. Kniskern was short and squarely built, somewhat overweight, his fair hair somewhat balding. A quick and crude artist's sketch of him would have made him look like Barney Rubble. Dressed in a short-sleeved shirt and a sports jacket, he more resembled an engineer than a businessman. He carried a leather briefcase embossed with his initials in gold, and had a rolled-up map under his arm. He wasted no time with small talk, shaking hands and then leading Novak to a corner table on the outdoor patio. A waiter walked up. Kniskern ordered Scotch, Novak a rum-and-tonic.

Kniskern began by sketching in his background. He came from a family of Fort Lauderdale real estate developers. He had retired from that business and become interested in Norman's Cay. He had flown there to inspect a piece of beachfront property near the airstrip and liked it enough to buy it. He had built three villas on the land, which he now rented out. The income that had begun to flow in had exceeded his expectations. His interest in Norman's had grown. He had leased space from the island management to open Dave Woodward's scuba shop; now he wanted to lease or buy the hotel and restaurant too.

Novak didn't like real estate developers. He hated what they had done to south Florida, and held them as a group partly culpable for the degradation of the state's marine environment. But he listened without negative comment; Kniskern's presentation was pleasantly low key, and so far his plans seemed inoffensive and small-scale.

Kniskern unrolled his map. "Norman's is special," he said. "It's like no other island in the Exumas, or in the whole Bahamas, for that matter. Ten minutes after landing, you can be bonefishing in the pond, or diving on the reef. And it's only nineteen minutes from Nassau, and a little over an hour from Miami."

Novak had a closer look at the map. He quickly saw that Kniskern's plans were grander than he had implied. Color-coded markings divided the island into what Novak took to be plots of land and strings of houses that existed now only in Kniskern's mind. But Kniskern didn't mention any of that. He began with the water.

Kniskern took a fountain pen and drew a ring around the north shore. Novak leaned forward. "There's more to this reef than anyone knows," Kniskern said. "No one's ever charted all the coral heads and formations, and there are wrecks down there that haven't even been dived yet." Kniskern spoke briefly of Norman the pirate and other buccaneers, including Henry Morgan and Blackbeard, who were rumored to have used the island. With the tip of his pen, he indicated possible wreck sites.

But Novak didn't like treasure hunters. They blasted, vacuumed, and demolished everything in their way. "I don't like treasure hunters," he said.

Kniskern surprised him. "I'm glad to hear that," he said. "They're not part of my plans."

"What are your plans?"

Kniskern ran his finger over the image of Norman's Cay on his map. "You must have noticed what an unusual shape the island has. It means that every resident could have his own private beach, as well as an anchorage in the lagoon. It's unique." Kniskern acknowledged that he wasn't the first to realize the implications of this. He told Novak about the development history of Norman's.

In the early 1960s, large portions of the island were bought for ninety thousand dollars by an American industrialist named William Smith. He sold his land in 1965 to a developer named Tom Perrine for one million dollars. Perrine, who had dug artificial lakes in the Midwest so that every buyer could have waterfront property, saw that this technique would be superfluous on Norman's. He tried to build a combination resort and housing development on Norman's at a time when a number of such schemes were at various stages of planning or construction on other out islands in the Bahamas. He invested about two million dollars in Norman's, building the hotel, marina, tennis courts, and a few model homes.

Perrine's commitment and execution were sound, but

his timing was bad. In 1967, the Bahamas received its independence from Britain. Lynden O. Pindling and his Progressive Labour party formed the first black government in the history of a nation whose population was ninety percent black. This may have been just, but it frightened investors, including those Tom Perrine had hoped to attract to Norman's. By 1972, he was bankrupt. He handed the deeds over to the big real estate company that held the mortgages, the Meridian Corporation, based in New York, which was an arm of DLJ, a large multinational based in Canada.

For a while, the Meridian Corporation had kept up desultory efforts to make a go of Perrine's idea. The island had even enjoyed a brief reputation in certain wealthy circles as a quiet refuge. But Meridian's interest in the island was never deep, and from the start the company tried to find ways to unload it. A deal with Howard Hughes almost went through, but Hughes demanded that he have the island all to himself, and when several landowners refused to sell he backed out. Later the fugitive financier Robert Vesco made an offer, but was turned down because of his reputation. A businessman from San Francisco with a vision of building a luxurious resort for homosexuals was also rejected. Meridian was still looking for a buyer.

Novak thought about what Kniskern had told him. The new black government was no longer quite so new. There had been no revolution, no bloodshed. After a brief period of nervousness, the tourists had returned, in greater numbers than ever. "Perrine's plan still makes sense," he said.

The remark brought a pleased expression to Kniskern's face. "I think so too," he said. "That's why I'm trying to make a deal with Meridian right now. I have plans for Norman's Cay. I love the place."

"What kind of plans?"

"I'll tell you all about them if things work out. But one of the things I see is Norman's becoming a center for marine research."

Novak could see that too. His pulse quickened.

Kniskern rolled up his map. "I've made some calls about you," he said. "To Lauderdale and Key Largo."

Novak wondered what Kniskern had been told. Had he heard only about Novak's penchant for getting into trouble, running poachers and souvenir hunters off the reef, hounding politicians for their laxity in enforcing environmental laws? Or had he also learned of Novak's expertise—that he had captained the largest scuba training boat in Florida and spent thirty years as a dedicated, if independent, researcher of underwater life?

Whatever Kniskern had heard, he asked only one question: "Why did you leave Key Largo?"

Why did he leave Key Largo? It was the sight of kids on the highway selling sea fans and chunks of coral; it was the scum out on the reef slaughtering sharks with bangsticks in order to sell their fins for soup, or just for the hell of it; it was the lying politicians and the second-rate dive shops with their murderous unconcern for safety, and the bloated hotels and restaurants spewing their waste into the sea. All this pent-up frustration came spilling out of Novak. Perhaps he raised his voice. He might even have pounded his fist on the table. Kniskern was looking at him. Novak sipped his rum-and-tonic to calm himself. Maybe he hadn't given a totally truthful answer. He had no intention of divulging anything about his personal life, nor did he mention the heart attack, but he did decide to own up to some of the business mistakes he had made.

First, he told Kniskern, he had been wrong to attempt running a basic dive trip operation and conducting research at the same time. He had wanted to study the habits of hammerhead sharks, for example, but had always seemed to end up teaching the fundamentals of diving, and doing the books. Second, the *Reef Queen* had been the wrong kind of craft for what he wanted to do. The *Reef Witch*, though much smaller and less well equipped, was more suitable. It was also all he could afford, and perhaps to say that he could afford even it was overly optimistic. Third, his business had been too big. Not that it could be called big in any sense that the present-day buccaneers of Norman's like Howard Hughes or even Phil Kniskern would understand, but what he really wanted was to run a small affair with an emphasis on research rather than recreation.

Novak regarded Kniskern, wondering briefly how Kniskern might take his answer. But not for long; Novak was not the kind of man who dwelled much on how others saw him. Is it an oversimplification to say that in the past that had been his weakness but in the coming months it would prove to be his great strength?

Kniskern smiled. "Dave Woodward is leaving. I'm looking for someone to take over the dive shop and the marina." Then he pressed the decisive button. "The man I want has to be as dedicated to protecting the character of the island as he is in protecting the ecology of the reef. I think that man is you."

How did Novak react? The one person who seemed to be capable of making his dream come true had just done so. But Novak didn't exult or wonder. That wasn't in his nature. Instead he replied: "I couldn't consider your offer unless it comes with complete control. I'm not interested if running that shop interferes with research."

"That'll be up to you," said Kniskern. "I'm not looking to hire you. I want a partner."

A dream come true. But how could he be a partner? Partners had money to invest, and Novak did not. This didn't appear to be a problem to Kniskern. They made a deal: Kniskern offered Novak a retainer of a thousand dollars a month against a half-share in dive shop profits; he offered use of his Boston Whaler, his Aero Commander 34, one of his villas on Norman's, and the present contents of the dive shop, all until Kniskern bought the hotel. At that time, they would renegotiate the deal, but Kniskern made it clear that Novak would become island manager, running the hotel and a center for marine research.

A dream come true. And so quickly. There were questions Novak might have asked. How likely was the possibility that Kniskern's purchase from Meridian would go through? Did he have any competitors, other potential buyers in the field? Did he anticipate any problems? What was the attitude of the residents?

But Novak didn't ask them.

Instead he decided on the spot to tender his resignation at Concordia and leave after the fall semester. Then the two men unrolled the map and began doing something they both enjoyed: making plans. Making plans was just a precise form of dreaming, and they both had dreams, two dreams that fed on each other quite conveniently. In the course of their discussion it was agreed that Novak would soon return to Norman's for a reception at the hotel. That would give him a chance to meet some of the new residents. It seemed that there were a number of these, all rich and influential, who had recently decided to make Norman's their home. Novak might have asked questions about these new residents, but he did not. Even if he had, it was unlikely that he would have learned the truth. Phil Kniskern wasn't the kind of man who admitted unpleasant truths, even to himself.

The two dreamers shook hands and parted in a state of mutual satisfaction.

6

$\approx\approx\approx$

Carlos Lehder was a charismatic man, and well aware of the fact. The knowledge gave him the ability to look forward to confrontations that others might be uneasy about, or even dread.

He had known from his first day on Norman's Cay that the Fat Man was a drug smuggler. Even if there had been any doubt, the Fat Man himself soon took steps to dispel it. One day, not long after Lehder's arrival on Norman's, the Fat Man had come calling. "Hi," he'd said, in his affable, middle-American voice. "I'm Ed Ward, your neighbor. Got a minute or two?"

They'd gone outside to the beach, and in that same style, the open easy manner of a good salesman, Ward had come right to the point. "I think you're a drug smuggler, Mr. Lehder. The reason I know's cause I'm one too." He'd glanced at Lehder with a little smile, waiting for some sort of reaction. When none came, he continued: "There's two kinds of people look like drug smugglers—that's drug smugglers and drug agents. I just didn't want you to think I was a drug agent, that's all." Again, he waited for reaction.

Lehder said, "Thank you." They shook hands. That was that.

Weeks passed before they met again. Lehder had much to do. He began bringing some of his people to the island. He visited the Nassau office of the Guardian Trust Company, and enjoyed the commotion that resulted when he opened an attaché case containing one million dollars in U.S. currency. It amused him that the sight of the object of all their labors caused bankers so much consternation. Just the proper amount of consternation, though: not quite enough to prevent them from opening seven accounts for him in various corporate names. Perhaps they believed his story about being a money-changer from Colombia with hopes of turning Norman's Cay into a yacht haven. At the Bank of Nova Scotia on Paradise Island, management was a little less credulous—they instituted a counting charge of one percent on all his currency deposits. But they cooperated all the same. Through the bankers, he began chanelling his money into legitimate businesses, like industrial parks and marinas; and into the public sector, too, via the election campaign chests of various Bahamian politicians.

So weeks passed before Lehder and Ward met again. This time, Lehder went to Ward's house. Again, their conversation was straightforward, free of dishonesty, hypocrisy, or even euphemism. And why not? Lehder told Ward that he dealt only in cocaine; Ward admitted what Lehder had already assumed, that he smuggled only marijuana. That lead to a discussion of the comparative merits of the cocaine and marijuana businesses. The discussion may have seemed spontaneous to Ward, but it followed a path predetermined in Lehder's mind. And nothing Ward said caught Lehder by surprise. He had foreseen every response.

Ward began by shying away from the idea of cocaine smuggling. The penalties for getting caught were Draconian, relative to marijuana sentences. The people involved in the cocaine business had a reputation for guns and violence, while the marijuana business was run on handshakes. And cocaine was known as a hard drug; Ward said he hadn't even tried marijuana himself, although he was living off it, until very recently.

Lehder made no attempt to counter these arguments. Instead, he gave Ward some financial insights into the cocaine trade. Ward was currently flying 1,200-pound loads of marijuana from Colombia into the U.S. at a markup of about $200 a pound. Lehder could buy cocaine for $25,000 per kilo in Colombia, and sell it for $50,000 in the U.S.—a markup of just over $12,000 a pound. Lehder allowed Ward to ruminate on the difference between $200 and $12,000. Then he pointed out how much safer the actual flying of cocaine was, with no need to mess with cumbersome bales of weed, crammed into overloaded planes. Cocaine was nicely packaged in plastic, and a 250-kilo shipment, less than half the weight of what Ward now carried, was plenty. That appealed to Ed Ward: he was a tidy, well-organized man. He was also a family man, with two children from his previous marriage and three from his wife Lassie's, and he understood the subtext when Lehder said things like: "I see no problem with both of us operating on this island, as long as there's cooperation, do you?" And Ward was a greedy man; otherwise he wouldn't be doing what he was. So when Lehder said, "I'd like you to think about working for me," he could see in Ward's eyes that the answer was yes, even if the man would need time to think about it.

"I'll think about it," Ward said.

"Fine," said Lehder, and presented him with a vial of cocaine to assist him in that process.

A week later, they met again to talk specifics. This time Carlos Lehder and Ed Ward negotiated a deal they called the Ten Point Agreement, as though they were diplomats in Geneva. Ward agreed to go to work for Lehder. Lehder promised to ensure supplies at the Colombian end. Ward would take responsibility for transportation and ground crews for unloading at the U.S. end, with Norman's Cay as a transit station. Loads would be limited to 250 kilos. Lehder would front Ward $600,000 to buy a faster, safer plane—a turboprop. He gave Ward a draft for $100,000 to cover the down payment; Ward would repay the loan at a rate of $100,000 per trip. He agreed to make ten trips. In return he would get a profit participation of ten kilos per trip. And he would be paid a fee of $400,000 each time, out of which he had to pay all his salaries and expenses. Ed Ward's experience at Sears had taught him how to do quick number work in his mind, but it didn't take a mathematician to multiply ten times $400,000, subtract $600,000 from the total and conclude that Ed Ward was on the road to real wealth.

There was only one problem. Ward had not yet mentioned any of this to his associates. Lehder supposed that he was not optimistic about their reactions. Indeed, Ward had admitted that although in the end she had acquiesced, his own wife was opposed to any involvement in the cocaine business, and Ward had suggested that the wives of his associates probably would be too. In his entire relationship with Ward, this was the only surprise: Lehder was amazed at the decision-making power of American wives. It reinforced his contempt for the whole society.

On September 6, Carlos Lehder knocked on the door of Ed Ward's octagonal house. Ward, smiling his salesman's smile, opened it himself; the smile might have been in place, Lehder saw, but Ward's eyes looked worried. This man would never be a threat.

Ward ushered him into the house and introduced him to his associates—the von Eberstein brothers, Lev Francis, the chief pilot, and three or four others from the Jacksonville group; but none of the wives, Lehder thought with amusement, imagining the man hurrying back to their suburban homes to make their reports.

"This is Joe Lehder," Ward said. Joe had once been an alias; Lehder still encouraged Americans to call him by that name—it seemed to put them at ease. "He's going to tell us how we can make a lot of money."

"We're already making a lot of money," someone muttered; one of the von Ebersteins.

"It's diddley-squat," Ward said, "compared to what Mr. Lehder's talking about. Guys. Are we going to give him a listen or not?"

They gave him a listen. In fact, Lehder let Ward do most of the talking. He described the amount of money involved, and how easy it would be with their transportation system already in place. Lehder studied the men's faces as Ward spoke. He saw that the initial reaction of all of them would be negative. Negative, but not deeply negative. These men were the kind who needed time to adapt to anything new. They had already crossed the line into drug smuggling; now it was only a question of product. They would come around; or at least enough of them would to make the proposition viable.

"Why's he need us in the first place, Ed?" said one of the Jacksonville people.

"Can you answer that, Joe?" asked Ward.

Lehder smiled. The real reason was that he didn't want to be in the position of ever having to enter the U.S. again. Falling into the hands of the U.S. law enforcement system was the only possibility he feared. Nothing else could hurt him. "That's a good question," he replied. "And there's a simple answer—I want U.S. pilots, familiar with U.S. aviation rules. I want to blend right in, like fish in the sea."

"Fair enough?" asked Ward.

His associates nodded. That made sense to them. But in the end, no amount of Ward's cajoling could persuade them to go along with the arrangement. "Guys. I don't understand you." Ward was getting nervous. Maybe he thought that the whole deal was collapsing, and with it his dreams of money, big and quick. At that point, Lehder assured him, in front of the others, that he had no reason to worry on that account. They would go ahead as planned. He advised the others to think it over, but put no pressure on them. That could come later, if necessary.

"That's enough of this, Ed," Lehder said. "Why don't we go over to the villas and relax a little?"

Ward had rented two of Phil Kniskern's villas to house the Jacksonville visitors. Lehder, Ward and Ward's associates drove over to the villas. They played a little cards. They drank a little booze. They snorted a little coke, courtesy of Joe. Lehder took some too, breaking one of his rules, although it wasn't as strict a rule as it had once been. He wanted to appear polite. Besides, he enjoyed it. A little coke couldn't hurt him. To tell the truth, it made him feel even more charismatic than usual.

That night, back inside Volcano, Carlos Lehder had a visit from Steve Francis. Francis handed him a manila folder. Inside were several photographs of a tanned, stocky man, one of them shot from an aircraft. The man looked slightly familiar. Had Lehder seen him before? "Who's this?" he asked.

"Novak," said Francis. "The hammerhead guy."

"Oh yeah. The hammerhead guy. Let me know if he shows up again."

"Sure."

Lehder stared at the photographs for a few moments. When he looked up, Francis was still there. Lehder realized that he must still be a little stoned: time was warped. Francis must be waiting for some kind of payment, Lehder supposed, cash or cocaine. Francis was scum, but useful scum. "I'm thinking of putting you on retainer, Steve," Lehder said.

"Retainer?"

"How does ten grand a month sound?"

"What you say?"

"Ten thousand a month, U.S."

Francis was speechless. Lehder peeled the first installment off the roll in his pocket. Francis left, trailing a vapor of obsequious good-byes.

It was quiet inside Volcano. Lehder thought of switching on John Lennon, possibly the "Imagine" album, but he decided to listen to the sounds of the sea instead. He was at peace, safe and at peace on his island refuge. He took out the cocaine left over from the party at Kniskern's villas and sniffed a tiny bit more. He felt good. Feeling good, with the sea whispering all around him, he studied the pictures of the hammerhead man. A man of science, Lehder thought; well, everyone has his place.

7

Richard Novak had no difficulty getting to Norman's Cay the second time. He was flown over by Phil Kniskern's pilot in Kniskern's plane on September 7. At the airstrip he was met by Victor Forbes, who immediately ushered him into one of the hotel shuttles to take him on a tour of the island. It was hurricane season. The air was still and the sun hot, beating down with enervating force. Novak hardly noticed the thin black man leaning against a motorcycle near the boarded-up customs shed, doing nothing in particular.

The meeting with Kniskern had changed Novak's perspective. He saw Norman's Cay in a new way now, observing things on the tour that he hadn't before. How private the houses were, he thought, separated by dense growths of pine, sea grapes, lignum vitae, casurinas, and mahogany. Narrow flower-lined paths led down to the houses from the road. As they passed each one, Forbes would slow down to tell Novak about the residents. Novak learned that most of them had other houses in Florida or Nassau and spent little time on Norman's. They flew over in their private planes to party at the hotel or do a little bonefishing in the pond. Take, for example, the octagonal house less than a mile from the strip. Its owner, the Fat Man, had another house in Fort Lauderdale. He also had two twin-engine Beach Bonanzas; they were identical, painted white with brown trim. Forbes talked a little more about the Fat Man, telling Novak that his name was Ed Ward and that he was an airplane mechanic and former Sears appliance salesman. Novak wondered momentarily how someone like that could afford a beach house on Norman's Cay, but what really interested him about the Fat Man was the radio antenna outside the octagonal house. It was as tall as the one at Nassau International Airport. Novak was about to question Forbes about it when he heard a motorcycle behind them. As he turned, the motorcycle dipped behind the crest of a hill, but not before Novak recognized its driver: the thin man who had been hanging around the airstrip, doing nothing in particular.

"Who's that?" Novak asked.

"Who?" replied Forbes, glancing in the rear-view mirror and seeing no one.

"The fellow on the bike. With the gold chains around his neck."

"Oh," said Forbes. "That be Francis."

Stephen Francis, Forbes went on, came from a family of Exuma builders. Forbes made no effort to disguise his contempt when he told Novak that some of the residents gave Francis money to refrain from burglarizing their homes.

"They pay him not to rob them?" Novak said.

"As a service," Forbes said, making a little joke perhaps, as Stephen Francis shot by on his motorcycle and disappeared around a curve. Novak didn't like euphemisms, and he didn't like extortionists either. His mind remained on Francis while Forbes continued to point out houses and expostulate on their owners.

Owners such as Floyd Thayer, retired ship captain and electrical engineer who had made millions with his inventions. Years ago he had sought shelter in the pond during a hurricane. Now he could afford to live there. Thayer's house seemed deserted. "Does Francis look after his house too?" Novak asked.

"Kniskern he be the one to discuss the politics of the island," Forbes said.

Owners such as Jack Reed, a race car driver and the best pilot on the island. Forbes had heard that Reed had spent time in jail because his mistress was underage. And Terry Knight, a record producer and manager of rock bands, the most famous of which was Grand Funk Railroad. He enjoyed spending the profits of his heavy-metal years on wild parties out on the pond. Novak wasn't much interested in rock music. He was interested in all the antennae and concrete-block guardhouses he saw. He asked how many residents there were, but Forbes didn't have the answer. Not long ago, he had known each one. That was before the real estate boom had brought in all the newcomers.

Soon Novak had his first look at the eastern arm of the island. Wild animals, including sheep, peacocks, and an enormous pig named Judy, ran free in a section of the eastern arm that had been designated a national park. Forbes talked about the park and its abundance of flora and fauna, but his description had much less effect on Novak than the glimpse of a lone cormorant on a rock in the pond. When he had first come to Florida, cormorants had been a common sight; now they were rare. That cormorant on a rock in the lagoon at Norman's Cay meant more to Novak that any rock music producer, jet pilot, or self-made millionaire. Was there anyone else on the island who felt the same way, or was the beauty of the island wasted on its inhabitants? Novak didn't ask himself questions like that.

But he listened closely enough to Forbes's description to realize that almost all the houses on the eastern arm had changed hands in the past three months. One of the most notable had a conical central section. It had a view of the lagoon on one side and of the sea on the other, guaranteeing spectacular sunrises and sunsets, and a cooling breeze all day long. It was Novak's favorite of all the houses he had seen; the kind of house he himself would own if he could afford to. Forbes explained that the owner was a South American businessman named Carlos Lehder. It seemed that he had paid for it in small bills; when the money was counted, the sum proved to be ten thousand dollars in excess of the agreed price.

"I don't understand," Novak said.

Forbes gave no further explanation.

Novak might have made more of an effort to understand had he not spotted a red Scarab racing boat in the pond. It was the kind of boat someone who had spent time at sea didn't forget easily. Novak had seen it before, in several Florida marinas and in Nassau.

"The *Fire Fall*," Forbes said. "Lehder's boat." And Lehder, it developed, was the host of the reception at the hotel scheduled for that night. The dark-haired man standing in the cockpit at that moment was Lehder, Forbes said. Lehder was too far away for Novak to distinguish his features. "Worth two hundred thousand dollars, man," Forbes said. "That boat." As Novak watched, the *Fire Fall* cut a circle in the pond and sped toward its entrance. There Novak saw an armada of pleasure craft cruising in from the open sea: big and beamy boats that had one thing in common—they all cost more money than Richard Novak had made or would make in his life. They had motored in for the party. Novak knew at once that he had nothing in common with the people on those boats. Nature on Norman's Cay fascinated him more than ever, but at that moment he decided he had no interest in the politics of the island.

This decision was not realistic, for three reasons. The first was the size of Norman's Cay. It was too small to permit the neutrality of any resident on any issue of importance. Second, Novak wasn't the kind of man who could keep his own counsel when it came to anything that conflicted with his beliefs. The third reason had to do with the character of the man who was hosting the party. Perhaps Novak was half aware of the improbability of his sticking to the decision when he made it. In any case, his awareness grew at the party.

Novak entered the dining room of the hotel early in the evening. Outside, the sun was going down and the sky was ablaze. Inside, the air was full of cigarette and cigar smoke and the dining room and bar were full of people, most of them men, a few women. One of the women was Paulette Jones. She welcomed Novak and led him to a buffet. The food looked as good as anything he might have found at a hotel in Nassau or Miami—spiny lobster, shrimp, barbecued steak, conch fritters, fresh fruit—but Novak wasn't ready to eat. He wanted to circulate first. Kniskern had said this would be a good opportunity to get acquainted with some of the new residents. As Novak mixed himself a rum-and-tonic, Paulette said:

"Here is someone you should meet."

Novak turned and found himself looking into the alert and intelligent eyes of the dark-haired man he had seen at Treasure Cay months before. Novak recognized him at once, partly because he was a keen observer with a good memory, partly because of the other man's presence, sensed from a distance at Treasure Cay, felt much more strongly now, up close.

"Mr. Novak," said Paulette. "This is Mr. Lehder."

There was no sign of recognition in the alert and intelligent eyes. Novak held out his hand and felt it gripped by one of about the same size. "Welcome to my party," said Lehder.

"It's Mr. Lehder's birthday," Paulette explained.

"Congratulations," Novak said. "How old are you?"

"Twenty-nine," Lehder replied.

He looked even younger. With his long hair, unlined face, trim and muscular body, Lehder could have passed for a contemporary of one of Novak's sons. But Novak knew right away that Lehder far surpassed them in self-assurance, poise, and worldliness. He absorbed all that just from being on the receiving end of Lehder's smile. At that moment, maybe simply because of the sight of the bared white teeth, Novak made a connection in his mind between Lehder and the hammerheads he hoped to research on Norman's. This was not necessarily a negative image. Novak didn't fear hammerheads; he respected them and was fascinated by them.

"Enjoy yourself, Professor," Lehder said, gesturing to the buffet. Then he moved off. He had nice manners and spoke English without an accent, although his speech couldn't be called cultured. Novak watched him. He saw how Lehder moved with a certain grace, and saw also how finely, tastefully dressed he was compared to most of the others in the room. The men seemed to favor flashy jackets and lots of gold jewelry; Lehder wore a silk suit that whispered what all the others were trying to shout.

Novak walked around the room. He was introduced to a few people, including Ed Ward, the Fat Man. Ed Ward wasn't fat in a grand sense, like Sidney Greenstreet; he was fat more in a K-mart clerk sense. But neither Ed Ward nor the others showed any interest in Novak; indeed, they were almost unfriendly. The only person who did pay attention to him was Stephen Francis, who stared at him several times from behind the bar, where he ladled conch chowder from a tureen. After a while, Novak was sitting by himself at one of the dining room tables. This was not the kind of outing he enjoyed. It was loud, it was smoky, he didn't care much for the look of the people, and everyone seemed to be drinking heavily, everyone except Carlos Lehder, that is, who didn't touch a drop. Novak was thinking about slipping out for a walk on the beach when Phil Kniskern sat down beside him.

"Having a good time?" Kniskern asked.

Novak said something noncommittal. A well-built blonde woman walked by. When she was out of hearing, Kniskern said: "Have you met Lehder? That's his German teacher. And his mistress."

"His mistress?"

"His wife stayed home tonight."

"Home on Norman's?"

"Yes. Although she spends most of her time in Florida."

"How does he handle that proximity?" Novak asked.

"He handles it," Kniskern replied. "They say he has another woman at his house in Nassau, and another in Florida."

"That takes money, if nothing else."

"Oh, he's got money," Kniskern said. He told Novak that Lehder was president of Titanic Air, an international plane brokerage. He had told residents on Norman's that he bought passenger planes, refitted them for cargo, and sold them to transport companies in Florida.

"And there's a lot of money in that?" Novak asked.

"Seems to be," Kniskern replied. "Apparently he's recently decided to relocate in Nassau. That's why he bought on Norman's. He wants a nice place to raise his children." Kniskern didn't have to mention the lack of a Bahamian income tax, or the confidentiality of Bahamian banking procedures. They formed the subtext of much of what happened in the nation.

"He speaks German?" Novak said.

"Yes."

"So do I."

"The two of you should have a talk some time," Kniskern said.

The two men lapsed into silence. Novak felt like an outsider; then he noticed that Kniskern himself didn't appear to have an easy relationship with the new residents. He wondered if Kniskern was in some way an outsider too. He had no opportunity to get into that, because Kniskern, his voice full of optimism and enthusiasm, began to talk about the wonders of the reef off Norman's.

"I have no problem with the reef," Novak said. "It's the rest of the island I'm having doubts about."

Kniskern's smile faded, but only slightly. "My fault. I should have put you in one of the beach houses."

"It's not that," Novak said. "The hotel is fine."

"The scuba shop?"

"It's fine too." Better than fine. It would make a perfect

base for what Novak wanted to do. It had its own generator, powerful enough to run a good-sized compressor, and the underground storage tanks would hold all the fuel the *Reef Witch* would need for months. Novak's difficulties arose not from what Kniskern had told him about Norman's but from what had remained unsaid. "I thought I had a handle on everything when we talked in Nassau," Novak told Kniskern. "Now I get the feeling that there's a lot more to this."

"In what way?"

"I don't know. Things are a bit strange here, that's all."

"How do you mean?"

"It's hard to describe," Novak said.

"Does it have to do with Forbes?" Kniskern asked. "I've been meaning to talk to him about his manner with the guests."

"It's not Forbes." Novak hesitated for a moment and then all his worries about Norman's, until then unexpressed even to himself, came pouring out. He began by telling Kniskern about the trouble he had had first getting to Norman's, then how hard it had been to get a room at the hotel.

"It's no secret that there have been management problems at the hotel," Kniskern said. "That's one of the things I hope to eradicate. With your help."

"Maybe it's that," Novak said. "But what about all the private pilots flying in and out? There's almost as much air traffic as in Nassau. And what about the plane I saw last time with a photographer shooting pictures out the side? Not to mention another photographer on the beach the next day. And there was the steamer making a run around the north shore, miles from the shipping lanes."

"That's not so unusual," Kniskern said. "This is one of the best harbors in the Exumas."

"I know that," Novak responded impatiently. "But how do you explain the way that man followed Forbes and me around the island today?" He nodded toward Francis, behind the bar.

"Francis?"

"Yeah."

Kniskern looked skeptically at Novak. "Are you saying it's all my imagination?" Novak asked. "Well, it's not my imagination that no one on this island except you, Forbes, and Paulette have said more than two words to me. That's not what I call a warm welcome."

Kniskern didn't speak for a moment. Then he rose, picked up his drink, and said, "Let's go outside."

Kniskern, Scotch in hand, lead the way out of the dining room and onto the hotel patio. He didn't appear to notice that some of the partygoers watched their exit, but Novak did. The two men sat on comfortable deck chairs overlooking the harbor. The night was warm and quiet. Bobbing lights shone from the boats in the harbor and the sky was full of stars. It was beautiful.

Kniskern sighed. "I guess I should have told you a little more about what's been going on around here."

"Like what?" Novak asked.

Kniskern raised his glass to his lips and took a big swallow. "How can I put this?" he said. "Some of the residents—not all, but some—don't seem to care for the plans I have in mind for Norman's."

"Like Francis," Novak said.

"Like Francis," Kniskern acknowledged. "And others. They've gone so far as to make trouble at the hotel and around the island."

"What kind of trouble?" Novak asked.

Kniskern took another drink. "Like you, I thought it might have been my imagination at first. Little things. Residents of my houses complaining that the water in the cisterns had gone bad. People not feeling welcome in the hotel. The generators shutting down, not just sometimes, the way it is in the islands, but too often. Same thing with the phone service. And the mail not being delivered."

Novak thought of a few things he could add to Kniskern's list. He said, "Does all that have anything to do with Dave Woodward leaving?"

"I'm not sure," Kniskern said. "But I do know that he became one of those residents who no longer felt part of the island."

The sounds of people singing "Happy Birthday" drifted out onto the patio. Novak turned and through the window saw the party guests ringed around Carlos Lehder, toasting him with raised glasses and bottles. "Are you telling me that you have competitors?" Novak asked.

"Competitors?" said Kniskern.

"For buying the hotel. Developing the island."

Kniskern drained his glass. "I'm not really sure."

"Could Lehder be one of them?" Novak asked.

"I can't answer that either. There's no evidence. The only evidence points to Kehm, but he doesn't have the connections." Novak hadn't yet met Chuck Kehm, but he had seen him and his tall wife, Lexi, aboard their thirty-six-foot Crocker ketch, where they lived with their two little children in the lagoon.

"I thought he was no longer island manager," Novak said.

"That's true."

"What's he doing now?"

"I can't honestly say."

There was a silence. When Kniskern spoke again he had somehow fueled himself with another dose of optimism. "Look," he said, "the fact is I've got the hotel negotiations locked up. Plus there isn't anyone else who's even in a position to compete."

"Really?" said Novak. "I've seen some of the houses that have been sold recently. Judging from the prices, there must be a dozen people in a position to buy the hotel, and more."

"I didn't mean just financially," Kniskern said. "I've got the only realistic development proposal. Anyone who thinks that Norman's can become a big resort like something in Nassau or Freeport doesn't know much about the islands. The banks are aware of that, and so is Meridian."

Some of Kniskern's optimism rubbed off on Novak, but

not all. He had seen real estate battles before, had seen what they did to Florida, to the Keys. Kniskern pulled his chair a little closer. "I've been in the real estate business a long time, Dick," he said. "I've developed an instinct for how deals are going to turn out. My instinct tells me that this is going to turn out fine. In another month or so, I'll have finished the negotiations and we can start turning plans into reality."

Novak said nothing. He thought about putting plans into reality.

Kniskern sat back, relaxing on his deck chair. He pointed out a strip of land north of the marina. "That's one of my favorite parcels on the whole island. Protected from the ocean and close to the beach. Not to mention the scuba shop. An ideal spot to put up a house, really."

Novak got the hint. His mind stopped raising questions about Norman's and began to occupy itself instead with visions of a rosy future: long days spent on the reef or out in the pond in a paradise partly of his own making; and peaceful evenings spent in harmony with his reunited family.

8

Richard Novak was the kind of father who related best to his children while they were little. The closer they got to adulthood, the more his rough edges rubbed them the same way they rubbed most other people. Novak had not really thought this out, and so was less than fully prepared for his first conversation in three months with his son Chris, now on the verge of adulthood.

The day after Carlos Lehder's birthday party, Phil Kniskern flew Novak back to Nassau. Kniskern talked the whole way about his plans for Norman's. His words provided a soothing sort of background music for Novak's thoughts about reuniting his family in a happily-ever-after life on the island. It never occurred to him that even if Kniskern's plans were realized, it might be too late. After all, two of his sons were in their twenties, and the third, Chris, was nineteen.

In Nassau, Novak sent a telegram to Chris in Fort Lauderdale, asking his son to meet him in Miami. Novak wanted to tell Chris all about Norman's. He didn't spend much time thinking of the best way to make his presentation. The idea was obviously wonderful, and no one could fail to see that.

They met in the hall of the main terminal at Miami airport and shook hands. Chris seemed a little bigger, a little older, than he had the last time Novak had seen him. He was a good-looking young man; Novak thought there was a resemblance to his own teenage self. Perhaps there was, but any observer would have been more conscious of the contrast between them. Novak's skin was lined and toughened by wind and sun; Chris was fresh-faced. And Novak had the look of someone who had been kicking around the islands for some time. He wore sun-faded jeans and a worn polo shirt. There was nothing seedy about Chris—he wore a shirt and tie, and neatly pressed chinos.

"How was your trip?" Chris asked.

"Fine."

"No problems at customs?" Chris asked.

"Not this time," Novak replied. Chris was referring to an earlier trip when Novak had attempted to clear customs while bearing some organic marine specimens. A dispute had ensued, probably a noisy one, Novak thought, but why had Chris raised the issue now, and in such a barbed way? It reminded Novak of Chris's mother: Dorothy, his wife. Was his son going to be a man who looked like his father and acted like his mother? This was an uncomfortable thought for Novak, and he shied away from it.

"Let's eat," Chris said. They walked across the hall and into a cheerless cafeteria.

As they sat down at a Formica table with their dismal trays of food, Novak realized he should have invited his son to eat somewhere nice, out of the terminal. He was wondering if it still wasn't too late when Chris said that he had tried to reach Novak in Nassau, only to be told that his father had gone to Norman's Cay.

"Norman's Cay," Chris repeated. "I couldn't find it on the map."

And thus Richard Novak began this important meeting, if such a word can be used to describe a conversation between father and son, on the defensive. "Well," he said, "Norman's isn't labelled on most maps. What of it? It's small, and the locals like their privacy."

That was the truth, but it did nothing to wipe the skeptical expression off Chris's face. Richard Novak could sometimes be self-absorbed, and unaware of what might be happening beneath the surface, but this time he knew what was on Chris's mind. Chris and the rest of the family thought that Novak had taken a summer leave from Concordia to conduct a seminar in marine science in Nassau. They believed that because he had led them to do so. Chris and the others weren't happy about his spending the summer away from Dorothy and the young ones. Neither were they happy about the way the Key Largo operation had ended. They also knew that the doctors wanted Novak to restrict his marine activities to what could be done in the classroom.

But, in Novak's mind, all those problems would be resolved in one stroke when Kniskern's negotiations were concluded. So, rather than dealing with them one by one, or mentioning them at all, he began to tell his son about Norman's Cay: the reef that ran for eleven miles, the lagoon where the hammerheads came to mate, the perfect hurricane hole, the pristine water, the unique shape, so ideal for privacy, the wild animals that roamed the eastern arm, the beautiful beaches, the long airstrip. It was a paradise, yet nineteen minutes from Nassau. Was he getting the point across? Novak didn't know. He wasn't good at communicating that kind of thing, except to a fellow dreamer like Kniskern. Chris was not a dreamer, or possibly any dreams he might have shared about Norman's were squelched by familial resentments. But Novak, talking on, didn't realize that. Chris waited until he reached the end of the spiel. And then all he said was:

"How's the dive shop?"

To which Novak had to answer: "It's closed until the new management's in place."

A vague answer; an answer that exposed him to another skeptical look. All his talk of the wonders of the diving on Norman's had had no effect. That hurt: he had taught Chris to dive, had seen that his son had a special aptitude for it, had watched him grow to love the sea as he himself had grown to love it as a boy on Long Island Sound.

"Look, Chris," he said, "things are still in flux. But this is an enormous opportunity. For all of us."

"All of us?"

"This is a chance to start over," Novak said. "It couldn't be better." He went on to describe Norman's Cay as the perfect place to conduct the kind of research he had always wanted to conduct, and, although he didn't say it, to live the kind of life he had always wanted to live. He began expounding on the hammerhead question, but Chris cut him off.

"Teaching is what you're supposed to be doing now. For your health. And for everything else. Isn't it taking a big risk to give all that up for an island that's not even on the map?"

At some level, Novak knew that his son's question had merit. But he didn't want to spend the rest of his life in a classroom. It might have struck him that his son was more settled than he was.

For a while, neither of them spoke. They busied themselves with their unpalatable food as conversations in Spanish rose around them. Then Chris put down his plastic fork and said: "When was the last time you had a checkup?"

"I'm in great shape," Novak told him.

"But you're supposed to see the cardiologist regularly."

"I feel fine."

"Do the doctors know you've been diving?"

"No, but I'm fine. Better than ever, really."

Chris gave him a long look. "Okay," he said, almost brutally, "where are you going to get the money to open a dive operation on a place like Norman's Cay?"

"That part isn't going to be a problem," Novak replied. "I've got a partner. And I don't see it as a dive operation—it's going to be a research center." Novak told his son about Kniskern and his plan to live in one of Kniskern's beach villas until the deal went through and he could build a house of his own, sell the trailer in Key Largo, and move permanently to Norman's.

If Novak expected this news would please his son, he was disappointed. There was nothing to see on Chris's face but resentment. Too late, Novak realized that this all had to do with Chris's loyalty to Dorothy. He hadn't understood how deeply Chris, and probably the other boys, felt that he hadn't treated Dorothy fairly. That came as a shock. It also shocked him to see that his talk of starting over and reuniting the family had made such a small impression. He wondered for a moment how much his son blamed him for Dorothy's diving accident, or, for that matter, how much guilt Chris felt about it himself. Both of them had been on the *Reef Queen* when it happened. Perhaps that accident had wiped out any possibility of Dorothy ever going near the sea again, or becoming involved in anything that had to do with his marine plans. Was that the case? Had Dorothy already told Chris something like that? It occurred to him they they must have conversations he knew nothing about. Did Dorothy have plans of her own? What were they? He tried to guess the answers in the expression on Chris's face, but all he saw was a cool stare. He thought again of how his son had matured. In some ways, he seemed more mature, as the world judges these things, than his father.

Novak tried again, more conservatively this time. "I'm approaching this very cautiously," he said. "For the next while, I'll only be going to Norman's on short trips to map out the reef and organize the shop. I won't bring the *Reef Witch* over until I'm sure that the deal's going through."

Chris said nothing.

Novak felt his temper begin to stir. He took a deep breath. "I promise you," he told Chris, "I'm not going to make a big investment of any kind—not money, not time—until everything is certain."

Again Chris was silent; he stared down at the table top. Novak watched him, a young man who had once been a boy who loved nothing better than snorkeling or scuba diving with his father on the reef; a boy who became the best student that Novak ever had.

"How's flying coming along, Chris?" Novak asked quietly.

Chris reached into his pocket and dropped some papers on the table. Novak looked at them for a moment before realizing what they were: brand-new pilot certification credentials. His nineteen-year-old son was licensed to fly private and commercial light planes. Novak looked up, pride beginning to swell inside him.

"I graduated from F.I.T.," Chris said, referring to a noted pilot school outside of Fort Lauderdale. "That's why I called you in Nassau. Tried to call you, that is."

"Congratulations," Novak said. "That's great." But perhaps—because he was feeling a sudden pang of guilt that he hadn't been there for Chris at such an important moment, and then when they did meet, had spent the whole time talking about his own plans—perhaps his words weren't as full-bodied as they should have been. "It really is great, Chris. You've done a good job."

That brought a faint smile to Chris's face. He pointed out the window. "See that Piper? It's mine, at least partly."

"It is?"

Chris nodded.

"It's a beauty," Novak said. He reached out, maybe a little late, and shook his son's hand. It was the moment to forget about Norman's and make Chris aware of how proud he was. And Novak did spend the rest of their time together at the airport trying to put what he felt into words. But all the while, in the back of his mind, a new thought was struggling to be born: once he and Kniskern were in charge at Norman's, they would certainly need a pilot. And who would be better than his son? Novak even had a vision of Chris flying Dorothy down for the first time, of her liking the island, of her running the shop while he handled research on the reef. It was a vision of personal and familial fulfillment. He smiled happily at his son. His son smiled back. Chris would love Norman's Cay once he saw it, Novak thought. He was sure of it.

9

Phil Kniskern had said that he needed a month to complete his negotiations with Meridian. A month passed. Richard Novak heard nothing from Kniskern. During that time, he returned to his professorship at Concordia. He tried to concentrate on his courses, German 201 for intermediates and German 310, *Die Deutsche Novelle: Realismus und Naturalismus*, for advanced students. He tried to instill in them an appreciation for writers like Gottfried Keller and Theodor Storm, Gerhart Hauptmann and Adalbert Stifter. But his mind wasn't really involved. His mind was on Norman's Cay.

On the first long weekend of the term, Novak packed his regulator and his tanks and flew down to Norman's. Half an hour after landing, he was cruising over the northern approach to the reef on Victor Forbes's Whaler. A strong breeze was blowing and the air was fresh and salty. Novak forgot everything but the sea. He hadn't even stopped to check into the hotel.

Standing in the bow, Novak suddenly leaned forward and called out, "Slow down."

Forbes pulled back on the throttle. Off to the right, Novak got a clear look at what he thought he had spotted: two young hammerheads, each about three feet long, swimming close to the surface. "See them?" he said.

"Yeah," Forbes answered.

"Keep them on your right."

"Okay."

They followed the sharks along the edge of the reef and out into open water. There the hammerheads dived and disappeared. "They'll be back," Novak said. He explained that hammerheads and other sharks were possibly responsive to the earth's magnetic signals, and used that sense to orient themselves. It was likely that there was some sort of magnetic anomaly deep under Norman's Cay which allowed the hammerheads to home in on the island from great distances in mating season. "Next time you see those two they'll be ten feet long."

"Not me, man." Forbes didn't appear to share Novak's interest in theories of magnetism, and he was afraid of sharks. But Novak knew he was going to need a local assistant, and Forbes, although illiterate, knew the waters, so he continued to talk about hammerheads as they swung around and headed back to the reef. After a minute or two, Forbes interrupted him. "Best we go in," he said, and pointed at the horizon. Dark clouds were on the move.

"One more drop," Novak said. He didn't want to leave the reef; he didn't want to go back to Concordia. All he wanted to do was live his new life.

Grudgingly, Forbes tossed the anchor over. He kept looking at the clouds, coming quickly now across the sky. "Ten minutes," Novak said, donning his gear. He was about to plunge over the side when something in the distance caught his eye. It was a long black shape silhouetted against the white beach of a little cay off Norman's shore. At first he thought it was a tree. Then he thought it might be a boat. He measured it against some of the nearby palms: a big boat; in fact, a ship. "What's that?" he said, pointing.

"Just a cay," Forbes replied. "Ain't got no name. Nothin' on it but land crabs," he added, in case Novak was contemplating an expedition.

"Then what's that on the beach?"

"What?"

"The thing that looks like a ship."

Forbes barely glanced at it. He shrugged.

"Let's take a look," Novak said.

"Why?" Forbes asked. "Ships be running aground in the Exumas all the time."

"Maybe there's someone on board," Novak said. "Maybe they need help." Plus he was curious by nature; even nosy. He doffed his gear and packed it in the stern. "Come on."

"No time," Forbes said, gesturing at the sky. The storm was coming fast. The wind began to blow hard and the sea grew rough.

Novak pulled the anchor. "There's time," he said.

With a sulky expression on his face, Forbes turned the wheel and headed for the nameless cay. It had a semicircular harbor fringed by a shallow reef. Novak had learned that Forbes knew every cut in every reef in the northern Exumas, so it surprised him when Forbes took so long to find the cut in this one. Perhaps he was hoping that Novak would give up. But Novak didn't. Forbes found the cut and glided through, into calmer water. He guided the bow of the whaler onto the beach and Novak jumped out.

The ship lay canted, partly on the beach, partly in the water, its keel stuck deep in the sand. There was no one aboard and the deck was bare. Novak's first thought was that he had seen it before. He looked more closely at its white superstructure and reddish hull, and remembered the steamer he had wondered about on his first trip to Norman's. He couldn't be certain, but he thought this was the same ship.

"How long has she been here?" he asked.

Forbes shrugged.

Novak couldn't believe that the beaching and apparent abandonment of such a large craft would not be news in a small place like Norman's. "Are you saying this is the first you've heard about it?" he asked.

"Don't know nothin' about it, man," Forbes said, looking anxiously at the sky.

"I don't understand how it got here," Novak said. Forbes was silent. Novak ran his hand over the hull. It was unmarked, giving no evidence of any battering. He tried to imagine some storm that would have carried the ship safely through the reef and onto the beach. It was almost an impossibility. If the skipper had lost control in a storm, the ship would surely have been dashed against the coral. Therefore it had steamed deliberately through the narrow cut and just as deliberately onto the beach. But why?

The first drops of rain speckled the water. "Let's go, man," Forbes said. Reluctantly, Novak returned to the Whaler and Forbes wheeled around, heading for home. It was only then that Novak noticed that the steamer's stern bore neither a name nor a port of call. He could make out the layer of fresh white paint where the words had been obliterated. Novak was just about to ask Forbes to go back in case closer examination might reveal what was written underneath the paint when a bolt of lightning burst across the sky, and thunder boomed. Novak's heart began beating wildly and he flinched as though he had been struck.

Richard Novak was terrified of thunder, had been since he was a child, and had never outgrown it. Richard Novak, a man who swam with hammerheads and dove deep in the sea, had this secret fear. "Hurry up," he barked at Forbes. Forbes regarded him with amazement, but he pressed the throttles all the way down. The Whaler surged toward the reef. Novak crouched in the bow the whole way back to Norman's, clutching the rails with all his might.

The storm had passed by the time they tied up at the dock. Novak walked up to the hotel with the intention of making a telephone report about the steamer to the police. He entered the lobby and found it exactly the same as on his first visit: deserted. "Hello?" he called. "Hello?"

There was no response. He picked up the phone on the reception desk and tried to place the call to the police by himself. He was unable to get a dial tone. Novak reached for the registration book, turned it around and began leafing through. It appeared that there had not been a single hotel guest since his last visit. He was still going through the book when Paulette Jones entered through the front door.

They looked at each other in surprise. Her manner was less than welcoming. "I didn't know you were coming back," she said, moving behind the desk. "I'm afraid there's no room at the hotel. We're booked solid." She slid the registration book away from him and closed it firmly.

Novak was amused that she would try running him through the identical paces that had ended in failure the first time. "That's all right," he said. "I'll be staying in one of Mr. Kniskern's beach houses."

"Oh."

"But first," Novak continued, "I'd like you to put me through to the police in Nassau."

Paulette's eyes narrowed. "The police?"

Novak described what he had seen on the nameless cay. "I don't think the police would be interested in something like that," Paulette said. "Boats go aground all the time in the Exumas."

"So I hear," Novak said. "But I think the police will be interested in this one."

"I doubt it. In any case, it's not possible right now. The phones are out."

"What about ship-to-shore?"

"We don't have the range."

Novak remembered the tall antennae he had seen here and there on the island, and suggested they approach a resident who could at least reach Highbourne Cay.

"That is not possible," Paulette said.

"Why not?"

"It just isn't." She opened a drawer and took out a ring of keys. "Here," she said.

"What's that?"

"The keys to the Smuggler's Beach Villas—Mr. Kniskern's houses," Paulette replied.

"You told me there were no locks on Norman's," Novak said.

"There are now."

"Why?"

Paulette hesitated. "There's been a little trouble at some of the houses."

"What kind of trouble?" Novak asked.

"Minor trouble," Paulette answered. "Nothing to be concerned about. Have a nice visit, Mr. Novak." She turned, walked into the office, and closed the door.

10

Richard Novak, asleep in the cool and comfortable beach house that belonged to Phil Kniskern but that he already considered his own, dreamed he had left the compressor running. He awoke in the middle of the night to engine sounds.

Although the villa had fine ocean views, the bedroom where Novak slept looked out on the airstrip, not more than fifty yards away. The engine sounds came from that direction. Novak rose and fumbled in the dark for a pair of shorts. As he pulled them on, a car door slammed, not far away. Novak peered through the slats of the storm shutters.

He saw the yellow headlights of a pickup truck shining across the runway. The beams focused on an airplane, sitting on the strip. Novak could hear its idling engine, see the dust raised by its spinning propellers, see the red and green glow of its taillights. The plane had either just landed or was about to take off. Both actions were improbable. The airstrip on Norman's Cay had no lights, no radar, no control tower. Novak wondered briefly whether someone had fallen seriously ill and had to be evacuated. Knowing CPR, he thought he might be of some use. He was about to dash outside when he noticed a number of shadowy figures moving between the plane and the nearby boarded-up customs house. Whenever one of them happened to step into the beam of the pickup's headlights, Novak saw a shotgun in silhouette. He stayed where he was. After a while, he thought he recognized the plane: it was the one that had circled over him on his first day on Norman's, with a photographer leaning out and snapping pictures. He thought about that for a few minutes, but it led him nowhere, and no amount of peering through the storm shutters brought further revelations. Novak was baffled, and he didn't accept bafflement easily. He groped around for the rest of his clothes.

Dressed, he entered the living room, found matches, and lit a kerosene lamp. He carried it to the front door, intending to go outside, walk around the house and over to the airstrip. He got as far as opening the door. There he stopped and stood motionless for a few moments. Then he blew out the lamp, went inside, took his shark-emergency pistol from the drawer in the bedside table, tucked it into the waistband of his shorts, and moved cautiously out into the night.

The air was warm and smelled of the exhaust of burning airplane fuel. Novak walked softly along the porch that ran beside the beach house, down the stairs and into the cover of the scrub that lined the runway. He was being very quiet, but not so quiet that the crabs weren't aware of him. He could hear them brushing against dry fallen leaves as they scuttled away. Novak knelt in the sand behind a small pine that grew on the edge of the strip.

From there the plane was less than twenty yards away. Novak could see a man sitting behind the wheel of the pickup, and three more standing around the plane. Of these, the first pumped fuel into the plane from a tank on the back of the pickup, the second hefted bags that looked like mail sacks from the truck into the plane, and the third talked on a hand-held radio to unseen others who responded in crackly voices. Novak recognized this third man: Ed Ward, the Fat Man, at one time—or was he still? Novak couldn't remember exactly what Forbes had told him—appliance salesman for Sears. No one appeared in need of CPR, not even the man toting the sacks, which were heavy and numerous.

Novak remained where he was, kneeling behind the tree. The fuel pumper finished pumping and uncoupled his hose. The sack carrier loaded his last sack. With a grunt audible to Novak, Ed Ward climbed into the pilot's seat of the plane and revved the engines. The other men got into the pickup. It drove to the head of the runway, turned, and stopped. The driver flicked on the highbeams, projecting a cylinder of light along the strip. Meanwhile, Ed Ward taxied to the other end of the strip and circled. After a pause, the plane rolled forward, gathering speed. It roared past Novak in a boiling cloud of dust, shooting toward the pickup. He kept expecting the wheels to lift off the ground, but they did not until the very last moment. Ed Ward's plane barely cleared the pickup, and its red and green taillights wobbled as it rose into the sky. Novak realized how heavily loaded it was.

The taillights disappeared in the darkness. The pickup drove back along the runway, passed Novak, and stopped at the customs shed. Several shadowy figures jumped into the back. The pickup turned off the runway, bumped onto the road, and was gone. The sound of its motor slowly faded to nothing. Then there was only silence.

Novak rose and walked onto the runway. He searched the night sky for any moving lights and saw none. He stood there for a little while, thinking about what he had witnessed. How smooth and well rehearsed the whole operation had been! It had not seemed like something being done for the first time. And yet, what risks were being run, taking off in a small overloaded plane from an unlit dirt strip at night. People took risks like that when they were making money in illegal ways, and Novak had seen evidence of such activity before. In the Keys, he had sometimes encountered soggy bales of marijuana lying on isolated beaches, and once he had helped Gus Holleran and other narcotics agents investigate a sunken plane that had gone down with a cargo of cocaine. So Novak knew that Ed Ward had flown a shipment of illegal drugs out of Norman's Cay a few minutes before, and given the size of the load, he suspected that it had been marijuana: the profits from the sale of a similar amount of cocaine would have permitted the former Sears salesman to acquire the whole chain, and Novak couldn't imagine drug dealing on a scale like that.

Standing on the dirt strip, he thought about Ed Ward. Now he understood a few things. How, for example, an appliance salesman could afford to set himself up on Norman's Cay. And why he would want to. Then he remembered the locks that had been installed since his last visit, and Paulette's intimation that there had been trouble on the island. How compatible were his plans for building a research center with Ed Ward's narcotics business and his shotgun-toting companions? How could his dream of reuniting his family on Norman's, how could Kniskern's entire concept, coexist with Ward's activity? As a practical matter, the island was much too small. And as a moral matter, Novak could not stomach anything to do with illegal drugs. Novak was not the kind of man to stick his head in the sand in circumstances like these. Real estate wars were bad enough. Real estate wars that had their roots in nighttime drug runs were intolerable. Ed Ward would have to go.

A twig snapped in the scrub. The sound made Novak jump, and his hand went to the gun in his waistband as he scurried into the shadows at the edge of the runway. Crouching in the bushes, he listened with all his concentration, but heard no more snapping twigs, nor any other menacing sounds. All he could hear was the sea, never far away on Norman's. Nevertheless, when he returned to the beach house, it was as noiselessly as possible.

Rounding the porch, he saw that the front door was open. Hadn't he closed it? He thought so, but couldn't remember. And even if he had, wasn't it likely that a breeze had pushed it open? Of course, but Novak drew his pistol as he went inside anyway, and pointed it around the darkness like an actor in a made-for-TV movie. No one saw this performance. The beach house was empty.

Novak returned the pistol to the drawer of the bedside table. He considered going back to bed, but knew he wasn't sleepy. Instead, he lit the lantern and brewed a pot of coffee. Then he sat on the porch, sipping from his mug, and watching the stars fade in a lightening sky, thinking.

There was only one thought, really. Ed Ward had to go.

11

A combination of coffee, sleeplessness, and the nocturnal activities he had seen on the airstrip on Norman's Cay made Richard Novak feel jittery the next morning. He was scheduled to meet Victor Forbes for a reef dive after breakfast, a prospect he would normally be regarding with anticipation, but now he found himself almost ready to cancel it. His heart was beating too rapidly; he could feel it. His mind was in turmoil. To calm himself, although he would not have put it that baldly, Novak opened his Bible.

Save me, O God; for the waters are come into my soul. One of the Bible's attractions for Novak was its abundance of sea imagery. *I sink in deep mire, where there is no standing: I am come into deep waters, where the floods overflow me.* Novak, on the porch of the villa on Smuggler's Beach—how picturesque the image of smuggling in bygone days compared to the realities on the airstrip—read Psalms until it was time to meet Forbes.

They motored out to the reef. The water was calm and blue. Golden shards of reflected sunshine sparkled all around the boat, and when Forbes cut the engines there was nothing to hear but the sea sucking gently at the hull. Novak, donning his gear, was doing what he loved best in surroundings of perfect beauty, but he wasn't happy about it. He spent the morning mapping the reef. He was very quiet; no lectures for Forbes today on reef ecology or the mating patterns of hammerheads. Forbes noticed. As he prepared to raise anchor for the last time, he paused and said, "You sick, man?"

Novak, sitting in the stern with pen and notebook, looked up. He almost made some routine reply; almost. But he couldn't quite control himself. Perhaps a few more Psalms would have done the trick. In any case, he barked at Forbes, "Your Fat Man is a drug smuggler."

Forbes grunted, a grunt that another Bahamian might have been able to interpret, but Novak could not.

"I'm talking about Ed Ward," Novak said. "He's flying drugs out of Norman's at night. I saw him with my own eyes, so don't bother arguing about it."

Forbes shrugged. "I'm not arguing."

"So you admit you know about it?"

"Everyone be knowin' about it, man."

"What do you mean, 'everyone'?" Novak said, his voice rising.

"Everyone on Norman's. The residents. Mr. Kniskern."

"Kniskern knows about it?"

"It's no secret," Forbes said.

"I don't believe you."

Forbes shrugged.

"I can't believe Kniskern would proceed with his plans for the island if he knew something like that was going on."

Forbes's strong hands closed around the anchor line. "Forget about it, man."

"Forget about it?"

Forbes nodded and began pulling the anchor. Novak put down his notebook and rose. "Forget about it?" he repeated, moving toward Forbes.

"It's just the way it is," Forbes said. "They been here for a long time."

"I don't understand."

"Since seventy-six."

"What are you talking about, Forbes?"

"The Fat Man," Forbes replied. "And his people."

"His people?"

"You've seen them," Forbes said. "At Mr. Lehder's party."

"Is Mr. Lehder one of his people?"

This question brought a little smile. "No, man," Forbes said.

"What's so funny?" Novak asked.

The smile vanished. "Nuthin'." Forbes went on to explain who Ed Ward's people were: Paul Alexander, in charge of ground control; the bearded Greg von Eberstein, pilot, and like Ward a former Sears clerk; von Eberstein's older brother, Ernest; and Lassie, Ward's wife, a former dental assistant. All of them came from Orange Park, a suburb of Jacksonville, Florida. They were completely middle American in everything but their occupation. And of course they now had more money than most middle Americans. Lassie Ward sported a necklace of gold beads; she added a new one after every successful flight. Ward's group had been using the airstrip before the construction of most of the houses on the island. In the beginning, Ward had appeared for no more than one flight a month. Then Kniskern had built the Smuggler's Beach houses, and Ward and his people had leased them, becoming part of the year-round community. Now Ward had built his own house, the octagonal one with the enormous antenna, and the von Ebersteins owned another house nearby, the first one up from the airstrip. Sometimes, other associates took rooms at the hotel. And now too, Forbes said, there was more than one flight a month.

All this was unacceptable to Novak. Just as unacceptable was Forbes's attitude. "It's our history," he said. "We've had pirates and bootleggers and gunrunners. Now it's weed. So what?"

"So what? Something like this could ruin the whole island. I've seen it happen in Florida."

"This is different," Forbes said. "No one cares about a little weed down here."

"This isn't just a matter of a little weed," Novak said.

"And I care, for one. And so will the police in Nassau when they find out."

Forbes looked at him closely. "You going to tell them, man?"

"I don't know what I'm going to do," Novak answered. "But something has to be done, doesn't it?"

Forbes stowed the anchor in the bow. "Just forget about it, Mr. Novak. It's no good to get mixed up in island politics. Island politics is very complicated."

"This has nothing to do with politics."

Forbes made no reply. They returned to the dock in silence. Novak studied the map he had sketched of the reef. It was almost complete. The shop was in pretty good shape too. In another month he would be ready to bring the *Reef Witch* over from Florida, and soon after he could start bringing in groups of divers. If things went smoothly. And they were going smoothly, on the surface. If only he hadn't seen what he had last night. But he had. Did it really matter? Was it his problem? Novak struggled with the dilemma. Hadn't he promised Kniskern to stay out of island politics? Maybe Forbes was right, after all. And if something should be done about Ed Ward, wasn't it more Kniskern's responsibility than his? Yes, but according to Forbes, Kniskern knew all about Ward, and had done nothing.

Novak entered his villa on Smuggler's Beach and slammed the door. His heart was racing again. He paced the floor, in a miserable mood. Then he heard a plane coming in. He went out onto the back porch and watched it land.

The plane touched down on the strip, slowed, turned, and rolled to a stop by the customs house. It was a Beechcraft Bonanza, white with brown trim. It looked a lot like the plane he had watched taking off less than twelve hours before. This judgment was confirmed when the door opened and Ed Ward stepped down with a big smile on his round face. The pickup drove onto the runway, braked sharply beside the plane. Lassie Ward jumped

out and gave her husband a big kiss. Then Ward shook
hands with a few others who had been in the truck.
Novak recognized Greg von Eberstein. There was a bit of
whooping and high-fiving, as though Ward were a football
hero who had just taken one into the end zone for State.
Then everyone piled into the pickup and sped off toward
the hotel.

Novak walked onto the runway. He stood under the sun
for a few minutes, staring at the plane. Then he pivoted
and started for the hotel. His stride quickened as he
neared it. His heart was racing again, but there was nothing he could do about it.

Novak entered the hotel. Paulette was standing behind
the reception desk. She turned to him. Was there appre-
hension in her eyes? Novak wasn't sure, and he was going
too fast inside to deal with the problem. He barely noticed
Victor Forbes and Steve Francis standing by the kitchen
door, almost failed to apprehend that they had been talking
in low voices when he came in and had now fallen suddenly
silent. Novak caught the glint of Francis's gold chains as
he went by, and then he was in the dining room.

A few of the wealthy homeowners were lingering over
lunch. At the back of the room, several tables had been
pulled together, making a surface the size of something
that might be found in a corporate boardroom. Seated
around the table and already into their second drinks were
members of Ed Ward's corporation. Novak recognized
most of their faces, although he could put names to only
a few of them: Ward, Lassie, Greg von Eberstein. One or
two glanced up at Novak, then ignored him. Novak
paused. Once more, he faced the strong temptation to do
nothing. All the arguments ran again through his mind,
at fast-forward speed. And he might have done nothing—these people were criminals, after all, and he was
just a civilian in a foreign land—when someone at the
celebration laughed a braying laugh. Novak knew then
that even if it proved futile, he couldn't live with himself
if he said nothing. It was the laugh that did it. Perhaps

his dilemma was of a kind not subject to ratiocination; perhaps it demanded an emotional response.

Novak stepped forward and looked right at Ed Ward. "I want to talk to you about last night," he said. His voice sounded steady enough.

Ward turned to him. He had an amiable, down-home face, and a loose smile to go along with it. His eyes, Novak saw, were tired and bloodshot. Flying drugs at night through DEA cordons was not a stressless vocation.

"Do I know you?" Ward asked. "I don't think I do."

"The name's Novak," Novak told him. "We met at the reception here last month."

"Well, how do," said Ed Ward.

Novak moved a little closer. He was aware of Steve Francis slipping into the room behind him. "I saw what went on at the airstrip last night."

"Last night?" said Ward. "I'm not sure what you're talking about, fella." This was a delaying response, and not a very clever or original one. It was quite possible at that moment to picture Ed Ward at Sears, trying to cope with a dissatisfied customer. It was much harder to see him as a drug smuggler, and almost impossible to think him dangerous. Emboldened, Novak raised his voice.

"You're running narcotics off this island. I saw everything. Don't waste my time denying it."

The room fell silent. Novak was aware of staring eyes, not just at Ward's table, but also from the homeowners scattered around the room. He felt like the first person to voice an unpleasant truth secretly known by all, about the nonexistence of a caring God, say, or the impossibility of winning the war in Vietnam. The implication of this was that Forbes had told the truth: all the legitimate residents knew about Ward's operation, and were complaisant. This was an implication he should have examined, but there was no time.

Ed Ward, still smiling, although the amiability was gone from his expression, said, "You're mistaken, fella. I'm in the construction business. We flew a load of supplies to

Nassau last night. Not that I can see it's any of your concern, exactly."

Maybe Novak should have left it at that. He had said what he had come to say. But he couldn't leave it. "That's false, Mr. Ward," he said. "No one flies construction supplies at night from a strip with no lights and no radar." A feeling of power, perhaps unreal, surged through Novak and he went on. "I don't tolerate drugs. Not on my boat. Not in my classroom. And there's no place for them on this island, either. I intend to go to the police."

No one spoke. The resultant pause was perfectly timed for Novak to wheel and march out the door.

He walked out into the sunshine on a high that got higher and higher as the scene played itself over and over in his mind. He had freed himself of an enormous weight, and at the same time, he had done the right thing. Norman's Cay was a great place. What's more, the island needed him, Richard Novak, in a big way. Hadn't he just made that very clear? In the same sense that it was his duty to protect the reef from poachers and souvenir hunters, it was also up to him to protect what was above the high-tide line from Ed Ward and his like. Now he understood the nature of the trouble on Norman's: it was like a frontier town of pioneers cowed by an outlaw they didn't know how to handle. Well, Novak knew how to handle Ed Ward.

Drug smuggling was a police matter. That's what police were for. Why did societies organize themselves, anyway? Wasn't one of the main reasons to afford institutional, safe protection from criminals? Of course it was. Police headquarters were in Nassau. Novak flew to Nassau that day. He fully expected to return soon with a detachment of police, and half expected that Ward and his gang would have already fled by then, making Norman's once again an island fit for his dreams.

12

In their spiffy white jackets with red trim and brass buttons, the members of the Bahamian police force would not look out of place in a Gilbert and Sullivan chorus. Novak understood why such decorative outfitting was probably wise in a nation that depended so heavily on tourism. But as he climbed the stairs to police headquarters in Grosvener Square in Nassau, he hoped to find the sort of underlying efficiency promised by the neo-fascist uniforms worn by their colleagues in certain American cities.

"I have evidence," he said to a constable behind a tall counter, "of a large ongoing criminal operation centered in the Exumas."

He was given a form to fill out.

Novak spent some time with the form, trying to shape his story to fit its little boxes and categories, better suited for recording the details of a parking lot scrape or a purse snatching. He handed it in, inwardly pleased with the succint, fact-filled job he had done. The constable laid it on a pile, unread.

"Aren't you even going to read it?" Novak asked, his temper starting to fray.

The constable's eyes narrowed. "All reports are read," she said, "in due course." W. S. Gilbert might have spun a line like that into a zany number. Novak was angered.

"This is important," he said. "I'm not talking about some pickpocket in the market. This is a big drug-smuggling operation. People are carrying weapons around in the open. I've got names, dates, aircraft descriptions, and tail numbers. There must be someone in this building who wants to know about it. Someone higher up."

The constable gave him a look somewhere between a stare and a glare. Then the report was taken away. Novak sat.

Not long after, he was ushered into a cramped office overlooking a traffic jam. A sign on the desk said: "Dudley Hanna, Assistant Commissioner." Dudley Hanna had alert, intelligent eyes and a pencil mustache. He regarded Novak closely for a moment, then tapped the report on his desk with a pencil and asked a question Novak didn't like: "What's your interest in this?"

Novak didn't see what that had to do with anything. "I live on Norman's," he said, adding, "part-time," to head off any line of inquiry about residency requirements. "There's been some trouble on the island lately, and it's all traceable to these dope smugglers." He related everything Paulette had told him about the recent troubles, and recounted in detail all he knew about Ed Ward's operation. He gave the assistant commissioner names, nationalities, and descriptions of everyone involved.

Dudley Hanna didn't look shocked. He didn't even look particularly interested. If anything, he appeared mildly annoyed. Novak saw no reason for that, so doubted his own perception. After Novak finished talking, Hanna rose and walked to a wall map. It showed a big blue sea dotted with specks of green: the Bahamas.

The assistant commissioner pointed with his pencil. "One hundred thousand square miles," he recited. "Seven hundred islands and cays. That's on one side, Mr. Novak. On the other are three ships, thirteen patrol boats, one fishing smack, and two planes. Plus a department of three hundred men and women. Do you know how many places there are where a ship can be unloaded, or a light plane landed?"

"Many, I'm sure," Novak said. "But Norman's Cay is a

little different. For one thing, it can accommodate both ships and planes." He thought suddenly of the nameless tramp steamer beached on the nameless cay, and wondered exactly how big Ed Ward's business might be. "For another," he continued, "patrols won't be necessary, at least not for a long period. With the information I've given you, you should be able to make arrests soon."

Hanna looked at him impassively. "You're right," he said, snapping the eraser end of the pencil against the map, near, or maybe smack on the spot where the dot representing Norman's Cay must have been, had Novak been able to see it. "Norman's is different. It's always been controlled by foreign banks and foreign investors. A rich man's playground. And oh, so private. Privately owned. Privately managed. A remnant of colonialism, you might say."

"I don't see how that affects things, even if it's true," Novak said.

"No?" said Dudley Hanna, returning to his desk. "But you want me to spend public money in the interests of this private retreat, a private retreat providing no benefit to the Bahamian citizen, other than the few no doubt employed there in servile capacities."

Novak felt his temper beginning to rise. He tried to stay calm. "But something has to be done," he said. "Surely you accept that."

"Maybe," responded Hanna. "But not necessarily by us."

"Not necessarily by you?"

"It's not our problem. These are American criminals, flying into Florida. It's a matter for the police up there, and the famous DEA."

"But it's happening here," Novak said.

"I'm well aware of that, Mr. Novak. These islands are full of drug scum from your country. They come in their racing boats and their private planes. Is it our fault that the U.S. has a drug problem and we're on the shipping route?"

There was an answer to that question. Did the assistant commissioner really imagine that all the drugs brought into the Bahamas left for the U.S.? Some of them were going to stick. And drugs brought the same wads of dirty money and its attendant corruption that had done such sickening work in Florida. According to Gus Holleran, the customs inspector, it was already happening—vast amounts of cash were moving into Nassau banks. But there was more to it than corruption and dirty money. Drugs brought violence. He recalled that coroners in Miami had been forced to lease special trailers to store the bullet-ridden corpses awaiting autopsies. So the answer to the assistant commissioner's question was that the drug problem had already arrived. Novak kept this lecture to himself. He had a feeling that uttering it would be counterproductive. Instead, he said, "Look, commissioner, you're right, the situation in Florida is terrible, way beyond our control. But Norman's is a little place. Let's not allow one group of hoodlums to wreck it."

Hanna looked at him for a few moments, then shook his head. "There are priorities, Mr. Novak."

"What do you mean?"

"Norman's Cay is remote. There are so many other islands much closer to Florida in need of surveillance."

Novak's voice rose a little. "Remote? It's nineteen minutes from Nassau and an hour from Miami. And the police work on Norman's is more advanced than on these hypothetical other islands. The surveying part is over. I've done it myself. All you have to do is waltz in and take the glory."

For a moment, Dudley Hanna seemed ready to raise his voice too. Then he looked away, almost like a man ashamed of himself. "All right, Mr. Novak," he said quietly. "I'll take this up with my superiors."

"That's not good enough, commissioner," Novak said. He couldn't stop himself.

"Not good enough?"

"It sounds too slow. This is an urgent matter."

"That's why I am bringing it to the attention of my superiors. Are you telling me how to do my job?"

That's what Novak wanted to do, but he didn't say it.

"Good," said Hanna, relaxing slightly. He rose to signal the end of the meeting. Novak stayed where he was. The assistant commissioner stared down at him. "There will be an investigation, Mr. Novak. I promise you that."

Wasn't that promise the most Novak could have expected from this initial meeting? Probably, he thought, and got up. Dudley Hanna held out his hand. "Don't you want to know how to get in touch with me?" Novak asked.

"Oh, yes," said the assistant commissioner. He took down the information. The two men shook hands.

Novak left the police building in Grosvener Square and walked outside. It was a gray day, and a wind, raw for that time of year, was blowing. The tourists were in T-shirts but the market women were wearing their sweaters. Novak stood still for a little while, trying to come to terms with what had happened inside police headquarters. In the end he told himself that the situation on Norman's Cay was out of his hands now. He had unleashed the forces of the law.

The volume was turned up to the max. John Lennon's voice shook the walls of Volcano. For that reason, some time passed before Carlos Lehder heard someone calling, "Hello? Anybody home?" He turned down the volume and let Steve Francis inside.

"Mr. Lehder?"

"Yes?"

"You said for me to keep my eyes and ears open, right?"

"What is it?"

"The hammerhead man. He came back. He made some trouble at the club."

"What kind of trouble?" Lehder asked.

Francis told him how Richard Novak had boldly walked up to Ed Ward and his group and accused them of drug running.

"What did Ward do?" Lehder asked.

"Nothin'."

Lehder snorted with contempt. "And where is he now?" Lehder asked.

"The hammerhead man?" said Francis. "He gone. Off the island. I don't know where."

"Don't worry. He'll be back."

"He will?"

"So keep watching."

"Yes, Mr. Lehder."

Francis went away. Lehder thought about the hammerhead man. For a while, he had considered the possibility that Novak was a drug agent. Drug agents look like drug dealers, the Fat Man had said. But Richard Novak did not. And no drug agent would have pulled a scene like the one Francis had just described. Why then, Lehder wondered, had Novak done it? He, Lehder, had no fear of Ward and his gang, but most ordinary citizens would. What sort of citizen was Richard Novak? And what did he want on Norman's Cay?

13

Richard Novak returned to Concordia College and finished teaching the fall semester. The problems of Norman's Cay faded somewhat in his mind; the promise of Norman's did not. As soon as his last class was over, he flew down to Key Largo and began making preparations for his scuba and research center.

The *Reef Witch* had been on shore, outside Novak's trailer, for ten months. Novak cleaned it, oiled the machinery, and began loading his gear—tanks, regulators, weight belts, wet suits, masks, fins, snorkels, books, his motorcycle. He also cleaned and packed the gear that Chris had used in the past, and kept enough room in the stern to sleep an extra person. Chris hadn't been returning his phone calls lately, but perhaps he would before Novak set out. Time passed happily; he was doing real work, and that made Norman's real. More than ever, he let himself think of Norman's as his island, or at least he thought of himself as belonging to it. He found expression for that feeling too: one of the last things he did was paint the words "Norman's Cay" in big blue letters across the stern of the *Reef Witch*. The *Reef Witch*, out of Norman's Cay. He could almost see it slicing across the pond.

While the paint dried, Novak went inside the trailer and took out his charts. He plotted the course to Nassau, and then to Norman's Cay. After that, he stared at the phone for a while, thinking about Chris and hoping it would ring. When it did not, he took out stationery and wrote Chris a letter. It began with an admission that he intended to retire early and spend all his time on Norman's. It ended with an invitation, almost a plea, that Chris would join him. He was licking the stamp when the phone rang.

He laughed as he picked up the receiver, but it wasn't Chris.

"Dick?" said a voice. "This is Phil Kniskern."

"Hello," Novak said, with unmasked enthusiasm, generated partly by the excitement of his preparations, partly by his positive feelings about their last talk on Norman's.

There was a pause. When Kniskern finally spoke, Novak realized that this time the enthusiasm was one-sided. "The situation on Norman's is beginning to concern me, Dick. Some of the residents are starting to talk."

"Have you run into a snag?" Novak asked with some anxiety, assuming that Kniskern was referring to his real estate proposals, and knowing that his plans—*Reef Witch*, Norman's Cay—depended on the acceptance of those proposals.

"No," said Kniskern. "Nothing insurmountable, that is. Negotiations shouldn't take much longer, in fact."

"Great."

There was another pause, longer than the first. Novak heard Kniskern clearing his throat. "But that's not the reason I called," he said.

"No?"

"No. The thing is, Dick, the situation on Norman's is delicate right now. Not just for me. For all the residents. It just doesn't strike me as a good time to stir up trouble."

"I'm not sure I understand," Novak said, genuinely puzzled.

"I'm talking about the little chat you had with Ed Ward and his friends. I don't think it was very discreet. And neither do most of the other homeowners."

"Discreet?" Novak said, his mind filling with questions there was no time to consider. How had Kniskern found out about the confrontation? From someone on Norman's? Ward himself, maybe? Or from the assistant commissioner in Nassau? And in that case, did it mean the police were taking action? He plunged ahead. "I don't see what discretion has to do with it. Everyone on the island seems to know about Ward. Forbes told me the whole story."

"That wasn't very discreet of him, either," Kniskern responded.

"Phil. I don't understand you. Those hoodlums are flying drugs in and out of Norman's and they're making trouble on the island, too—the broken cisterns and all that. Hasn't it occurred to you that they might want Norman's all for themselves some day?"

Kniskern was silent again, and when he spoke, his tone, usually mild, had developed an edge. "I don't have any proof that there are drugs on Norman's. And neither—" Novak began to interrupt and Kniskern raised his voice—"neither do you. It's all hearsay, and making wild claims that can't be supported isn't going to do anybody any good right now. I'm having enough problems closing this deal without having to handle a lot of worried owners."

"But Phil, I think they've got legitimate reason to be worried."

"You're not hearing me, Dick. There is no proof. Just a lot of rumors. And now there's talk about investigators coming to the island."

"There is?" Novak said, unable to conceal his pleasure.

"Yes, damn it. Nassau police called me in Lauderdale."

So, his complaint had brought results, after all. "That's good, isn't it?" Novak said.

"Are you joking? It's terrible. We've got a reputation to maintain. Reputation is everything when it comes to real estate values."

Novak was baffled by Kniskern's attitude. "But your reputation will be in the mud if you let people like Ed Ward use your airstrip to smuggle drugs. Haven't you seen what happens? In the Keys, and all over south Flor-

ida? You might as well know it—I was the one who went
to the police in Nassau."

"God damn it, Dick. God damn it. Couldn't you have
spoken to me first?"

Novak hated the taking in vain of the deity's name. With
difficulty, he kept himself from reprimanding Kniskern, and
replied, "I didn't think it was necessary. I thought I was
doing the right thing. I still do. This kind of activity has
to be nipped in the bud, for practical reasons. And, for
moral reasons, I think we have to take a stand."

Kniskern responded to this speech only in part. "I'm
glad you see the importance of being practical, Dick. The
practical thing is to stay out of island politics right now.
Didn't you promise me you would do that?"

"Yes, but—"

"And there's a good reason for that. You're just not in
a position to understand the situation on Norman's. You're
a newcomer. You don't seem to realize that I've known
these people for quite a while. They were on the island
before I came."

"Are you talking about Ward and his gang?"

"I'm talking about Ward, his wife, his kids, his friends.
That's who I'm talking about. I think I know them and I
think I know the kind of life they're hoping for on Norman's. What right have we got to make trouble for them?
None that I can see, not without solid proof. So let's be
more discreet in future. That's all I'm asking. I can't run
a hotel and build Norman's into what we both want with
a lot of narcs snooping around the island."

At that moment, Novak knew that he would get nowhere with Kniskern, and he felt nothing but contempt
for the man. He almost lashed out at him, as he had
lashed out at Ed Ward. But that wouldn't have been fair.
Kniskern was innocent of everything but the desperate
need to protect his investment. And Novak himself had
an investment, an emotional one already and a financial
one in the future, in Kniskern's investment. He glanced
out the window at the *Reef Witch*, all ready for the jour-

ney across the Gulf Stream and all the way to its new home port. He already had a feeling it would be one of those important journeys in a man's life. And so, looking at the *Reef Witch* and thinking of the next stage of his life, Novak said: "All right, Phil. I'll let you handle island politics."

"Thanks, Dick. Wonderful. That's all I'm asking. I'll take care of this. You won't have anything to regret. I promise you that. Norman's will always be run on an above-board basis. That's the only way I can operate." He laughed. "And just having you there will make that for certain."

Those were soothing words, and they soothed Novak. He told Kniskern that he was on his way to the island, and would be there for Thanksgiving weekend. Kniskern replied that he would fly down from Lauderdale and meet him there. They spoke friendly good-byes. Then Novak folded his charts and went outside to his boat. He tossed in an English primer for Forbes. With luck, he could be in the water in a matter of hours.

14

Novak had a rough crossing. The Gulf Stream was choppy, and because the *Reef Witch* was heavily loaded—with ten full dive rigs, the Honda bike, underwater cameras, fishing gear, books, and the trunk of research material from which he hoped to write a book on hammerheads—Novak had to hold back on the throttle to avoid overheating the single Evinrude 175.

Arriving in New Providence, he dutifully reported to Bahamian customs, where the inspectors subjected the *Reef Witch* to a thorough search, opening everything he had so carefully packed and poking through his belongings in a way that seemed calculated to raise his blood pressure. Other men might have wondered whether this was a moment when a modest bribe might be in order; Novak did not. It was almost dark when they finished with him, and fully dark by the time he was safely anchored in the harbor. He warmed something in a can over the gas stove, swallowed it down with a glass of rum, and soon after zipped himself into his sleeping bag on the deck by the console. He thought about the next morning's journey to Norman's Cay. His eyes closed. The waves rocked him to sleep.

He awoke with a start; or perhaps he hadn't been sleeping at all. As he fumbled on the deck for his watch, he heard a splash. Then something bumped against the stern of the *Reef Witch*. What was it? A piece of driftwood? A big fish? Then came another bump, harder than the first. It was followed by the unmistakable sound of two hulls scraping together. Novak lay transfixed. His first thought was that the customs inspectors had returned. He rejected it: customs had rules about searchlights and loudspeakers, as much for their own protection as for that of the boating public. But who, other than customs and Phil Kniskern, knew that he was in Nassau? He was asking himself that question when a footfall sounded on the deck of the *Reef Witch*. Then two tanks knocked softly together, and there was a pause as though someone were feeling for a foothold in the dark.

Novak stayed where he was, perfectly still. He had heard the stories of piracy in the islands; he had heard more specific ones of thieves who made it their business to learn what kind of traffic was coming through customs. The *Reef Witch* would be a good target. It was carrying thousands of dollars in readily marketed gear; besides, Novak had five hundred dollars in cash and two thousand dollars in traveler's checks in the pocket of his jeans. Rumor had it that some of the thieves made it a point to leave no witnesses behind.

Novak crept forward, half out of his sleeping bag. There was a speargun in the bow but of course it wouldn't be loaded. And there was no time. Footsteps came purposefully across the deck. At the last moment—maybe he had been asleep, after all—Novak remembered the machete he kept in the storage compartment under the console. He had time to open the compartment, but that was all. A foot stepped into the side of his leg, then kicked again, experimentally. Novak rolled out of the sleeping bag and came up punching. He hit something; something hit him. Then Novak and another man were rolling across the hard gear that lay on deck.

Novak struggled free, free of the gear, free of his assailant, and jumped to his feet. His eyes had now adjusted to the night, and he could make out the man: a black man, somewhat bigger than he. As the man rose, Novak saw a gun in his hand.

Then came a shot, and the sound of a bullet ripping into the console. If this man was a thief, his method was to kill first and steal at his leisure. The man came closer. Novak hit the deck, rolled, grabbed the machete. Was there another shot? He couldn't hear because of the pounding in his ears. Now the man was standing over him. Novak lashed out with the machete, felt the blade strike flesh and bone. Then he and the man were doing the same thing: staring at the man's hand, dangling limply from his wrist, with dark blood spilling down from a wound that was beyond bone-deep; staring at that, and at the gun, still held, but now at a crazy angle, in useless fingers.

Neither spoke. The man made no cry. He shuffled backward, tumbled over the stern into his own boat. Novak saw that it was tied to his own. Without thinking, he cleaved the line with his machete, then ran to the bow and cut through his own anchor line. He hurried back to the console, turned the key, shoved the throttle all the way down, and roared out of the harbor, with a vulnerable feeling in the small of his back and panic in his mind.

It took Novak a while to settle down. Almost clear of the channel between Nassau and Paradise Island, he eased back on the throttle. He thought of going back, of reporting the attack to the police. But he recalled the frustrations of his last report to Bahamian police; this time all he had was a vague description of the attacker, and a slug possibly buried in the console. Based on these clues, the police would not get their man. Novak decided not to waste his time. The course to Norman's Cay was already charted and the *Reef Witch* was carrying plenty of fuel. He could always put into Highbourne Cay and make his report there. Novak got out the charts, checked them in the light of a torch, and turned for the open sea.

It was the kind of quick decision the sea is known to make mariners pay for. The night was clear and starry when Novak set out, but almost immediately, as though a decision had been made to teach him a lesson, the wind rose and thick clouds swept overhead, covering the dome from horizon to horizon. Rain pelted down in gusts, dampening the charts and soaking Novak before he could unpack his foul-weather gear. As the storm grew worse, he was forced to admit a fact that he had previously hidden from himself: the *Reef Witch* was underpowered. Underpowered and overloaded. The stern wallowed, spinning the compass wildly in the beam of his torch, and a few tanks worked loose and started crashing around the deck. Novak decided to put into Eleuthera. He kept watch off the port bow, waiting for the lights of the island to appear, but they never did. And neither, later on, did he see the lights of Highbourne Cay.

He was lost. Lost at sea in a storm at night, in a little open boat. Novak cursed himself; he hadn't even taken the simple precaution of listening to the weather forecast. Now he had put in jeopardy all his gear, his trunkful of research notes, even the money he had saved for the research center. He didn't think of adding the risk to his own life to the list until he heard the first crack of thunder.

He cut the engine. Had it been his imagination? No. Lightning shot across the sky, and thunder boomed again. Novak feared thunder, and there was nothing he could do about it. He began running about frantically—finding the spare anchor, securing it to the cleat, tossing it over; then dragging out tarpaulins, covering gearing, making a little tent over the console. He crouched down beneath the tent, hoping to wait it out. The storm intensified. The thunder and lightning closed in. Help me, God, Novak silently prayed. He began scrambling through the darkness, hunting for his wet suit, tank, regulator, and the rest of his gear. He jerked it on his body, tied a line to his weight belt, and wrapped it around a cleat. Then he jumped into the sea.

Novak hung suspended beneath the hull of his boat,

deep enough so that he heard nothing except the sound of his own bubbles, but not deep enough to escape the sight of the lightning, which from time to time flashed its white strobes all around, startling him with watery visions that disappeared before he could focus on them. Watery visions: a clump of seaweed like Medusa's head, a sinuous green moray on the nocturnal prowl, a big-headed shadow in the deep. Novak tried to take slow, even breaths to conserve air, but because of his fear he kept breathing much too rapidly and soon, much too soon, he thought, his tank was empty. Novak ascended reluctantly.

On the surface, rain still fell, but lightly now. The storm was passing, its fury muted and distant. Novak climbed into the boat. The wind had blown the tarpaulins off his supplies. Everything was in chaos. Novak didn't have the strength to deal with it. He shrugged off his tank, found a scrap of tarpaulin, wrapped it around him, and lay on the deck. He didn't even remove his wet suit. The cold and the dampness made him shiver. The rain stopped. He slept.

Novak awoke bobbing on a calm sea under a warm sun. There was no land in sight. He stripped off his wet suit and dove into the water, swimming for a few strokes and returning to the boat. He felt much better. The sun dried him as he tried to sort through the confusion on the deck.

It was messy, but there was little real damage. The charts were ruined, and there was a bullet hole in the console, but the rest of his supplies, including the trunk of research notes, were undamaged. Novak changed fuel tanks, then pulled anchor and headed east, knowing he would see land sooner or later.

Only a few minutes underway, he saw another boat, moving northwest. Novak changed course to cut it off, hoping to find out where he was and the correct heading to Norman's. In a few minutes, the boat was very close: a big Hatteras, fitted with tall outriggers for deep-sea fishing. Novak noticed how fast it was going, trailing a wake of boiling foam. He waved his hand in the air, hoping to attract the helmsman's attention. The Hatteras did not appear to slow down. Novak turned his wheel and steered a course that would take him directly into the other boat's path.

The Hatteras moved toward him. He could hear the sound of its engines, make out details on the deck. Although he could see no one on board, the helmsman must have been inside the glassed-in wheelhouse, must have been able to see him by now. But the Hatteras kept coming.

What was going on? It was daytime and there wasn't a cloud in the sky. Novak leaned on his boat horn, waved his arms, yelled at the top of lungs. The Hatteras bore down at him. Now he could read the make on its tournament rods. At the last second, he swung the wheel and avoided being run over. As the Hatteras roared by, almost within touching distance, Novak still saw no one on board. Furious and alarmed, he followed it, sounding the horn, yelling, waving. He even set off a flare. The Hatteras kept going, easily stretching the distance between them. Novak gave up.

He slowed the *Reef Witch*, looked around, suddenly saw land in the southeast, green humps on the horizon. The Exumas. He turned toward them, recognizing that he must be backtracking along the course the Hatteras had followed.

Not long after, he motored into the pond at Norman's Cay. Phil Kniskern was not there to meet him, as he had promised. Neither were there any other boats around. Novak tied up at the dock and walked toward the hotel. He saw no one. There wasn't a sound of human activity. The island seemed deserted.

15

"He's back."

"Who?"

"The hammerhead man. In that old tub of his."

"In the storm?"

"Yeah."

This was interesting. Not worrying, but interesting. Carlos Lehder was in a good mood. Everything was going well. For a while, his attempt to take over the hotel had stalled. Chuck Kehm was supposed to have delivered it for him. At the same time, Kehm had led Phil Kniskern to believe that he was supporting Kniskern's interest. Perhaps, thought Lehder, Kehm had become confused. Lehder had known brighter men. Of course, he had done what he could to help Kehm, had given him every chance to prove himself, by choking off the tourist trade. Still, Kehm had failed. He had outlived his usefulness on Norman's Cay. Lehder had taken the appropriate steps. Now he would deal with the hotel transaction himself. Initial negotiations seemed promising. And some of the old landowners, so reluctant to sell, were having second thoughts, second thoughts inspired, perhaps, by unsolved acts of vandalism on their properties. Soon he would be in a position to buy up large chunks of the island. Norman's Cay: refuge and haven—the island nation he had dreamed of as far back as Danbury. Imagine. Lehder switched on John Lennon and cranked up the volume.

*   *   *

Tired, caked with salt, in a bad mood, Richard Novak walked around the marina, searching for Phil Kniskern. They had a lot to discuss. But he didn't see Kniskern, or anyone else for that matter. He climbed the hill to the hotel. The first thing he noticed was that the power lines from the marina were down; they lay in coiled heaps by the side of the road. Then he saw that the hotel antenna was dangling from a single wire on the roof. The storm must have hit Norman's very hard, he thought. He reached for the doorknob, turned it—and found it was locked. Three months ago there hadn't been a lock on the island. Now locks were everywhere.

He knocked on the door. "Hey. Anyone there?" No one answered.

Novak walked away, down the road to the villa that he had come to regard as his own at Smuggler's Beach. He had a key, but he didn't have to use it. The front door was unlocked; open, in fact. And so were the sliding glass doors along the porch.

They had been dislodged from their tracks. Had the storm done that, too? And had the storm also taken all his possessions—books, clothing, diving gear—out of the drawers and off the shelves and scattered them across the straw rug in the living room?

Novak stood still in the villa, his villa, and felt what people feel at times like that: violated. Anger built inside him. He strode onto the porch, down the steps, out to the airstrip. No one was there, either, although three planes were lined up at the head of the strip, and a fourth had just taken off and was flying north. Had the storm been strong enough to knock down antennas and power lines but leave little planes upright? Novak tried to puzzle it out; thoughts of the storm, the locks, Ed Ward, tumbled through his mind. He neglected to include the armed attacker on the *Reef Witch*.

Novak returned to the marina and entered the dive shop. Relieved to find no signs of damage or forced entry, he began clearing space for the supplies on the boat. Victor Forbes came in.

"Hey, man," he said, with a big smile. "I was thinkin' you might not come back."

"I'm back. What's going on around here, Victor?"

"What you mean?"

"I mean the antenna on the hotel, the power lines, the break-in at my place. And why is the hotel locked up? Where is everybody?"

The expression on Forbes's face, so open moments before, grew guarded. "Nothin's goin' on, man. Paulette's on Highbourne for the day, that's why the hotel's locked."

"Aren't there any guests?"

"No more guests, man," said Forbes. "No more tourists on Norman's."

"What is that supposed to mean?" asked Novak.

Forbes shrugged. "Everything's cool, man. There's lot of new people around. The price of houses is sky-high." He laughed at the craziness of the prices.

"What kind of new people?"

"Residents. You know. You and me can make plenty of money taking them out to the reef, jukin' lobsters."

"I won't allow you or anyone else to denude these reefs, Forbes," Novak said, focusing all his frustration on the one source of irritation he could get a grip on. "I've already told you that. I don't want to have to say it again."

"Okay, man," Forbes said. "But they's rich. They'll be needing lobsters from somewhere."

Novak sighed. "Taking lobster is okay in moderation, Victor. That's all I'm saying."

Forbes smiled. Without being asked, he helped Novak in the shop. Later, they unloaded the *Reef Witch* together. When they were finished, Novak opened the trunk containing the hammerhead research and began spreading some of the papers out on the counter to show Forbes. Forbes seemed interested, and Novak wanted to encourage that. But he had barely started when the door burst open and a distraught-looking woman came in, followed by two small children who also seemed distraught.

"Victor," she said, addressing Forbes and not appearing to notice Novak at all. "Where is he?"

The woman was tall, dark-haired, slender. Novak had seen her before, although he hadn't met her. She was Lexi Kehm, wife of Chuck, the former island manager who was now a private real estate agent of some sort on the island, if Novak remembered correctly.

"Where is he?" Lexi Kehm repeated, her voice on the edge of hysteria.

Forbes couldn't meet her gaze. "I don't know. I haven't seen him since last night."

"No one has," said the woman. "No one. He didn't come home last night." Her voice broke. Behind her one of the children started to bawl. "I've been to every house on the island. He's not here."

Forbes looked pained. "Maybe he's gone out to the reef," he said in a soothing tone.

"The boat's still here," said Lexi Kehm.

"Then maybe somebody carried him over to High-bourne," Forbes suggested. "For supplies, like."

"He wouldn't do that without telling me," Lexi said. "And anyway, he promised to take us shopping in Eleuthera today. He promised."

Forbes had run out of ideas. He looked down at the floor. His submission to the force of her argument seemed to calm Lexi. Novak looked from one to the other, dimly aware that there must be some subtext to this conversation, but totally ignorant of what it was.

"He's been kidnapped, Victor," Lexi said. "You know it and I know it."

Forbes shook his head.

"It's all because of the goddamned hotel deal," Lexi said. "People warned him, but he's just so pigheaded. This was his chance to make big money." Her eyes filled with tears; they rolled down her face. "Christ," she said. "Some chance." Now both her infants were crying. Lexi Kehm swept them up and hurried away.

As soon as she was out of sight, Novak confronted Forbes. "What the hell is going on, Victor?"

"Nothin'. Nothin' I know about."

"You're not a very good liar," Novak said.

Forbes smiled shyly.

"Let's start with the hotel deal," Novak said. "What was she talking about?"

"Kehm's trying to be a real estate agent these days," Forbes said.

"And who was he acting for in the hotel sale? Meridian wouldn't want him. Is he acting for the buyer, is that it? Kniskern?"

"I don't know, Mr. Novak."

Novak looked closely at Forbes. He seemed to be telling the truth. "Maybe," he said. "But I think you do know something about the warning she mentioned."

"I don't know about no warning," Forbes said. Novak glared at him. " 'Cept last night, maybe," Forbes added reluctantly.

"What happened last night?"

"Him and Francis be fightin' down at the hotel."

"Who are you talking about?"

"Kehm," Forbes said.

"Fighting with Francis? You mean physical fighting?"

Forbes shook his head. "Arguing. But loud."

"What about?"

"The hotel sale. And the houses Kehm be selling."

"What did they say?"

"I didn't hear a lot," Forbes said. "They drove off to see some of the new residents."

Novak felt frustration growing inside him. He had been on Norman's Cay several times now, and learned a lot of facts about the place, but he had no pattern to fit them into; nothing made sense. An understanding of the island danced just beyond his grasp. For example, how was Kehm involved in the hotel sale? Wasn't Kniskern buying it from Meridian? The deal was supposed to be consummated any time now.

"Who are these new residents?" Novak asked.

"I don't know. But a lot of the houses have changed hands lately. The new people want them bad."

"What makes you say that?"

"They be payin' top dollar," Forbes said. "And they been persuadin' the old owners to sell."

"What do you mean?"

Forbes paused. Novak moved a step closer to him. "There been a few fires," Forbes said quietly.

"Fires?"

"And maybe some shots fired into a house or two."

"By whom?" Novak said, remembering the break-in at his villa. His voice rose. "Who's been setting fires and shooting guns?"

"I don't know," Forbes said, his face a mask. Novak couldn't tell whether he was too frightened to tell or really didn't know. He was about to try another angle, when Forbe's mention of gunfire finally triggered a connection in his mind, a connection between what was happening on Norman's Cay and the armed attacker on the *Reef Witch*. He searched his mind for any evidence to support such a connection, but found none.

"Let's go look for Kniskern," Novak said. All at once, he had huge doubts about Kniskern's ability to complete the sale. And if Kniskern failed, what happened to all his own plans? What happened to the research center? And the reunited Novaks, living in harmony, like the Swiss Family Robinson, on a tropic isle? "He's got to be told about all this."

"Mr. Kniskern's not on the island," Forbes said.

"Maybe he's flying in today. We can find out."

Novak and Forbes went outside. They didn't see Kniskern; they didn't learn anything about when he was expected. But on the road to the hotel, they encountered Steve Francis: Francis, paid by residents not to break into their houses; Francis, who had followed Novak around the island; and who had argued with Chuck Kehm the night before, when Kehm was last seen. Novak held out his hand to stop him. The thin man stood languidly in the middle of the road, his gold chains glinting in the sun. Novak felt Forbes standing nervously behind him.

"Where is Kehm?" Novak demanded.

"Kehm?" said Francis.

"You know what I'm talking about. What have you done with him?"

"Me?" said Francis. "I'm a friend of Chuck's. An old friend. Why would I do anything to him?"

"Where is he, then?"

"Off the island," Francis said, starting to smile. "The police arrested him last night and flew him out."

"What are you talking about? What police?"

"Why, the Royal Bahamian Constabulary. They're the law around here, in case you didn't know."

"But what did they arrest him for?"

"He's not a Bahamian."

"So?"

Francis smile broadened. "So he didn't have a work permit and he was selling real estate. Foreigners can't work here without a permit. It's an offense."

"Are you telling me the police flew all the way down here just to arrest one man on a work permit violation?"

"It's a serious offense."

"So serious they couldn't take the time to tell his wife?" Novak asked. "She's worried sick about him. Why didn't they have the common courtesy to tell her?"

"You'll have to ask them," Francis said.

Novak wanted to hit him. He stood before Francis, his chest swelling. Francis, younger, but much less powerfully built, did not back down. He was not at all afraid of Novak. "One more thing, Francis," Novak said. "Someone must have tipped off the police about Kehm. Who was it?"

Francis tried to wipe the smile off his face, but he just couldn't. Novak turned and walked away in disgust.

16

Phil Kniskern didn't come to Norman's Cay on Thanksgiving, and Novak was unable to reach him. The hotel remained closed; he couldn't make a phone call. One or two planes came in. They left with a few of the older residents and their possessions. It didn't look as if they were coming back.

On Saturday, the sky clouded over and rain fell; not hard, just steady and dismal. Richard Novak made a decision. It was irresponsible to set up on Norman's Cay at such a time. And not just irresponsible, but impractical as well. The island's infrastructure had fallen apart. How could he possibly bring divers to a place where there was nowhere to stay? He would think of this as a temporary retreat. After talking to Kniskern, he could be more definitive. In the meantime, he couldn't leave his boat or his gear on an island beset by unexplained fires and gunshots. He walked slowly through the rain to the dive shop and began packing up. Time dragged; he moved at half-speed and hadn't accomplished much when the door opened and Carlos Lehder stepped into the shop.

Lehder wore khaki shorts and a linen shirt. He looked fit and content. Novak hadn't seen him since the reception at the hotel, hadn't seen the *Fire Fall* either. He had assumed that Lehder was one of the residents who had left.

"Hello, Mr. Novak," Lehder said, extending his hand.

Novak shook it. "We seem to have the island to our-selves," he said. "Although not for long."

"No?"

"I'm leaving."

"Really?" said Lehder. "I'm sorry to hear that."

Novak looked at him with interest. "What else can I do? There's nowhere to eat, nowhere for divers to stay, nowhere to buy spare parts. I can't even make a phone call. Kniskern was supposed to meet me here. I don't have a clue where he is or what he's doing."

"No?" said Lehder, glancing down at the counter, cov-ered with research notes.

"No," Novak replied. "It looks like I'm going to have to study hammerheads somewhere else."

"Ah, yes," said Lehder. "The hammerheads. I've actu-ally seen them from the house."

This show of interest in the hammerheads caught No-vak's attention. No one else on Norman's had expressed any interest in the hammerheads themselves; not even Kniskern, who seemed taken merely with the prospects of having a continous supply of paying customers. Novak took a close look at Lehder. Lehder noted it and smiled.

"They're attracted to the lagoon, aren't they?" Lehder asked.

"That's what they say. I'd like to study the phenome-non. It makes Norman's very special, from my point of view."

"I think it's special too," Lehder said, with another smile, this one rather difficult to interpret.

"You're interested in hammerheads?"

"Yes. Although I know nothing about them. Why would they come into the pond?"

"To mate, probably," Novak said. "But the mechanism that draws them is poorly understood. It's an important object of research." Novak began to warm to his subject. "And the hammerheads themselves are wonderful crea-tures. Perfect killing machines, for one thing, if you want to look at them that way."

"How is that?" Lehder asked, his face intent. Novak proceeded with his hammerhead lecture, going into much more detail than he had with Forbes, and receiving a much more intelligent and engaged response.

"A lot of people—and I'm talking about scientists," Novak continued, "consider the hammerhead a primitive shark. Totally untrue." Novak shuffled through his papers, letting a few drop, ignored, in his excitement. "Look at this diagram. You can see there's nothing primitive about the shape of that head. On the contrary, it's highly specialized, highly evolved. It's perfectly designed for precise triangulation—no other shark has as good a sense of smell, or an equal ability to judge distance."

Lehder studied the diagram. "There really is something almost . . . attractive about them, isn't there? Once you get over the initial reaction, that is."

Lehder couldn't have chosen better words. Novak beamed. "Exactly. That's exactly right, Mr. Lehder."

"Call me Joe."

"Joe?"

"My friends call me Joe."

"And I'm Richard—or Dick," Novak said, almost shaking hands all over again. Lehder, he thought, was a charming, cultured man, much more mature than his chronological age. Then he remembered what he was in the middle of doing. Packing up. Clearing out. The thought must have registered in his expression, because Lehder said, "Something wrong?"

"It's too bad, that's all. There's work to be done here, valuable work."

"What sort of setup did you have in mind?" asked Lehder.

What was the point of going into it now? Novak didn't know, but he responded to Lehder's interest. He described his plans for the research center. On a map, he indicated areas in the pond and on the reef that he wanted to use for observation posts. He outlined his long-term plans for the shop, mentioning not just more space, more shelving, but the facilities of his dreams, like a map room, a photo lab, a lecture room with video equipment, a big generator to run a big compressor, even a recompression chamber. "Norman's could be important in marine science. On an international scale. I mean that." And if it was, wouldn't he finally gain the reputation that had always eluded him? And wouldn't the scientific community be forced to recognize him as an expert? Those thoughts Novak kept to himself.

Lehder's attention was focused totally on Novak's talk. Novak felt it; he felt the presence of the man. And when he had finished, Lehder had questions, smart questions:

"What about a second pier in the marina for a dive boat?"

"Would it be possible to build some sort of observation chamber on the bed of the pond?"

"Could you have a compressor right on the boat?"

Novak responded to all of them. Lehder had a few more. The conservation grew general. Novak mentioned his professorship. And then Lehder did something that made a great impression. He spoke to Novak in German. His German was excellent, far more cultured than his English. The two men spoke in German for a while. They had things in common: they liked some of the same restaurants in Florida, and some of the same back roads. They even seemed to agree on which housing designs on Norman's they liked best. Volcano was their mutual favorite. And both men could trace their lineages back to similiar little towns in Central Europe.

There was a pause. Lehder fingered the hammerhead diagram. "You know, Dick, you really shouldn't let these little recent difficulties upset your plans. They won't last forever. I'm going to weather them myself. It's too bad that a few malcontents are disturbing the peace here, but the answer to all this is good management, and I see good management coming in down the road."

"You do?"

"Absolutely."

Novak sighed. "I wish I could count on that."

"There are no guarantees in life, Dick," said Lehder. "You must know that. But I didn't think you were like the others."

"What do you mean?"

"I didn't take you for the type that cuts and runs when the going gets a little tough."

Novak bridled. "You're underestimating the problems," he said with some edge. But Lehder's remark had stung.

"I'm a businessman," Lehder said. "I know how to deal with problems. But you're very right about one thing, Dick—Norman's has the potential to be a special place. It's a question of leadership."

"Leadership?"

"The island needs a leader. To smooth out the problems. To set a course."

This impressed Novak. No one else associated with the island seemed to be able to think beyond his own interests. "Maybe you're right," Novak said. "But I can't wait."

Lehder rose. "Why not?"

Novak waved his hand. "Lots of reasons." He began enumerating them.

Lehder interrupted. "I'm willing to help you, Dick. I can help make the research center a reality. I could even put an observation chamber in the pond one day. And I could let you use the *Fire Fall* while you're getting started."

"That's very kind of you," Novak said. "But I really don't see how I could accept all that."

Lehder smiled. "I don't think you understand. I'd like to be your partner."

Novak didn't know what to say. From his observation, it was clear that Lehder had plenty of money, perhaps enough so that he could build the research center and bring in all the equipment quickly and with no pain at all.

"Really," said Lehder. "I insist. Just say yes and I'll speak to my banker first thing Monday morning."

At this point, Novak recalled that he already had a partner, the recently elusive Phil Kniskern. "You're very generous, Mr. Lehder."

"Joe."

"Joe. But first, I couldn't do anything without speaking to Phil Kniskern."

"Of course."

"And second, I can't promise any return on your investment."

"That's not important. If you want, think of it as a retainer for taking me out to the reef and teaching me about hammerheads."

Novak was reduced to repeating how generous Lehder was and how he would have to talk to Kniskern. Lehder laughed, shook hands again, and was gone.

Novak stood in the shop, motionless, for some time. Then he resumed work. But he didn't pack up. Instead he began unpacking everything already repacked. He had made another decision: he would make a trial attempt to bring one group of divers to the island. Why not? Wouldn't anything else be cutting and running, given the appearance of his new ally?

Back at Concordia, Novak had a lot of trouble reaching Phil Kniskern on the telephone. He finally got through to him in a hospital. Kniskern's voice was weak. He had had a heart attack, and bypass surgery was scheduled. Novak decided that this was not a good time to bring up the new developments. He made his expressions of sympathy and was about to say good-bye when Kniskern interrupted.

"Dick?"

"Yes?" He could hardly hear Kniskern.

"There's something you should know."

"What's that?" Novak asked, straining to hear.

There was a long pause. "I'm not involved in Norman's anymore. Except for the villas, and I don't expect to have those much longer."

"What do you mean? What about the hotel?"

Another pause, longer than the first. "It was sold."

"To whom?"

"Carlos Lehder. He bought the strip too. And the marina, with all the buildings. Including your dive shop. He's going to buy up the whole goddamned island."

Kniskern's voice was almost too weak to express the bitterness he felt.

17

In the weeks before Christmas, Novak worked feverishly to organize his group dive expedition to Norman's Cay. Eight divers, an ideal number, joined the group. Most of them were students he had from Fort Lauderdale. Each paid six hundred dollars, which wasn't bad, since it included everything but the round trip to Nassau. From there, they would be flown to Norman's on a Trans-Island charter, and would stay in rooms reserved for Novak by Paulette. Making these reservations had posed no problem, and neither had reaching Norman's by telephone. Novak gradually forgot about Phil Kniskern and his disappointment. Kniskern's dream had died, but Novak's, from which it had seemed inseparable, moved closer to realization.

The trip went smoothly. In Nassau, there were no mysterious delays or cancellations. Novak and his divers landed on Norman's on a January day that was all blue skies and soft breezes. They were met by Victor Forbes, who welcomed them warmly and drove them to the hotel. It was open. An immaculate private room awaited each researcher. The kitchen was fully stocked. Fuel and spare parts for the *Reef Witch* were already stored at the marina. Landscapers were at work everywhere, trimming, raking, mowing. No antennas hung askew; no power lines lay in coils on the ground. The whole island seemed to be quietly buzzing with efficiency. Novak was amazed; the change was almost too much. He remembered Carlos Lehder's prophetic diagnosis: all Norman's had lacked was a leader. He couldn't help but compare Lehder's accomplishments with Kniskern's. His respect for the young man grew.

But Novak didn't have time to reflect much on the changes. He didn't even see Lehder in the beginning. He was too busy preparing for dive trips, conducting dive trips, analyzing dive trips, sleeping. The students were especially excited to find caves in the coral on the northern section of the reef. Some of the caves seemed to extend deep into the rock. After a few days, when Novak was persuaded that he was dealing with a competent group, he allowed himself to be talked into some cave exploration.

Cave diving, even in shallow water, as this was, and remaining within sight of the mouth, as Novak planned to do, can be dangerous, and Novak took precautions. He made sure the divers were fully equipped; he lectured them exhaustively on the procedures, especially the importance of staying with one's buddy; he painted individualized stripe patterns on each of their tanks so that he could identify them underwater at a glance. Then, on a flat, calm day, he took the eight of them out to the reef and into a cave. Inside, they wondered at the coral formations. They made diagrams on their underwater slates of the locations of various tunnels, which Novak had told them not to enter. They noted and began the classification of the abundance of marine life. They had the kind of experience that would make the whole trip worthwhile. The only problem was that only seven of them came out.

Hollins. Hollins was the eighth. Novak knew that in moments, from an inspection of the tank stripes. Dougie Hollins. A good, confident diver, but young, and perhaps a little too confident. Oh, God, Novak thought. He had never lost a diver. What if he lost one now, on his very first trip on Norman's?

Novak motioned the seven divers to the surface. Then

he checked his watch and gauges and kicked back into the cave. He shone his torch all around the opening, picking out sea fans, starfish, bright little tropicals, and a fat green parrotfish, but no Hollins. He pointed the beam toward the back of the cave and followed it in.

The cave wasn't very deep, but at the back was a dark hole, the entrance to one of the tunnels Novak had told the divers not to enter. Novak glanced at his watch. He had to be right the first time. He grabbed a coral handhold and pulled himself into the tunnel.

The tunnel was short. It opened into a chamber that was less abundant in life than the cave opening. No sunlight penetrated the chamber. Novak shone his torch around, satisfied himself that Hollins wasn't there, and was about to turn back when he saw another opening in the far wall. He looked through. Beyond lay another chamber, also dark. He shone his light inside, saw nothing but the black spines of countless sea urchins that clung to the coral. Novak checked his dials. He had eight minutes of air left, less than that if he went deeper or was forced to exert himself. And he was already breathing fast, much too fast. He had to make a decision. Had Hollins entered a different tunnel? And if so, from where? The cave opening? The first chamber? Or this one? Maybe Hollins wasn't in trouble at all, but had already swum out, somewhere behind Novak, and was even now safely on the deck of Forbes's Whaler. With eight minutes of air left and deep in the coral, maybe Novak was the one who wouldn't come out. Things like that had happened before.

Novak decided to turn back, but before he did, he swept his torch around the second chamber once more. And this time, he saw something besides sea urchins: a Nikonos camera, lying on the rocky floor. Novak's pulse raced. He pulled himself into the second chamber.

Not far from the camera, he found something even more troubling: a weight belt. A diver without a weight belt might be so buoyant that he would be helpless in a cave like this, Novak thought. What would happen? He would . . . float right up to the roof. Novak jerked his beam up to the roof of the chamber. And there was Hollins, pinned against the sea urchins, saved from impalement only by the tank on his back. Novak swam up.

Hollins's eyes were wide with fear, but he was breathing and had air left in his tank. Novak grabbed him and swam him down toward the opening, fighting a current, which he hadn't noticed before, and fighting Hollins's buoyancy; at the same time, he had to handle the torch. Hollins was too far out of control to be trusted with it. Novak could feel him trembling.

Novak dragged Hollins through the opening and into the first chamber. They made a clumsy pair, the kind of team that raised lots of silt. It rose in clouds through the beam of the torch. Novak had trouble finding the right opening. He was about two minutes from the surface; and that was probably the amount of air he had left. And Hollins? He was panting into his regulator like a dog. But there was no time to fumble for Hollins's pressure gauge. If Hollins ran out of air, he was sure to let Novak know, probably by taking him in a death grip. Things like that had happened before.

Novak's light shone on an opening in the rock. Was it his imagination, or did luminosity glimmer faintly through it? Novak dragged Hollins toward it. Now Hollins saw it too, and tried to help. They struggled through the narrow opening, and into the short tunnel. At the other end shone daylight. Novak felt Hollins kicking frantically. Then, quite suddenly, the light was shut off. The tunnel blackened. Novak shone his torch on the spot where the exit had been; and saw a big hammerhead coming in. He felt Hollins panicking at his side. The hammerhead kept coming. There was only one thing to do, and Novak did it. He punched the shark in the snout. Novak had been forced to punch sharks several times before. Usually they went away. But once the shark had taken a bite out of his leg.

This one, because of the unexpected aggression, or because of the torch, or because it wasn't hungry, went away. Novak felt a surge from its powerful tail, and then it was gone. He swam Hollins into the cave opening, out beyond the lip and up to the surface.

In the boat, Novak began yanking off his gear. He told himself that what he had to say to Hollins should probably be said in private, but he was boiling inside, and the fact that Hollins seemed to be recovering rapidly from his scare—and more, was already assuming a kind of insouciance in front of his buddies—made Novak hotter. He turned to face him, and at that moment saw something that rendered him speechless.

A convoy of vessels, some that looked like pleasure craft but others that must have been mid-sized freighters, was steaming into Norman's Cay from the horizon. And that wasn't all. To the south, the sky was full of planes. It was like an invasion. The planes descended on the island and began circling the airstrip, waiting their turn to land. A stack-up over Norman's Cay. It was unthinkable. For the moment, Novak forgot about Dougie Hollins.

Carlos Lehder was not an empty talker. He had said that a leader could bring change to Norman's Cay. Now he was demonstrating how it was done. And with astonishing rapidity. But what kind of change, Novak wondered for the first time, would Carlos Lehder bring?

18

That night the pond at Norman's Cay was crowded with boats and the hotel was full of people. Novak, going in for dinner, recognized some of them: Dougie Hollins and the other diving students; Ed Ward and his associates; locals, including Forbes and Francis; and Carlos Lehder. There were at least a dozen pilots he had never seen before, wearing aviator jackets and fancy watches, and as many seamen, with deep tans and faded tattoos. And there were others more difficult to classify. Novak felt the excitement in the air, an elevated energy level not due only to the drink being served in quantity in the dining room and bar. The energy seemed to swirl around Carlos Lehder, who stood quite still near the bar, smiling, talking, looking every bit the solicitous host; everyone wanted contact with him—a word, a gesture—as though he were generating some irrestistible force.

Lehder saw Novak almost as soon as he entered the room. He gave him a big smile and beckoned. A little reluctantly, Novak moved toward him. He didn't like parties and he didn't like being summoned, no matter how charmingly.

"Richard! Good to see you. I hear everything's going great."

"Great" was not an adjective Novak would have picked to describe that afternoon's adventure with Hollins, but he just nodded.

"I knew it would," Lehder continued. "I have a lot of faith in you." He took Novak's arm and introduced him around: "Meet Professor Dick Novak," he said. "He's in charge of the entire scuba operation." Of those that Novak shook hands with that night, three stood out in his mind: Heinrich Rogol. "Island manager," Lehder explained. "In charge of real estate operations and all personnel." Rogol gave Novak a somewhat puzzled look, and greeted him in a thick German accent. He was a blond, muscular, hirsute man who seemed somewhat inappropriately turned out for a managerial type: his open jacket didn't quite conceal the shoulder holster and the .45 pistol inside it. Novak thought he saw the butt of another one tucked into his belt, but there was no opportunity for a better examination before he met Andy Havens.

"Hotel manager," said Lehder. Novak had seen Havens on the island before: someone had told him that Havens had flown for the RAF. Havens had a British accent and a smile rather fleeting for one who would be dealing with the public. Novak wondered what place Paulette Jones would have in the new regime, and was about to ask, when Lehder drew him up to a beautiful woman.

"This is Margit," Lehder said. "Margit Meie-Lennekogel. Margit has no official duties, except for improving my German. She's here just for pleasure—the sea and the sun."

The woman looked right into Novak's eyes, smiled, and slowly raised her hand to be kissed. Novak's reaction was a little slow. He was stunned—because she was stunning, because the word "pleasure" was stuck in his mind, because he had an unaccountable feeling that Margit was being offered to him.

He took her hand. It was warm. "I've heard so much about you," Margit said. Her English was excellent. "I'm looking forward to scuba lessons. Very much."

Novak was conscious of Lehder watching him. He was aware of undercurrents, but he couldn't read them. He let go of Margit's hand, stood there tongue-tied. With a laugh that also resisted Novak's interpretation, Lehder came to his rescue. He clapped his hand on Novak's back and said, "Remember the changes I promised? Come have a look." He drew Novak over to the end of the bar and began unrolling a thick roll of blueprints.

Novak examined the blueprints. As he studied Lehder's proposals, he grew transfixed. Lehder had plans: plans to triple the size of the hotel, to make it as plush as anything in the islands, adding a pool, an outdoor bar, central power, with lines to all the houses; plans for a grand new building to house the headquarters of Titanic Air; plans for a machine shop, a parts department and something else called "Special Projects"; plans for a supermarket, a bookstore, a cinema, a branch office of one of the major Nassau banks.

At first, as Novak worked his way through the blueprints, he was impressed—impressed by the strength of Lehder's commitment to Norman's, and by his resources, financial and organizational. The problem was that there was too much. The more he saw, the more his disquiet grew. He remembered what Kniskern had said: "Anyone who thinks that Norman's can become a big resort like something in Nassau or Freeport doesn't know much about the islands. The banks are aware of it, and so is Meridian."

But Kniskern was out of it now, and so was Meridian. And as for the banks, it looked like one of them was proposing to set up on the little island. Novak was wrestling with these thoughts when he came to the plans for the marina. And there Lehder's plans met his own, and he saw them clearly, in blue-and-white precision. He saw everything he needed: chart room, photo lab, video room, compressor room, recompression chamber, his own pier at the marina, with a new blue-and-white dive boat floating beside it. It was all there: Professor Richard Novak's big-time marine science research center. Courtesy of Carlos Lehder, benefactor. Novak's doubts receded. They remained unexpressed, and his disquiet withdrew into the background of his mind.

Novak did not remain long at the party. Too excited to sleep, he wandered down to the marina and looked at the silhouettes of all the boats and ships Lehder had brought to Norman's. Anyone could have blueprints drawn up, he supposed, but those vessels were real. The planes on the strip were real. And was Carlos Lehder, therefore, real as well? Novak turned and walked through the scrub where one day his research center would stand.

Novak had trouble falling asleep that night, and slept late the next morning. When he awoke, Norman's Cay was humming. Lying in bed, he could hear sounds of activity coming from every direction. He rose and hurried down to the marina.

Everyone else on the island was already there. Even Hollins and the other diving students were pitching in, helping to unload the ships that came one by one to the pier. There were enormous amounts of cargo; in one day, the entire infrastructure of the island was going to be changed. Crate after crate was swung onto the pier and taken away. Eight new jeeps came off a big steamer called the *Margaret Lee*. The next ship brought a fleet of trucks, all converted for hauling passengers. Then came another ship bearing endless coils of steel mesh and chain-link fence. The freighter behind it carried navigation and electronic equipment, including a big satellite transmitter that was quickly hauled up to the hotel.

Novak was amazed: amazed at the quantity, amazed at the efficiency, amazed at how quickly Carlos Lehder seemed able to move from blueprints to reality. The man himself sped around the harbor at the wheel of *Fire Fall* with a walkie-talkie in one hand, supervising everything without showing the least sign of stress. Novak could see his big smile all the way from shore. This, he thought, was a man who knew how to make things happen. And he had plenty of money; Norman's was suddenly oversupplied. What use would all those jeeps be? And the passenger trucks—there weren't enough houses on the island to shelter the number of people Lehder could now move from one end of Norman's to the other. And chain link? Steel mesh? What role would they play in a tropical paradise?

The last thing unloaded was a complete suit of medieval armor. Lehder came ashore and led the way as a laughing group of men carried it off the dock and all the way to the customs house by the airstrip. Novak followed. He watched as Lehder chose a spot next to the basketball hoop and had the armor suit set on its feet. Then Lehder walked around it and inspected it carefully. He seemed pleased. "Heinrich," he said to Rogol, who was standing nearby, "I need something to dub him with."

"Dub?"

"You know," Lehder said. "Like Robin Hood." He reached inside Rogol's jacket and took out his .45. Turning to the suit of armor, he tapped the barrel of Rogol's gun ceremoniously on one shoulder and then the other. "I dub you Sir Norman," he said, "Knight of Norman's Cay."

Laughing, the men started moving back to the marina. Lehder noticed Novak. "What do you think of him?" he asked, gesturing toward Sir Norman. "I imported him specially from Europe."

Sir Norman looked like a replica to Novak, but he kept that to himself. "Very nice," he said.

"I'm glad you like him," Lehder said. "Sir Norman is here to protect us."

"Are we in danger?"

There was a pause. Then Lehder smiled. "Got to get back to work," he said. "See you at the party."

"Party?"

"An all-island celebration on the beach tonight. I'm flying everything in from Nassau—steaks, beer, a band, maybe some girls. It's to show how much I appreciate your students and everyone else for all the help today."

"Thanks," Novak said, with no intention of going. He spent the rest of the day working in the dive shop, sorting gear, building shelves, collating notes. He lost track of time, and was only half-aware of nightfall, music, partying noise. He was repairing a regulator when the door opened and Lehder walked in.

"A hard worker, I see," Lehder said, smiling.

Novak shrugged.

"I admire hard workers. But there's a time for play, too. Come on."

"Come on?" said Novak.

"To the party. Everyone else is there."

Novak shook his head. "I've got too much to do here."

"It can wait," Lehder said.

"Not really."

Lehder came a little closer. "It's not just social," he said. "This is an important occasion, Dick. Symbolically. Team spirit is vital in every organization. I've brought some very capable people to Norman's. It's important to meet them, to get to know them. As part of the team."

Novak had little fondness for organizations and was wary of the concept of team play. "Beach parties aren't really my thing," he said.

Lehder was no longer smiling. "That's not the point. The research center is part of the organization."

Novak laid down the regulator. "Maybe," he said. "But it's something I have to build myself, in the way I see fit. That means when I think there's work to be done, there's work to be done."

There was a stillness. "You seem to forget, my friend, who has seen to all your needs," Lehder said quietly. "What more could you ask for?"

"That's just it," Novak said, his own voice rising. "I didn't ask for help and if it's contingent on me changing my plans to conform to some notion of what makes an island resort, then I'm not interested. I'm not a professional entertainer, and I don't need to be entertained either."

"I see," Lehder said, appearing not at all rattled by this outburst.

"What's that supposed to mean?" Novak said.

"I thought you and I had an understanding, that's all," Lehder replied. "I must have been wrong."

"You weren't wrong. But I don't tell you how to run your business, whatever it is, and I expect the same consideration."

"Whatever it is, Dick?" Lehder's voice grew still quieter. Novak looked at him, but said nothing. In truth, he didn't know why he had used the phrase. Lehder picked up the regulator. He didn't brandish it or wave it around; he just took possession of it. "You'd better understand something, amigo. There's no research center, no trips to the reef, no diving in the pond, unless I say so."

Although the two men were very close now, Novak didn't back away. "That sounds like a threat," he said.

That rekindled Lehder's smile. "Let's just say that everyone on Norman's has a role to play—and no one is more important than anyone else. No one's off the team. Everyone's on. Understood?"

Novak said nothing. Lehder looked him in the eye. His gaze was hard and penetrating. Novak couldn't recall ever being exposed to one so powerful. He had to exert all his will to keep from averting his own eyes. "Don't make this unpleasant for yourself," Lehder said. "Wouldn't you rather learn about the team approach from me, instead of from Heinrich and his boys?"

"What does Heinrich have to do with anything?"

Suddenly Lehder laughed. In the next moment, the tension in the room dissipated. Lehder turned and headed for the door. It was as though nothing had happened. "See you at the party," he said, going out into the darkness. "There's lots of time—it'll probably last all night."

But Novak didn't go to the party. He remained in the dive shop, although he was now too agitated to work. Later, he made his way along an unlit path that ran parallel to the beach. He got close enough to see the fires, the band, the dancing; hear drunken laughter and hot music; smell marijuana. Then he returned to his villa, locked the door, and lay on the bed.

19

Phil Kniskern flew down to Norman's Cay on the morning the diving students were due to leave. He had called Novak a few days before, telling him he was feeling better and would be happy to fly the students back to Florida, since he had business to attend to on Norman's at the same time.

Carlos Lehder was waiting for Kniskern in the bar. No one else was present. Kniskern had met Lehder several times and had always found him charming. He had rented his villas to Lehder and his associates without any difficulties. So now he smiled and offered his hand.

Lehder shook it, but didn't smile. Neither did he ask about Kniskern's health or offer him anything to eat or drink. They sat down opposite each other at one of the little tables. A manila envelope lay on the tabletop, under Lehder's hand.

"You have a proposition for me?" Kniskern said.

Lehder nodded. "I want to buy your villas."

There was a pause, but not a long one, before Kniskern said: "I'm willing to sell. It depends on the amount."

"Two-fifty," Lehder said instantly.

"For all three of them?"

"That's my offer."

"It's too low," Kniskern said. He waited for Lehder to ask how much he wanted. But Lehder said nothing; he just tapped the manila envelope. Kniskern, growing uncomfortable, said, "I think they're worth a lot more than that, especially with the kind of development that seems to be going on here now."

"What kind of development are you talking about, Kniskern?" Lehder asked.

Kniskern. Previously it had always been "Mr. Kniskern" or "Phil." All at once Lehder's charm seemed to melt away; beneath it lay something hard and tough. "Just what I saw from the plane," Kniskern replied. "And on the way up to the hotel. You've obviously gotten things moving on Norman's. Congratulations."

"Congratulations?" said Lehder. "So you're pulling for me, then?"

"I'm pulling for Norman's, Mr. Lehder."

Lehder leaned slightly toward him. "I am Norman's now, Kniskern. If you're pulling for Norman's, you're pulling for me." Kniskern was silent. "But," Lehder continued, reaching into the envelope, "I have reason to believe you're not really on my side at all."

He drew a few blown-up photographs out of the envelope and turned them so Kniskern could see. Now, for the first time, Lehder flashed his charming smile. "Recognize anyone?" he asked.

The top photograph, shot with a high-powered lens, showed Kniskern on an airstrip talking to his pilot, a Bahamian named Ludlow Adams. "That's my pilot," Kniskern said.

"Who does he work for?"

"Me," Kniskern said. "And he does some charter work. What's this all about? I don't remember this picture being taken. Who took it?"

Lehder didn't reply. Instead, he slid the top photograph off the pile, revealing the next. It showed Kniskern on a street, walking beside another man. Lehder pushed it aside. The next photograph showed Kniskern at an outdoor cafe with the same man and another one. The last photograph was of Kniskern and the second man standing by Kniskern's plane. "How about them?" Lehder said. He

Richard Novak (*Credit: Eric Bergman*)

Carlos Lehder at the wheel
of his private plane.
(*Credit: Sygma*)

Carlos Lehder with his
second wife, Diane.
(*Credit: Sygma*)

Aerial view of Norman's Cay, Bahamas.

Norman's Cay Hotel and Yacht Club.

The airstrip on Norman's Cay, large enough to land a DC-3 cargo plane.

One of Lehder's armed men guarding the landing strip.

Richard Novak aboard the *Reef Witch*.

Schooling hammerhead sharks. (*Credit: Chip Matheson*)

Richard Novak diving off Norman's Cay.

Richard Novak with student divers on Norman's Cay Pier.

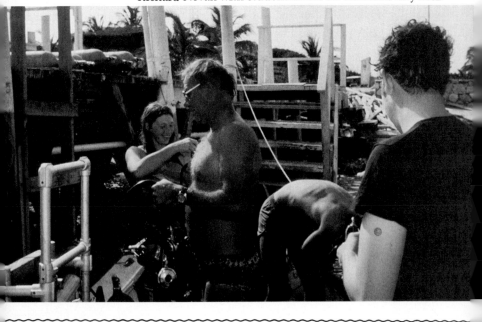

Planes used by Carlos Lehder to smuggle cocaine into the
United States.

Carlos Lehder's helicopter flying surveillance over "Volcano."

TOP: The remains of the plane that crashed behind the Norman's Cay Hotel. BOTTOM: The DC-3 that one of Lehder's pilots crash-landed in the Norman's Cay Harbor.

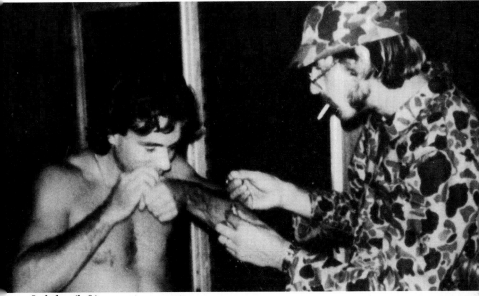

Lehder (left), snorting cocaine.

Loads of cocaine Carlos Lehder smuggled into the United States.

Carlos Lehder embracing his daughter. *(Credit: Manuel de Dios Unanue)*

Three of Carlos Lehder's girlfriends at the Yacht Club bar.

Home purchased by Carlos Lehder, known as "Volcano."

Philip Kniskern's beach house occupied by Richard Novak.

Ed Ward and his team of partners loading cocaine into the Merlin III aircraft Carlos Lehder purchased for their use.

Ed Ward and his partners at the Norman's Cay Yacht Club.

Caves in Norman's Cay lagoon where Carlos Lehder sometimes stashed cocaine.

Loads of cocaine hidden at stash site on Norman's Cay.

The remains of the recreation area in front of Norman's Cay beach bungalows.

The remains of the Norman's Cay police car.

The remains of the Norman's Cay Hotel after Carlos Lehder fled.

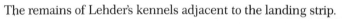

The remains of Lehder's kennels adjacent to the landing strip.

Carlos Lehder shortly after his arrest and extradition to the
United States. (*Credit: Sygma*)

was looking closely at Kniskern, closely enough to see the sweat forming on Kniskern's upper lip.

"Look," Kniskern said, "I really don't under—"

"Recognize them?" Lehder interrupted. "That's the question."

"Sure. They're investors from Lauderdale. I was trying to get them interested in Norman's before . . . before you came along."

"Investors, huh?"

"Yeah."

"Like the well-known Ludlow Adams, maybe? Your so-called pilot?"

"My pilot? You've lost me there, Mr. Lehder."

"I don't think so," Lehder said. "I think you know god-damned well that all three of them are pigs."

"Pigs?"

"Pigs for the DEA." Lehder let the words hang in the air. He watched the sweat forming on Kniskern's upper lip. "I see you don't even bother to deny it. That just leaves one more question: why are you so buddy-buddy with the DEA?"

"Jesus, Mr. Lehder, I don't know anything about the DEA. If any of these guys have anything to do with the DEA, this is the first I've heard about it. I swear. They never discussed any of that stuff with me, ever."

"What about your pilot?"

"Never. But you can be sure I'll grill him about this when I get back. I don't like being used, if that's what's been going on."

Lehder gave Kniskern a long look. Then he slipped the pictures back in the envelope. "You do that, Phil. If that's what's been going on."

Kniskern wiped his upper lip. Lehder rose. "What about the villas?" Kniskern asked.

"You've heard my offer," Lehder said. He picked up the envelope. "It stands." He started for the door, stopped, turned. "Oh, and Phil. I don't think you'd better land on Norman's anymore."

"What?"

"In fact, I'm sure of it."

"But I have every right to use the strip. I still own those villas."

"Then you wouldn't want anything to happen to them, would you?" Lehder walked out.

Richard Novak walked across the airstrip toward Kniskern's plane, camera in hand. Forbes was already there, helping the diving students load their gear. "Morning," Novak said. "I'd like to get a group photo before you all go." The students turned to Novak. He raised the camera and through the viewfinder saw that something was wrong. There were only seven faces in it.

"Where's Hollins?" Novak said. Again, as in the water, the missing eighth.

"Not here yet," Forbes said.

They all looked around, waiting for Hollins to come running up the path. He did not. "He must have slept in," Novak said. "Where's he billeted?"

"The Emlin house," Forbes replied.

Novak hurried to his villa, hopped on his motorbike, and sped up-island. On the way he passed a work crew clearing land for an extension of the airstrip, and half a mile up the road a second crew building a cinder block wall that was part of something called "Reception Station" on the blueprints. In reality, it looked like the border crossing to a totalitarian state.

The Emlin house, less than a mile from where the road curved toward the eastern hook, had a peaked roof and fine views. Emlin, the original owner, had recently sold out to Lehder and left the island on short notice. Novak knew that, but he didn't reflect upon it as he walked up the steps to the porch; neither did he reflect on the holes punched in the screen, or the spent shell casings scattered in the garden. His mind was on Hollins, who had become a nuisance now, and whom he wanted to see off the island forever.

Novak peered through the screen. He saw Steve Francis, framed in a rectangle of light from a room beyond; it shone on his gold chains, and on a diamond newly stuck in his left earlobe.

"Where's Hollins?" Novak called to him, wondering what Francis was doing in the house.

"Not here."

Novak looked past him, saw a trail of scuba gear leading toward a room off the main hall; scuba gear that should have been in the shop. Novak recognized the stripe pattern on the tank: the one he had given to Hollins.

"Get him up, Francis," he said. "The plane's waiting."

"He's not here, man. I told you."

Novak pushed open the door and stepped into the house. He walked toward the room off the main hall. Francis, in his underwear, blocked his path. He looked rumpled and seedy; Novak could smell him. "Get out of my way, Francis."

Francis wavered. Then Hollins spoke from inside the room. "Let him in, Steve." Francis stepped aside. Novak entered the room.

Dougie Hollins reclined on a sofa bed along the far wall. He still wore yesterday's clothes, and looked as though he hadn't slept. There was only one other place to sit, an easy chair at right angles to the bed. Heinrich Rogol was in it. What was he doing there? Novak glanced around. He saw empty bottles and full ashtrays—full of butts not only from tobacco cigarettes. Hollins's suitcase lay open on the floor. With his foot, Novak slid it toward the sofa bed. "Come on, Hollins. You've got time for a quick shower."

With effort, Hollins pulled himself to a sitting position. He looked terrible. Novak, not an expert in these matters, could tell nevertheless that he was stoned out of his mind. "I like it here," Hollins said.

"Me too," Novak told him. "But it's time to go."

"I like it here, is the thing, Mr. Novak. I don't want to leave. You know?"

"I know you're leaving. I brought you here, I'm making sure you go, as scheduled. This was an organized trip, with a beginning, middle, and end. I made that clear in Florida."

"This isn't Florida," Hollins replied. "Norman's Cay belongs to Joe Lehder now. And he said I could stay here as long as I want." There was a pause. Then Hollins, with an up-from-under look that might have been meant to show some sort of business acumen, but instead communicated only cunning of a low order, said, "There's room for more than one dive outfit on Norman's."

The remark enraged Novak. He moved toward the sofa bed, intending to grab Hollins the way he had grabbed him off the ceiling of the cave. But then he heard Heinrich and Francis moving quickly behind him. Novak stopped. Heinrich, he remembered, carried a .45. Or two of them. At that moment he thought of the spent shells in the garden. His anger faded, replaced by puzzlement. And Hollins, he remembered, was legally an adult, laughable though the concept was.

"Okay, Hollins. Suit yourself." Novak turned and left quickly, but not so quickly he didn't catch Francis's smirk, or hear the snickers that followed him out.

Back at the airstrip, the students were on the plane and Kniskern was waiting beside it. Novak climbed on board, told them that Hollins wasn't coming, and said good-bye. He had been planning to invite them back for the hammerhead migration, but he changed his mind. Instead he just thanked them for their hard work. That way he didn't have to think about the future.

Novak climbed out of the plane. Kniskern was still standing on the strip, watching him. Novak hadn't seen Kniskern for months. Kniskern looked pale, drawn, shrunken.

"I've got something to tell you," Kniskern said.

"Stay out of island politics?"

Kniskern didn't smile. He looked grim. "I'm leaving Norman's. I'm finished here. This is Lehder's island now."

"So I hear."

"He wants to buy the beach villas."

"Including the one I'm in?" Novak asked.

"Yes," said Kniskern. "But I'm not selling." He reached inside his jacket, took out a folded sheet of paper, and handed it to Novak.

Novak opened it and read. It was a contract, a contract between Kniskern and him. Kniskern had made Novak his representative on the island. The villas were in his sole care.

"All right with you?" Kniskern said. He had one hand on the plane, as though he needed its support to remain on his feet.

Novak nodded. "But there's one thing I don't understand. If you're finished here, why aren't you selling them?"

Kniskern sighed. Then he glanced around and lowered his voice, although there was no one in sight and the students in the plane couldn't hear them. "There are things about Norman's I haven't told you. I haven't been allowed to tell you."

"By whom?"

Kniskern glanced around again. "I'll get to that. But first you should know that all the trouble on the island was caused by Lehder and his men, not by Ed Ward. Ward's just a little fish. Lehder had the lines cut and the flights cancelled and the tourists driven off."

"Why? To screw up your deal?"

"That was part of it. He was the reason my negotiations got stalled, although I didn't know it at the time. And I probably wouldn't have believed it even if I had known it."

"Why is that?"

"Because everyone involved knew what Lehder is. I still can't believe they'd do business with someone like that."

"Yeah? Well I don't know what he is. Tell me."

"Lehder's a major cocaine smuggler, Dick. That's where all his money comes from. He's got a criminal record

going back to 1972 and he's been behind bars several
times. And his men have all served time. Arson, rape,
narcotics. You know Michelle, that girlfriend of Reed's?
He took her away from home when she was thirteen."

Novak's voice rose. "You knew all this and didn't tell
me?"

"Shh. I'm sorry, Dick, I really am. I tried to keep you
from getting involved."

Novak made no attempt to lower his voice. "The hell
you did. You got me here under false pretences. Do you
think I ever would have come if I'd known this?"

Kniskern hung his head, like a child. "I'm sorry. I've
made a mistake." He looked up, and when he spoke his
voice was bitter. "You've got to understand, I've been in
a horrible position myself. They swore me to secrecy."

"Who?"

Kniskern answered very quietly. "The DEA."

"I don't understand," Novak said.

"They're moving against him, in cooperation with the
Bahamians. They need absolute secrecy, that's all I can
tell you."

"What do you mean, they're moving against him? If
he's what you say he is, why haven't they already arrested
him?"

Kniskern hesitated. "Legalities, I guess. It's complicated."

Novak suddenly found himself thinking of the armed
man who had boarded the *Reef Witch* in Nassau harbor.
It didn't occur to him to ask whether Lehder already knew
he was being investigated. Nor did he think to ask if his
own presence had become known to the DEA, and if so
what role they thought he was playing. Instead he ran
his eyes over the contract and asked, "What's your angle?
Why are you putting me in charge of the villas?"

"Because I trust you, Dick," Kniskern said. "And frankly,
I haven't got the physical strength right now to . . ."

"To what?"

"To hang on here."

"You want me to hang on for you?"

"You could put it that way," Kniskern said. "Then, when Lehder's gone, we can continue as planned." But he didn't sound optimistic; his voice was weak and strained. "You don't have to stay on the island itself," Kniskern added. In fact, I wouldn't advise it. You should close the shop and wait this out in Nassau or Florida."

"You mean just run away?" Novak asked.

"It's not running away. It's simply being prudent while the authorities do what they have to do. There's nothing to keep you here in the meantime."

That wasn't true. There was Hollins for one. And Lehder for two. Lehder, who wanted him to be a team player. He had resisted, even before he had understood the nature of the game. Now, knowing it, he was outraged. The man had been trying to inveigle him—and when that failed, to threaten him—into joining a criminal conspiracy. The idea that he might have become even an accessory to drug dealing sickened him, and so did his realization of the clever pyschological techniques Lehder had used on him. All the little storms of his anger and annoyance, which now swirled separately around Kniskern, Hollins, the authorities, coalesced and focused all their force on Carlos Lehder. "I'm not leaving," he said.

"That's foolish."

"Maybe," Novak said, and then found himself echoing Hollins. "I like it here. This is . . . home. And I know how to handle men like Lehder."

Kniskern looked at him dubiously but said nothing. Novak was unshaken. Lehder, he knew, was like a dangerous animal—a hammerhead shark, say. You never turn your back on a hammerhead; that was one of Novak's rules. You face it. If necessary, you punch it in the snout. He could deal with hammerheads; he could deal with Lehder. The principle was the same.

The students were watching them from the windows of the plane. "I'd better get going," Kniskern said. He held out his hand. Novak didn't want to shake it—it was too soon for kissing and making up—but he did. Kniskern had shown poor judgment and behaved badly, but Kniskern wasn't his enemy. Lehder was his enemy. That's what he had to keep in mind.

"Good luck," Kniskern said, climbing into the plane. "And be careful."

Kniskern's plane rolled down the strip, turned, picked up speed and rose into the sky. Novak watched until it faded from sight.

Later, Novak saw Paulette Jones walking down the dock toward a waiting boat. She carried a big suitcase. "Hello, Paulette," Novak said.

She looked at him with embarrassment.

"Going somewhere?" Novak asked.

"Home," Paulette said. She wouldn't look at him. "San Salvador."

"Vacation?"

She shook her head. "I'm leaving," she replied. "For good."

"Why?"

Paulette bit her lip. "It's for the best. Leaving, I mean." Now she glanced at him, briefly met his gaze. "Aren't you?"

"No," Novak said. "I'm not."

Paulette stepped forward and gave him a quick kiss on the cheek. Then she got into the boat and didn't look at him again.

20

Gus Holleran, the American customs agent in Nassau who had originally told Novak about Norman's Cay and introduced him to the pilot Lawrence Ferguson, hadn't always been a customs agent. Previously, he had been a leading drug-traffic investigator in Miami. Novak knew that; Holleran had admitted it late one night in the bar at the South Ocean Beach Hotel. Novak didn't know why Holleran was no longer a drug investigator. He had asked, but Holleran had just said, "It's a tough business," and left it at that. Not long after Kniskern and the students flew out of Norman's, Novak went to Highbourne Cay and called Holleran.

"What do you know about Norman's Cay?" he asked.

"Norman's? Well, there're the hammerheads, like I told you, and—"

"I don't mean that," Novak interrupted. "I want to know why Norman's would appeal to someone like Carlos Lehder."

"Never heard of him."

"Then ask some of your pals at the DEA. I'll see you in a couple of days."

They sat far from anyone else at a table under the thatched roof of the South Ocean Beach Hotel beach bar, drinking tall rum-and-tonics. Holleran, a big man who looked like he could take care of himself if things got rough, turned to Novak and said: "It seems that Norman's is a hot topic these days. And hot is the operative word. You were smart to get out."

"Who said anything about getting out?" Novak replied. Holleran looked puzzled. "You're here, aren't you?"

"Temporarily. Naturally, I'm going back—I just opened down there and the hammerhead migration starts in April. But first I want to know what's happening."

Holleran gazed at him for a few moments, then took a long drink. "It's partly my fault, I guess. I should have looked into Norman's more carefully before recommending it to you. It's just not the kind of place for someone like you. I'm sorry."

"I wish people would stop saying they're sorry, like it's the end of an era or something," Novak said. "And what do you mean—someone like me?"

"A civilian, that's all," Holleran answered. "Norman's isn't an appropriate venue for a research center, or anything legitimate for that matter. Not right now."

"In your opinion," Novak said. "I'm already on the island. Maybe if you'd told me before things would have been different, but you didn't and they're not. I don't care anyway. That's the past. I want you to help me prepare for the future. Are you going to or not?"

Holleran laughed. "Christ, you're bullheaded." He finished his drink and ordered another round. He took another long drink, staring out to sea. "Okay. I'll say it for the last time, as clearly as I can. Don't go back to Norman's."

"Thanks for the advice," Novak said. "Now what's going on?"

Holleran played with the icecubes in his glass. "It's a complicated investigation, Dick," he said. "Not the kind of situation to get caught in."

"I thought you said it for the last time."

Holleran laughed again, and downed more rum. Novak didn't remember him drinking much in the past. "Ever heard of Bobby Eliot?" Holleran asked.

"No."

"He's one of the DEA's top men in Jacksonville. A tough little son-of-a-bitch. Looks like a dope dealer himself. He's in charge of the Lehder investigation." Holleran paused. "But there's no need for you to know all this," he said. "And it might be dangerous."

"You can trust me."

"I didn't mean that. I meant knowing might put you in danger."

"That's a risk I'm prepared to take. I've made an investment down there. I'm not going to give it up without a fight."

"Who said anything about fighting? Shit. That's exactly the kind of thing I was afraid of."

"All right, then. I'm not going to give it up easily. Is that better?"

"Not really." Holleran sighed. "Bobby Eliot wasn't investigating Lehder at first. Last year, he got a tip from the Lauderdale cops. Some Sears clerk or something, earning squat, was living high off the hog. Cars, planes, beachfront house, the rest of it. But paying no taxes, get it? That's a red flag at the DEA. Plus the guy was a pilot. Red flag number two. Eliot put a tail on him, a tail that led to Norman's Cay."

"Ed Ward, right?"

Holleran smiled. "Right."

"He's not dangerous," Novak said.

"Eliot knows that. I'm sure he's got plans for Ward."

"Like what?"

"You'll see. Anyway, Ward's a side issue. On Norman's, Eliot's people saw Lehder's planes from time to time, and punched the tail numbers into the computer in Miami. Out of curiosity. And of course the screen lit up. All those pilots, all those planes were in the data bank. As was Lehder. They've all got records a mile long. Lehder's setting up a little criminal paradise down there, like some pirate on the Spanish Main."

"But why Norman's?"

Holleran shrugged. "Off the beaten track. But convenient to Florida and Colombia. And there's already all kinds of talk in Miami about big shipments of powder coming through the Exumas these days. Plus it's a good place to hide out. He's not the only one down there."

"Ward, you mean?"

Holleran dismissed Ward with a wave. "Much more big-time than that. I'm talking about Robert Vesco."

"The financier?" Novak said.

"He's on Cistern Cay. Ten miles south of Norman's. Bought it for $180,000 a year and a half ago."

"Does he know Lehder?"

"There's no proof," Holleran said. "But there's no strip on Cistern. The best way to get there is to fly to Norman's and go by boat the rest of the way. And Vesco's no recluse. They get sightings all over the goddamn islands. So it figures they know each other. If that's true, then it's probable Vesco helped him set up the money-laundering end. And Vesco wrote the book on that. My sources say that Lehder's not the type to pass up an opportunity like that. He's an enterprising guy, apparently. When he was just another teenage punk in Miami the cops thought they'd soon be fishing him out of the river, like they do with most of them. Now he's the head of some coke operation that no one knows the extent of."

"He's enterprising, all right," Novak said, thinking of the changes on Norman's and how efficiently Lehder had managed them. The unloading of the fleet in the lagoon was probably the best-run operation he had ever seen in the islands, if you wanted to look at it that way. "But if they know all this, why aren't they arresting him?"

"I told you—it's complicated," Holleran said. "He's the subject of ten separate investigations now. DEA, FBI, CIA, Miami police, L.A. police—all stepping on each other's toes. And Bobby Eliot has to get action from the Bahamians. That means the State Department's probably involved, which makes it a nightmare. To say nothing about the Bahamians. Hanna's on his side, but—"

"Dudly Hanna?"

"You know him?"

"Yeah, but I didn't get much action out of him."

Holleran put down his drink and looked closely at Novak. "What do you mean?"

"I went to him about Ward." Novak described his conversation with Dudley Hanna.

"Who else did you talk to?"

"Just someone at the desk."

"And since you got back?"

"No one. I thought I should talk to you first."

Holleran nodded. "You did the right thing. It's best to keep a low profile right now."

"For how long?"

"Till Eliot and Hanna make their move."

"And when's that going to be?"

"Who knows? Probably just Eliot and Hanna, if they're smart. I've already told you everything I know. Against my better judgment. I hope it's changed your mind."

"About what?" asked Novak.

"Going back to Norman's. Now you know what's at stake down there, maybe you understand that the murder of a marine researcher wouldn't mean a hell of a lot."

"I'm there to run a dive operation," Novak said. And, he thought, he now had legal responsibilities on Norman's, thanks to the contract Kniskern had given him. "And that's what I'm going to do."

"So you want to be a hero," Holloran said.

Novak got angry. "I'm going back because I like it there and I have a right to be there. If that's not good enough for you, Gus, then think whatever the hell you want."

Holleran held up one of his big hands like a traffic cop. "Okay, okay. Just stay out of trouble, that's all. And Dick?"

"Yeah?"

"Keep me posted."

"Sure."

Novak hitched a ride back to Norman's with a pilot who had calls to make in the Exumas. After nineteen minutes in the blue, the plane descended over Norman's. The pilot circled in from the west, and low; so low that Novak could see his own house. And still lower, so he could see men standing on the porch. A lot of men. Some of them had guns. They were pointing them, in fact. Pointing them at someone standing by the sliding doors. At first, Novak, peering through the window, thought that the someone was Hollins. He was young-looking, young enough to have been Hollins, and Hollins had been on Novak's mind. But it wasn't Hollins. As the plane skimmed right over the house, just clearing the casuarinas, Novak saw that the man in the gunsights was his own son, Chris.

21

There were more armed men waiting on the airstrip. Novak's pilot, concentrating on his approach, hadn't observed the scene on the porch, but he did see the reception committee. Someone was pointing a rifle at the plane. "What the hell's going on down there?" the pilot said, and immediately raised the nose of the plane.

"What are you doing?" Novak said.

"What do you think, for Christ's sake?"

Novak grabbed one of his shoulders and squeezed hard. He yelled into the pilot's ear: "Land, or I'll put her down myself."

The pilot gave him a frightened glance. There was no time to think: he just obeyed, tipping the nose back down. The plane landed hard on the strip, thrusting Novak's body against his seat belt. It bounced several times, raising clouds of dust. Novak jumped out while it was still rolling. The plane never stopped; the pilot whipped it around in a tight turn, opened the throttle, and shot back into the sky, headed for Eleuthera.

The men on the strip approached Novak, but before they reached him, Chris, taking advantage of the distraction, hopped off the porch and ran to him. Heinrich Rogol and his men chased Chris with drawn guns. Novak took Chris's hand and pulled him close. He looked carefully at his son, saw that he was unharmed, but also saw the fear in his eyes. Fear, and something more, something accusatory. "Who are these guys, Dad? What have you gotten into?"

There was no time to explain. Heinrich and his men surrounded them. Novak recognized some of them. The others were new. Heinrich pointed his .45 at Chris.

"Put that thing away, Rogol," Novak said. "This is my son. He's here at my invitation."

"They think I'm some kind of drug agent, or something," Chris said.

"Get him off the fucking island," said Heinrich, jerking his gun at Chris's plane, parked near the customs house. "Now."

"I don't think you heard me," Novak said. "This is my son. I've asked him to help me set up the shop. The shop that your boss wants me to run, Rogol. If you've got a problem, talk to Lehder."

"No one lands here without permission. Those are Mr. Lehder's orders." But a wave of uncertainty seemed to roll over Heinrich and his men, and they lowered their guns. Still holding Chris's hand, Novak pushed his way out of the circle and walked toward his house. Chris had pulled his hand free before they got there.

Inside, Novak shut the door and closed the curtains. "Sit down," he said.

But Chris didn't want to sit. He stood in the middle of the room, arms crossed, glaring at his father. "Nice resort you've got here, Dad," he said.

"Don't be too quick to judge," Novak said. "There've been some unfortunate developments on the island, things no one could have foreseen. But they're temporary—I know that for a fact. And it's really not as bad as it looks."

"Don't tell me how it looks," Chris said; he was still scared, and it made him lash out at his father. "I flew into an armed camp because of you. They were all over the plane the second I landed. Your friend with the B-movie accent kept saying that he knew how to deal with DEA pigs. I thought he was going to shoot me."

Chris wasn't too far from tears. Novak spoke as gently

as he could. "I'm sorry, Chris." He realized that the stupid phrase was now coming from his lips. Everyone was sorry. It was a sorry situation. But temporary, he told himself again, and the thought buoyed him. "It's over now, son. I'll go talk to Lehder and make sure he understands."

Chris was not going to be easily mollified. "Lehder? He's the one that sent them. Didn't you hear what the guy said? Can't you just admit it? You've made a huge mistake. I don't know what's going on here, but whatever it is has nothing to do with your future. This place is nothing but trouble. Now let's get the hell out of here."

"Chris. Let me explain. This is just temporary. I promise you—everything's going to turn out as planned. Trust me."

Chris shook his head. "You're not thinking straight. I wasn't sure when we talked in Miami, but I am now. And I can't believe you don't see it too. Those goons could have killed me, Dad. What's wrong with you?"

Novak stood looking at his son. He couldn't think of anything to say, not anything that would help. Chris only wanted to hear that he would leave, and Novak couldn't bring himself to say that.

Sounds entered from outside. Chris pulled back the edge of the curtain. Looking through the trees, they could see Heinrich's men rolling Chris's plane onto the strip. "God damn it," Chris said. "What are they doing with the plane?"

"I'll go talk to Lehder," Novak said.

"What's that going to accomplish?" Chris replied. "Get packed, Dad. We're going."

Novak stood where he was, arms akimbo, miserable. "I can't, Chris. I'm just getting settled here. This island has great potential. It's going to be everything I told—"

"Forget it, Dad," Chris said, his voice rising toward hysteria. "Are you going to spend your time taking people like that out to the reef, for God's sake?"

A horrible thought, and Novak pushed it out of his mind. "I'm not going to let them run me off the island, Chris," he said. "That's that."

Chris stared at him. Novak looked away. "Good-bye,

Dad," he said, his voice quiet now, under control. "Call when you change your mind. I'll come get you." He opened the sliding glass door and walked quickly to the strip, without another word, without looking back. Novak went outside, took a few faltering steps toward the strip, halted. He watched Heinrich's men silently make way for Chris, watched Chris get into the plane, watched the smooth takeoff. Heinrich and his men dispersed. Then silence descended on Norman's Cay. Novak went back inside, sat on the bed, did nothing.

Night fell. It brought new sounds from outside. Reluctantly, Novak rose and looked out. He saw plumes of smoke rising into the clear night sky. He went out onto the porch. From there, he could see shadowy figures lighting smudge pots up and down the airstrip. Quietly, he crept through the bush, toward the customs house. He heard the crackle of portable radios, heard trucks rumbling along the road. A big fuel pumper crossed the strip and stopped near the customs house. By the glow of the smudge pots, Novak could see the driver, lighting up a cigarette. Once or twice, the driver glanced up at the sky.

Avoiding the road, Novak made his way down to the beach. Orange lights shone through the trees. A string of bonfires burned along the beach as far as he could see. The whole island seemed to be ablaze. Novak listened hard. He heard the rumble of trucks, the crackling of the bonfires, the crackling of the walkie-talkies. And then, very faintly at first, came the drone of an airplane.

Treading carefully, Novak returned to the scrub near the customs house. The fuel truck had been moved to the side of the airstrip. There were lots of men around the customs house now, and more along the edges of the runway. They were quiet and and made no unnecessary movements. From time to time, light glinted on a weapon in someone's belt.

Then the plane came down out of the northeastern sky, touched down, rolled to a stop. The men sprang into action. They ran to the plane and coupled a hose to it from the pumper. Another truck appeared out of the darkness, braked to a quick stop by the cargo door, raising dust that glowed burnt orange in the light of the smudge pots. The men threw open the back door of the truck, unloaded cardboard cartons sealed with duct tape, loaded them into the plane. The cartons were of the size and type that might be used for shipping a stereo system, say, complete with speakers. The cargo door of the plane was closed and locked. The plane took off, heading northwest, toward Florida. The whole operation had taken two or three minutes.

The next plane landed before the sound of the first one had faded away. Novak watched the procedure repeated, more quickly, if anything, the second time. This second plane flew away in the same direction as the first. Then came the third.

Crouched in the bushes by the side of the runway, Novak watched the process repeated ten times that night. How different this was from Ed Ward's operation. Novak remembered the noisy scene on the same strip, the little single-engine plane barely clearing the the trees, the almost giggly celebration when it was over. Amateur night.

Now he had seen the pros. Carlos Lehder was building a machine for pouring cocaine into the U.S. The bonfires and smudge pots were only temporary, Novak knew. Soon all the navigational equipment that Lehder's fleet had brought would be installed; navigational equipment that had seemed purposeless until now, but would render night flying safe and efficient. The drugs too must have come to Norman's by sea. Did Lehder have some special place to cache them on the island? A good question, Novak thought.

Later, he thought of another one: Lehder knew he was on the island. Why hadn't he bothered to keep him from seeing what he saw that night?

Much later the same night, Carlos Lehder lay wide awake in his bed in the Volcano house, too excited to sleep. His first big shipment from Norman's had gone without a hitch. Once all the navigation and communications equipment was installed, there was no reason the procedure couldn't be repeated every night of the week. Seven shipments a week. His mind roughed out the numbers. They were fabulous. Lehder smiled, and reached for the woman lying beside him.

"I'm tired," she said in Spanish. This was not his wife Jemel, who never came to Norman's now, nor was it Margit or Chocolata. She was Liliana Garcia Osorio, a pretty, middle-class woman from Armenia, his home town. He intended to marry her, too. When? Soon, he thought, although he had made no move to divorce Jemel. Would that jeopardize the status of his marriage to Liliana? Lehder didn't occupy himself with that concern for more than a moment. After all, Liliana was five months pregnant with his child.

He reached for her again. This time she turned toward him obediently. "What are you smiling at?" she asked.

"Everything," he replied.

There was a knock at the door.

Francis. Lehder let him in, with some annoyance.

"What is it?" he said.

"Sorry, boss," Francis said, shifting his weight nervously. "Sure moved a lot of coke tonight, huh?"

"I told you never to use that word."

"Sorry. Children, right? Coke is children and the island is the farm." He grinned foolishly. "Moved a lot of children, then. Sounds funny."

"What do you want, Steve?"

Something in his tone made Francis avert his eyes. "Here," he said. "I thought you'd want to see this." He handed Lehder a photograph of two men talking at beachfront bar. Lehder knew them both. One was a man he had done some business with in the past. Gus Holleran. The other was a man he was doing business with now. Richard Novak.

Lehder didn't go back to bed.

22

The next morning Novak went to the hotel for breakfast as he usually did. But as he entered, he saw Heinrich Rogol and a group of Lehder's pilots digging into hearty portions; almost a parody, in his mind, of honest laborers chowing down after a hard shift. Novak turned and walked out. He decided at that moment to avoid eating in the hotel.

But he had to eat. Later that day he put to sea in the *Reef Witch*, en route to Harold Albury's market on Highbourne Cay for supplies. It was a beautiful day, radiating the kind of blue perfection of sea and sky that had drawn Novak so magnetically to the region in the first place. Now he didn't notice any of it. Some men might have asked themselves at that moment if the fight was worth it. Novak did not.

Harold Albury, a white Bahamian, had a phone in his store, and so served as a one-man bulletin board for the northern Exumas. "Message for you," he said as Novak walked in.

"Who from?"

Albury fished through a pocketful of crumpled papers and handed him one. "Call Gus," it said.

Novak reached Holleran at the South Ocean Beach Hotel. "What's up?" he said.

"Hangin' in?" Holleran asked.

"Yeah."

"I've got someone who wants to talk to you."

"Who?" Novak asked.

"One of Bobby Eliot's men."

"Good," Novak said. "I've got plenty to tell him."

Holleran named a time—ten-thirty the next morning; and a place—a little beach east of Nassau, away from the tourist hotels.

Novak went down to the dock. A thickset white Bahamian was gazing at the *Reef Witch*. "You out of Norman's Cay?" he said.

"What about it?" Novak said.

"Nothin'. I don't know you, is all. And I know just about everybody around here." This was the moment to introduce himself, but Novak did not. "The name's Welles," the man said. "Elvis Welles." Novak nodded and boarded his boat.

Novak hitched a ride out of Highbourne early the next morning and arrived in what he thought was plenty of time. But it took him much longer than he had anticipated to find where Kniskern had left his car. That made him drive impatiently. It had been raining all morning and traffic was slow. Novak pulled out to pass a truck and plowed through a deep puddle. The car stalled and he pulled over to the side of the road. It was after ten, and he was still miles from the rendezvous. Novak turned the key, pumped the gas pedal. Nothing. Just let it sit for a while, he told himself. But he was unable to let it sit for more than ten or twenty seconds. He kept turning the key, pumping the gas.

Kniskern's car didn't start until the sun came out and dried everything out. By then it was eleven o'clock and Novak was in a fury. His first thought was to turn around and go to the South Ocean Beach, find Holleran, and arrange a second meeting. But then it occurred to him that Eliot's man might have been delayed by the rain too, and he drove on toward the eastern end of New Providence.

The beach Holleran had picked wasn't the kind shown

in tourist brochures. Narrow, covered with seaweed and litter, it was used mostly by Bahamians from Over-the-Hill on weekends. But this was a work day and no one was around. Novak parked by the side of the road, not far from two pink cinder block bathrooms, one for men, one for women.

He walked onto the beach. There was no one else on it, and no sign that anyone else had been. Of course, he thought, a DEA agent was unlikely to leave a note for him, pinned to a tree, or stuck in a bottle. Novak walked down toward the water. The rain had smoothed the dark sand; for that reason, the footprints he suddenly came upon were very distinct. They weren't the prints of a typical beachgoer—whoever had made them had been wearing shoes. Novak followed the prints for a few yards, before noticing that in fact there were two sets, both men's, from the size of them, and both shod. He followed them. They led down to the water, where they had shuffled around, obliterating any clear markings, and then turned back up the beach, toward the men's bathroom. Novak went inside.

The men's room was small and dirty. Novak smelled rotting fish, rotting fruit, urine. The room was deserted. He walked over to the sink. It looked like someone had cut himself shaving—there were splashes of blood in the sink. A bad cut—a red hand print was smeared on the tile next to the broken mirror. Novak went back outside. Now he saw more blood, a trail of red drippings that led him away from the men's room and into a thicket of pine trees. In the middle of the thicket, on a bed of damp pine needles, lay the body of a man. Novak knew at once that he was dead—an ice pick had been stabbed deep into his head, through the right ear.

Novak bent over the man. He was white, in his early thirties, casually dressed. Was this Eliot's man, the man who had been sent to meet him? And was there some sort of message in the fact that he had been stabbed in the ear? Novak occupied himself with these questions for a moment or two. And then the horror of it hit him. He was tough and rugged, but still, after all, a German professor and student of marine life, not a cop or drug agent. Murder and corpses weren't part of his existence. All at once, his gorge rose; he felt faint and his heart started beating wildly. He walked unsteadily out of the pine thicket, into sunlight that made him even more lightheaded. Then he ran to the car, jumped in, locked the doors, and sped away.

Novak braked to a squealing stop in front of the South Ocean Beach Hotel. He hurried into the lobby and asked the receptionist to call Holleran's room.

"Mr. Holleran checked out, sir."

"Checked out?"

"He left for the airport an hour ago."

Novak ran outside, got back in the car and raced to the airport. He entered one of the hangars where the charter pilots gathered, and there the first pilot he asked told him that Holleran had flown out with Lawrence Ferguson.

"Where to?" Novak asked.

The pilot shrugged. No one else knew either—not the other pilots, not the mechanics, not the customs agents. Confused, Novak sat on a chair and tried to piece everything together. Why hadn't Holleran waited to find out the results of his meeting with Eliot's man? And what about Ferguson? He remembered how closely Ferguson had questioned him about his interest in Norman's on his very first trip. Now he saw those questions in a different light. Was Ferguson a DEA agent? That would explain his concern about Novak's intentions. Then Novak had an appalling thought: Ferguson would have shown the same concern if he was working for Lehder. And, following that line, where would that put Gus Holleran? An even more appalling thought. Novak was trying to cope with it when another question arose in his mind, one that drove everything else away: what would have happened if he hadn't stalled Kniskern's car—if he had arrived at

the rendezvous on time? Now Novak was not just confused, but frightened too, although he probably wouldn't
have admitted, it, even to himself.

"Dick Novak?"

Startled, Novak looked up. A man with a big head and
dark curly hair was standing over him. He looked familiar.
"Hi," said the man. "Josh Berger. Gus Holleran sent me."
Novak got to his feet. Where had they met before? At
some hotel, Novak thought. Had Holloran introduced
them? "Where did he go?" asked Novak.

"Norman's Cay," Berger replied.

"Norman's?"

"Yeah," said Berger with a smile. "You know the place?"

Novak nodded somewhat absently. His mind was racing
to process this new information.

"I can drop you there, if you want. I'm on my way to
Highbourne."

A few minutes later—not nearly a sufficient interval for
Novak to sort through his thoughts—he was in Berger's
plane, three thousand feet over the northern edge of
Exuma Sound. Berger was at ease at the controls, obviously an experienced pilot. Novak relaxed slightly and
glanced around the plane. His gaze fell on a manila envelope stuck in a compartment in the passenger-side door.
He wouldn't have looked at it twice, except that his name
was written on it: "Novak."

Novak took the envelope and opened it. He glanced at
Berger. Berger was watching him, with a grin on his face
that Novak didn't like at all. At that moment, Novak
remembered where he had met Berger: not at Holleran's
hotel in Nassau, but at the hotel on Norman's Cay; Carlos
Lehder's hotel.

He removed the contents of the envelope. Berger made
no move to stop him. The contents: a set of photographs
on thick color stock, and a bound report. The pictures
were all of himself: Novak on the *Reef Witch* at Norman's,
Novak with Kniskern, Novak with Forbes, Novak in front

of his beach villa; and finally, the most important one—Novak at the beach bar with Gus Holleran.

Novak looked through the report. It was a résumé of his life. He glanced at Berger. Berger was still watching him, still seemed amused.

"Your only mistake was getting caught with Holleran," Berger said. "Up till then the reef story was holding up nicely."

"What the hell are you talking about?" Novak said. "It's not a story."

Berger's grin broadened, but he said nothing.

"You'd better turn around," Novak said. "I'm not alone. People are going to start wondering where I am. Then Lehder won't be happy with you."

Berger gave him a look—puzzled? wary? sly?—that defied Novak's powers of interpretation. But he didn't alter course, and there was nothing Novak could do about it—he was unarmed and didn't know how to fly.

Ten minutes later, they were circling Norman's. From the air, Novak could see the magnitude of the change taking place on the island. There were clusters of heavy equipment at different places in the interior, and construction sites at the far corners of the island where structures that looked like look-out towers were being built. As Berger brought the plane lower, Novak saw men—Lehder's men—dropping what they were doing and hurrying toward the airstrip.

Berger lined up with the airstrip and made his approach. Novak saw that trucks and jeeps were parked across the strip, blocking it. He assumed that Lehder's men were moving to clear them, but as he watched he saw that they were driving more vehicles onto the tarmac. Berger said, "Lehder doesn't think I've got the balls to land," a remark that made no sense at all to Novak. Why would Lehder not want his own operative to land?

After that, things happened quickly, too quickly for Novak to do anything but react. A series of images impressed themselves on his mind: Heinrich Rogol on the ground, drawing his pistol and pointing it at the plane; Berger, cutting power and dipping the nose of the plane down, straight at the line of vehicles; men scattering in all directions. Then Berger said: "Hang on," and the next moment they hit something, bounced, spun, and careened down the strip shooting off a rooster tail of sparks. It seemed to go on and on, like a roller coaster gone mad.

The plane finally came to rest in a sand bank to the side of the strip. Before Novak had a chance to collect himself, the doors were thrown open and someone grabbed him and shoved him to the ground. He looked up, saw Heinrich pointing his .45 into the plane, heard him say, "Berger, you're a dead man, you son-of-a-bitch."

A man with a rifle said, "No, Heinrich."

Heinrich turned and said, "What the hell are you talking about?"

"Not here," said the man with the rifle. "Don't be a fool." He came forward and pulled Berger out of the cockpit. Berger, pale and scared, fell on the sand. Then strong hands dragged Novak to his feet, pushed him into the back of a truck.

The truck stopped in front of the customs house. Novak was hustled inside. Lehder, wearing a silk suit, was waiting for him. Heinrich handed Lehder the manila envelope from Berger's plane and left them alone.

Lehder regarded Novak coolly for a moment, then sat down at a table and began going through the contents of the envelope, leaving Novak standing before him like a servant. Novak used the time to take stock of himself. He wasn't hurt, just shaken up. Glancing around, he saw that the customs house had been transformed into a communications center; the walls were banked with radio equipment.

After a minute or two, Lehder rose and gazed out the window at what was left of Berger's plane. He shook his head. "You disappoint me, Novak," he said.

"I haven't a clue what you're talking about."

"No?" Lehder said. He went to the table, picked up the photograph and flicked it like a playing card at Novak. It landed at his feet. He looked down, saw the picture of Holleran and himself at the beach bar.

"I knew Holleran long before I even heard of Norman's," Novak said. "We stay at the same hotel in Nassau."

"This isn't a good time to lie," Lehder said. "And it doesn't work at this level. I have my own intelligence capability, Dick, as you can see. I know all about Bobby Eliot. I know he's been sending Berger and others like him down here to spy on me. I know everything that happens in the Bahamas." He smiled and added, "Before it happens."

Novak's head filled with questions: Berger worked for Eliot? Then why had Berger brought him here? Could Berger have thought that he, Novak, had been involved in the killing in the pine thicket? And what was Holleran's role?

When Novak spoke it was not so much to mollify Lehder, although he must have known that his life was at risk, as it was to try to understand what was happening. "I don't know this Eliot guy from Adam," he said. "But Berger seems to think I went to Nassau to set Eliot up. Or Holleran. I'm not sure which."

Lehder saw something funny in this. He laughed, not sarcastically, sardonically or cynically, but with genuine amusement. "Holleran set Eliot up," he explained. He looked at Novak as though he expected him to get the joke and start laughing too. Some men might have been afraid of Lehder at that moment. But Novak was not, perhaps out of bravery, more likely because he was too preoccupied with the constantly twisting details of what was going on. Was Holleran working for Lehder? And if so, why would Lehder care whether Novak had met him at the beach bar? Or could Holleran be a double agent, working for both sides? Is that what Lehder had learned from the photograph? And if that was the case, wasn't it possible that Eliot—and Berger, surely—suspected him of being in league with Lehder? Novak couldn't answer those questions. All he knew for certain was that he felt used. The craziest part was that the only one giving him information was Lehder.

Lehder was watching him, amusement still on his face. "You see, Dick, this isn't the kind of thing someone like you should get involved in. I hoped you would've seen the opportunities here. The protection I can provide. The encouragement for your endeavors. And a home in this very special place. I can be trusted. Those others—Eliot, Holleran, Berger, Kniskern—cannot." He stared at Novak. The amusement slowly left his face. "Eliot is sending someone to pick up Berger. You can stay or go, as you like." Lehder walked out of the customs house.

A few minutes later, a single-engine plane appeared over Norman's. Novak went outside, saw Lehder ordering his men to clear the strip. The plane made its final pass and landed. Heinrich advanced toward it, gun in hand. The cockpit door opened, and a tall man climbed out. He was carrying a gun too. He and Heinrich regarded each other warily. Lehder, standing near the customs house, motioned, and armed men brought Berger out from behind the building and walked him to the plane.

The tall man nodded to Berger. Berger, still looking scared, said, "What the hell kept you?" Heinrich laughed. Berger shot him a look filled with hatred, then boarded the plane.

Lehder turned to Novak. "Well?" he said.

The tall man looked at them. "The hell with Novak," he said. "My instructions don't say anything about him."

Berger, through the open door, spoke quietly to the tall man. Some of his words carried in the still air. Novak thought he heard Berger say, "There's been a mistake."

"All right," the tall man said. "Move it, Novak."

Everyone looked at Novak. Both possibilities, staying and leaving, were unpalatable. But it was time to make a choice; an irrevocable one, he knew. Novak crossed the tarmac and climbed into the plane.

* * *

"Okay," Novak said, when they were safely in the air, "would you guys mind telling me what's going on?"

The tall man turned from the controls. "You shut the fuck up," he said.

Not another word was spoken. The plane landed safely in Nassau, and Berger and the tall men left Novak there, standing by himself outside the terminal.

23

Norman's Cay was finished for him. Novak, staying in Chris's tiny apartment near the flight school in Melbourne, Florida, knew that after only a day or two. It wasn't just that he could no longer safely return. The truth was that the Norman's he had first seen and fallen in love with no longer existed. That virginal island had been violated, ruined forever by Carlos Lehder. Even if Lehder was somehow eliminated, Novak knew he could never see the island in the same pure way again. His memories would prevent that. Norman's Cay was the site of his humiliation, the place where Lehder had fooled him completely, exposing his naiveté and powerlessness. So Norman's was finished, Novak told himself; more than once. The logical, analytical part of himself listened and believed. But somehow the dreaming part remained untouched, and his dream of a future on Norman's Cay did not die. It lay dormant, unacknowledged; a hidden and secret well of motivation.

After a few weeks in Melbourne Novak also knew that he didn't want to return to teaching. Norman's and the hammerheads might be in the past, but that didn't mean he had to turn his back on the sea. He decided to set up a small dive operation in Nassau. The problem was that the *Reef Witch* and all his gear were still on Norman's.

That meant he had to go back one last time. It was his

boat, after all, his property. He had every right to claim it, didn't he? Besides, he couldn't afford to reequip himself.

"But what if he decides to make trouble?" Chris said.

"Why would he bother?" Novak responded. "Anyway, what choice have I got?"

Chris sighed. "Just don't lose your temper," he said. "Whatever happens."

"Yeah, sure."

Chris sighed again. But, relieved that Norman's no longer played a role in his father's plans, he agreed to fly Novak down. On a sunny morning in April 1979, with clear visibility and no wind, Novak and Chris strapped themselves into the cockpit of Chris's Piper and took off from Florida. They had made careful preparations. Mechanics had inspected the plane thoroughly the day before. En route, they stopped in Nassau to top up the tanks, making any refueling on Norman's unnecessary.

A few minutes after noon, Christ started his descent, coming down out of the sky and circling the familiar green fishhook. From the cockpit, the island looked deserted. Novak could see the construction projects, further advanced now, but there were no crews at the sites. No boats were moving in the pond, no one was sunning on the beach, no cars were parked at the hotel. For a moment, Novak entertained the wild thought that Lehder and his gang had gone.

Chris landed smoothly and swung the plane around, leaving it poised for a quick takeoff back to Nassau. Novak climbed out of the plane, his eyes on the customs house, waiting for someone to emerge. But no one did. Novak and his son walked past the tennis courts to the marina. The road was rutted now by the passage of heavy equipment, and stacks of lumber and crates of equipment waited on the pier. Novak unlocked the shop and went inside. Chris kept watch on the steps.

Nothing in the shop had been touched. Even his shark pistol was there, under the counter. Novak put it in his pocket.

Dust had gathered on the tanks, regulators, wet suits, and on Novak's research notes, open on the desk in the corner where he had left them. He sat down and gazed at his own handwriting for a while, and thought how close he had come. Then he roused himself, opened a steamer trunk, using a little more force than necessary, and dropped his notebooks inside. He was sprinkling talc on the wet suits when he heard Chris's urgent call: "Dad!"

Novak ran outside in time to see a passenger truck and hotel shuttle squealing to a stop. Five or six armed men, led by Heinrich Rogol, jumped out of the truck and came toward him. Heinrich drew his .45. "This is private property," he said. "You're trespassing."

Hot words rose in Novak's throat, all about his right to be on Norman's and his contract with Kniskern. But Chris was giving him a warning look, so Novak stifled them and merely said, "I'm just closing up shop. We'll be gone in a matter of hours."

Heinrich glanced at the shuttle bus. Novak saw Lehder sitting quietly in the back, watching like a spectator at a play he had already seen: not bored, but in no suspense about the ending. Heinrich turned back to Novak. "Mr. Lehder owns this island and everything on it. That includes the scuba shop and its contents."

"The hell with that," Novak began. "No one's going—"

"Dad!" Chris interrupted. Novak fell silent. Chris stepped between his father and Heinrich. "We're not here to take anything that doesn't belong to us, or to cause any trouble."

"You being here causes trouble," Heinrich said.

"We'll be packed and gone in an hour," Chris said.

"You're going now," Heinrich said, wrapping his hand around the butt of his gun. "Or never."

That was too much for Novak. He strode past Heinrich, toward the shuttle bus. Heinrich's men quickly blocked his path. Over their shoulders, Novak could see Lehder through the window. Now the play seemed a little more interesting: he was smiling. It was Novak's impression at that moment that Lehder knew he had a gun in his pocket and was hoping he would reach for it.

"Dad!" Chris called. "It's not worth it. Everything can be replaced."

Novak knew that wasn't true—Lehder was taking everything he had. Too late, he realized how much he had sunk into a dream that wasn't going to come true. The knowledge filled him with violent urges, but he didn't reach for his gun. He had no right to risk Chris's life. Moreover, he was not a killer. Novak turned away from Lehder in the shuttle bus, away from Heinrich's goons, walked to Chris, took his hand, and started for the airstrip. Behind him a shot rang out, and a bullet tore into side of the shop, making a sound that must have sounded like triumph in Heinrich's ears.

Lehder and his men followed Novak and Chris to the airstrip. When they reached the plane, Heinrich jerked his .45 at Chris and said, "Start her up." Novak saw with pride that Chris wouldn't be rushed. He went through his preflight routine, checking the prop, opening the hood to inspect the spark plugs. Novak grew aware that Chris was taking a long time, but he didn't know why. He glanced again at the shuttle, saw Lehder—now watching with complete absorption.

"Hurry up," Heinrich said.

Chris had moved under one of the wings and was shining a pocket flash into the tank. He turned slowly to Heinrich. "You've siphoned the fuel," he said with disbelief. Now Novak saw what his son must have been aware of almost at once: damp stains on the tarmac.

Heinrich waved his gun; his gestures with it were growing freer. "Get in," he said.

"Why?" asked Chris. "I don't think you left me enough to clear the strip."

Heinrich smiled. "There's enough for that."

Chris didn't move. Heinrich raised his gun, fired a shot over Chris's shoulder. The bullet struck the customs house. The next moment Novak was charging at Heinrich, heedless of the weapon he was so clearly itching to use. Heinrich backed away. Someone stuck out his foot, tripping him. Novak fell on the strip. He lay there for a moment, long enough to feel the momentum of events, to know with certainty that he and his son might be shot in the next minute or two and end their lives on the airstrip of this little island. He had to control himself, had to be calm.

Novak picked himself up. When he spoke his voice was quiet. "Give Chris fuel," he said to Henrich. "Let him go. Lehder and I can settle this later."

Heinrich glanced at the shuttle bus. Lehder's face was impassive. Heinrich pointed his gun. "Get in."

Novak almost reached for his own pistol. But what was the point? He and Chris were outnumbered, outgunned. Lehder wanted him to reach for the pistol. That's what this was all about. And Novak knew at that moment that he never again would do anything that Lehder wanted. He nodded to Chris. They climbed into the plane.

"Oh God," Chris said.

"What is it?"

"They've taken the radio too."

Lehder wanted them to die, die an accidental death. Planes went down from time to time in the islands. No one would be surprised. Novak opened his door and shouted in the direction of the shuttle bus: "You're going to jail. I promise you that."

Chris primed the engine. The propeller caught. Chris released the brakes and the plane began to roll. Now for the first time, Novak saw a man standing in the shade of the customs house with a short length of hose in his hand. It was Victor Forbes. His apprentice and pupil, now repaying him by siphoning their fuel. There was time to do no more than register the fact.

The plane picked up speed, rose into the air. "How much fuel have we got?" Novak asked.

"I don't know."

"Approximately."

"Teacups, Dad," Chris said. "It's a matter of teacups."

Chris pointed the nose up high. The plane shook with the effort. "What are you doing?" Novak asked. He had assumed Chris would stay low, hoping perhaps to see a ship and ditch as close to it as he could.

"Shut up, Dad. Just find us a place to land."

Novak grabbed the sectional maps. He realized what Chris was doing, knew that Lehder hadn't taken Chris's flying skills into account. Chris was planning to fly the plane as high as he could, then use the air currents to stay up long enough to find a strip. Novak fumbled through the maps, then called out the coordinates of a strip on the southeastern end of Eleuthera. Chris adjusted his course. Moments later the engine coughed, then sputtered. Chris rocked the plane, allowing the pump to suck out the last drops of fuel. Eleuthera appeared in the distance, low and green.

"It's no good," Chris said. "We're not going to make it."

"Yes we are," Novak told him, proud as never before of his son, thinking of so many things he should have told him. "You can do it."

Less than a minute later, Novak saw that the prop was no longer just a blur. He could see its turning blades. A bad sign. They spun slower and slower; then not at all. It was silent in the plane, except for the sound of the clock ticking on the control panel.

Now Novak could distinguish details: the brown of the reef, the white of the beach, the black of the airstrip not far inland. Not far inland, and no more than three miles from where they were. But they were coming down fast.

"Promise me one thing," Chris said suddenly. "You'll never go back to Norman's."

Novak said nothing. If they lived, he would have to go back, wouldn't he? Lehder had taken too much of him, of his life, back there on Norman's Cay.

The plane dropped down over the reef. Novak could see the spume on the wave tops, the ripples the breeze made on the water. It all shot by at frightening speed. Then they were over the beach, headed for the rocky bluff that separated it from the landing strip.

They almost made it. Novak saw the strip clearly now; Chris was headed toward it perfectly, leveled and balanced. Then the rocks reached up and ticked the tires. It was enough. The plane swung sideways, bounced down into a field of sea-grapes, bounced again, spun, bounced, hit something hard, hard enough to fill the cockpit with the sound of ripping, twisting metal, and finally came to a stop, tipped up on one bent wing. Chris was slumped forward over the controls.

"Chris, Chris!" Novak said. "Are you all right?"

Chris looked up, nodded. He was as white as chalk. An aching was born in Novak's heart, and began to grow: an aching for revenge.

24

"No real harm done, as far as I can see," said Dudley Hanna, Assistant Commissioner of the Royal Bahamian Constabulary.

"I beg your pardon?" said Richard Novak, seated on the other side of Hanna's tidy desk at police headquarters in Nassau.

"No one got hurt," Hanna replied. "No injuries to you or your son. Not even a scratch. He must be an excellent pilot."

"That's beside the point," Novak began. "What you've got to—"

"Of course, there's the question of the aircraft itself," Hanna interrupted. He ran his eyes over a report lying on the desk. "Bent landing struts. They'll have to be rebuilt. Other damage, some structural." He flipped through the pages of the report. "But fixable," he continued. "It looks like an insurance matter."

"Insurance matter?" Novak was on his feet. "That thug tried to kill us. Kill us and make it look like an accident. He's a murderer—can't you understand that?" Breathlessly, Novak blurted out a disorganized account of the attack on the *Reef Witch* and his discovery of the body in the pine thicket. Hanna regarded him with distaste.

"Please sit down, Mr. Novak."

Novak sat.

Hanna paused, almost like an elementary-school teacher

making sure that order was restored. "Assuming for the moment," he said, "that what you say is true—"

"Assuming?" With difficulty, Novak remained in his seat. "Are you calling me a liar?"

Hanna regarded him with annoyance, but when he spoke his tone was still smooth and polite. "Not at all, Mr. Novak. But there are one or two little details I don't quite understand."

"Like what?"

"Like why you imagined you had a right to remain on Norman's Cay, for example."

"What are you talking about?"

Hanna's tone hardened slightly. "I'm talking about the fact that you're not an official resident of Norman's," he replied, turning quickly to a page of the report. "The beach villa in question is registered in the name of Philip Kniskern, is it not?"

Novak fumbled through his briefcase, found the contract between Kniskern and himself, could not restrain himself from flipping it onto Hanna's desk. "Kniskern left me in charge."

Hanna didn't even glance at the contract. "Why would he do that?"

"Because Lehder ran him off the island, that's why. Just like he ran the other legitimate residents off. And me too, Mr. Hanna. What I don't understand is why I'm the one getting the third degree."

Hanna smiled in a way Novak found maddening. "This is hardly the third degree, Mr. Novak." He turned to the last page of the report, where a list of Novak's possessions on Norman's had been appended. After a few moments, Hanna raised his eyes and looked at Novak without expression. "I'm not sure you appreciate the legalities of the situation," he said. "Mr. Lehder owns the entire marina on Norman's, including the shop you think of as yours. He can open and close it as he pleases. And no one is allowed on those parts of the island he now owns without his permission, the same way I couldn't enter your house without an invitation."

Novak's voice rose and he did nothing about it. "Legalities? You want to talk about legalities? Then what's your reaction to the fact that an international dope smuggler has taken over one of your islands?"

Now Hanna's voice rose too. "Hold it right there, my friend. Just what gives you the right to make a serious accusation like that about Mr. Lehder?"

"Are you kidding me?" Novak said. "It's no secret. There's an investigation going on right now and you're supposed to be part of it. Are you saying you don't know Josh Berger or Bobby Elliot?"

"Those names," said Hanna, his eyes blank, "are unfamiliar to me."

"Yeah?" said Novak. He rose and started for the door. "Maybe they'll become a little more familiar when you start seeing them in the Nassau *Tribune* and the Miami *Herald*. I'm sure their reporters will find all this very interesting."

"Wait a minute," said Hanna, before Novak reached the door.

Novak turned.

"Come, Mr. Novak, sit down."

"Why should I?"

Hanna sighed. "I know how this must look, Mr. Novak. But believe me—this is not a good time to go to the press."

"Maybe not for you," Novak said. "But you've left me no choice."

Hanna gave him a long look. "How do I know you can be trusted?" he said.

"Because I came to you in the first place," Novak said. "Would I do that if I was on the other side?" Had he been closer to Hanna's desk he might have pounded it. "Use your head, man."

Hanna looked angry for a moment. Then he sighed again. "All right, Mr. Novak," he said. "The truth is that an investigation is in progress, a confidential investigation with complex international ramifications. Do you really want to risk its success?"

"What kind of an investigation?" Novak asked.

"The kind that's going to lead to a big raid on Norman's, the arrest of Carlos Lehder and his incarceration for life. I repeat: do you want to risk its success?"

Novak returned to his chair. "No," he said.

"Good. Then go home and keep your mouth shut."

"When is this raid going to happen?"

"I can't tell you without breaking security."

"But I want to help," Novak said. "I know the island. I know Lehder, his goons, the whole setup."

"This is a police matter," Hanna said. "You'll be safer reading the accounts in the papers."

"I want to go down there," Novak said. "With you, when you raid him."

Hanna sat back in his chair. "Is this something personal?" he asked.

"What do you mean?"

"You have the look of a man spoiling for a fight."

"Nonsense."

"Be careful, Mr. Novak."

"Of what?"

"Of becoming like your enemy."

"That's a ridiculous suggestion."

"Is it?"

"And a waste of my time," Novak added. "Now, how about telling me exactly what Holleran and Ferguson are doing in your investigation."

"I can't do that without breaking security."

"I suppose it would be breaking security to tell me the name of the man in the pine thicket."

"Not only that. It might be dangerous for you."

"That's a risk I'm prepared to take."

Hanna shook his head. "Just go home, Mr. Novak. I'll call you when I need you."

"When will that be? I can't wait forever. I've got a boat on Norman's and a shopful of gear."

Hanna reached into his pocket, took out a business card and handed it across the deak. "See this man. He'll help with your things."

Novak examined the card. "Ian Davidson," it said. "President, Titanic Air." There was a Nassau address. "Who is he?" Novak asked.

"A local accountant," Hanna said. "And Lehder's business manager and representative in Nassau."

Novak took the card and left. He was outside in the summer heat when it struck him how handy it was that the assistant commissioner of police had happened to have the card in his pocket.

Ian Davidson had a prosperous-looking office and a haughty-looking secretary. She kept Novak waiting for a long time. While he waited, a black man came in and sat nearby. He seemed nervous, as though about to attend a big meeting and unsure of his preparation. He kept opening his briefcase and glancing through the contents. Soon that wasn't good enough; he removed them and spread them on his lap for a better look. Novak had a good look too, and what he saw made his pulse race. The man had a briefcase full of photographs, all taken at Norman's Cay. Novak recognized Kniskern, Berger, Paulette; and himself. There were lots of pictures of Richard Novak.

The man with the pictures was sent into Ian's Davidson's office ahead of him. After an hour, he emerged, walked through the waiting room without a look at Novak, and left.

"Mr. Davidson will see you now," the secretary said.

Novak entered Davidson's office. Ian Davidson was a white Bahamian who wore an expensive tropical suit and an unfriendly frown. "Hello," Novak said, "I'm Richard Novak."

"I know who you are," Davidson said, making no attempt to be civil. Novak glanced at his desk and saw the photographs arrayed across it. "Your equipment and your little boat will be delivered within a week. My office will be in touch. Is that what you wanted?" Davidson's phone buzzed. He reached for it. "Good day, Mr. Novak." The interview was over. Novak moved toward the door. "Oh, and Novak," Davidson said, phone in hand. "I wouldn't go back to Norman's Cay if I were you."

"No?"

"I'd wipe it out of your mind. There are many other beautiful islands in the Bahamas. Get to know them. For your own good."

Novak bristled. "I'll rely on my own judgment about that," he said.

"Suit yourself," Davidson said. "But if you think Hanna or any other cop is going to help you, you're in for a big disappointment."

Bahamian forces under the command of Assistant Commissioner Howard Smith raided Norman's Cay a few weeks later, on September 14, 1979. It was an impressive performance. Novak read all about it in the papers, as Dudley Hanna had suggested.

Operation Raccoon. Ninety officers, including twelve detectives. Three gunboats. One DC-3. The strike force swept down on Norman's just after dawn. The police met no resistance. They seized 8 handguns, 2 automatic rifles, 1 shotgun, 2 tear-gas launchers, 35 sticks of dynamite, 618 rounds of ammunition. They also seized marijuana and cocaine, but in amounts that seemed surprisingly small to Novak. They arrested thirty-three people and flew them back to Nassau on the DC-3. Novak scanned the list of prisoners. It included Ed and Lassie Ward, Margit, and some of Carlos Lehder's men. It did not include Lehder. He was scarcely mentioned in the reports. The police claimed with pride that they had hooked their big fish: Ed Ward, charged with illegal possession of weapons and drugs; the drugs in question being a little marijuana found in his son's bedroom. But Ward, as Kniskern had said, was just a little fish. Now Novak saw why Lehder had allowed the Fat Man to remain on the island: in case someone had to take the fall. The newspaper shook in Novak's hands.

The fishes were out on bail of two thousand dollars each in a day or two, or freed without charge. Most of the charges concerned work permit violations; most of those arrested were the construction workers. Disturbing but unconfirmable details began to leak. The raid had been scheduled for September 1, and postponed at the last minute for unknown reasons. Everyone on Norman's with the possible exception of the Wards had known it was coming. One of the gunboats had chased the *Fire Fall* around the island. The commander claimed that Lehder had been on board and had been observed dumping bags of white powder into the sea, just before allowing the gunboat to catch up. There was also a story about eighty thousand dollars found by a constable in a garbage bin, and handed over to Assistant Commissioner Smith, and a further forty thousand dollars found in Margit's bedroom that was also conveyed to the assistant commissioner. Neither sum was mentioned in the official account of Operation Raccoon.

Four days after the raid, Carlos Lehder arrived in Nassau and called a press conference. He was in an ugly mood. He told the reporters that he was a legitimate businessman who had invested $5 million in the Bahamian tourist industry and had plans to invest much more, injecting money into the islands and creating jobs. But if this was the way the government welcomed investors, he was no longer interested. Unless police harrassment ceased immediately, he would sell his entire holdings in the Bahamas and pull out. To show he was serious, he placed an ad in *The Wall Street Journal*: "For Immediate Sale: The Norman's Cay Yacht Club, Norman's Cay, Exumas." The whole development, including airstrip, marina, clubhouse, villas, twenty cars, eight boats, and two planes could be had for $2,932,000.

It was a bizarre spectacle, but wasn't seen as such by Nassau's business community. With few exceptions, the bankers and merchants rallied to Lehder's side, calling on the police to leave him alone. Lehder flew home to Norman's a hero.

Richard Novak was sickened.

25

Richard Novak returned to Concordia College, took up his teaching duties once more, and settled into the familiar patterns of his married life. He kept to himself the story of what had happened on Norman's Cay, telling Dorothy nothing of the attempt on his life, drug smuggling, Carlos Lehder, or of the disorientation of living in a corrupt world where no one could be trusted. Did his reticence stem from a desire to protect Dorothy from harm? Or did it mean that he was still reluctant to admit the impossibility of a future on Norman's Cay? Perhaps it was a bit of both; in any case, after a few months up north, Novak began making trips back to the Bahamas, like a hammerhead at the mercy of magnetic forces, returning to the lagoon.

Sometimes with Chris, sometimes hitching rides with other pilots, Novak visited different Bahamian sites, looking for a spot to transplant his diving operation. They all paled next to his memories of Norman's. Listlessly, he went from one to another, wasting his long weekends and brief holidays on depressing expeditions to vacation spots where relentless gaiety was the rule. Early in 1980, he even found himself back at Treasure Cay on Abaco, which he had crossed off his list once already, before he had seen Norman's at all. Treasure Cay was also the place where he had first encountered Carlos Lehder.

Novak checked into the Treasure Cay Hotel and went

into the restaurant for lunch. Tired and preoccupied with his thoughts, he took no notice of his surroundings until after he had ordered. Then, looking around, he saw Carlos Lehder seated at a table on the far side of the room. Novak's heart started beating furiously.

Lehder was having a sumptuous lunch with a group of Hispanic men. They were older than Lehder and looked like prosperous businessmen, well barbered, well manicured, well dressed. Lehder said something, inaudible to Novak, but the laughing response of the businessmen carried across the room. After a few moments, Novak's gaze was drawn to another table, where some rougher-hewn men were eating. This group did not seem as talkative or relaxed as the first one. The rough-looking men kept glancing at Lehder's table, like baby-sitters on an outing. One of them was Heinrich Rogol. Novak turned back to Lehder's table, in time to catch Lehder looking straight at him. Their eyes met. Without the least hesitation, Lehder smiled, raised a hand in casual salute, and resumed the conversation with his companions, all before the flustered Novak could react.

Novak left the rest of his meal untouched. Why had Lehder seemed so friendly? Why had he acted as though nothing had happened, as though he hadn't tried to have Novak and his son killed? Novak was almost ready to believe that Lehder had mistaken him for someone else when Lehder, leaving the restaurant, made a detour to his table and said, "Don't be a stranger."

"What?" said Novak.

"We should talk," Lehder replied, and then he was gone.

When Novak went to pay his bill, he found that it had already been settled.

His mind in turmoil, Novak walked along the beach. It was cold and windy, and he had it to himself. After a while, he sat down on the sand and stared out to sea, watching the white caps. What had Lehder meant: that he could return to Norman's and carry on as before, once again with Lehder's support? But Novak could never do that, not knowing what he now knew about Carlos Lehder. What's more, Lehder, through Ian Davidson, surely knew that Novak knew. Why would he invite trouble onto the island? Did he think he was invincible?

Novak, his jacket zipped up against the wind, was pondering these questions when he saw a man approaching across the sand. As he came closer, Novak observed that he was short, wiry, tough-looking. He had long blond hair and an untrimmed beard, wore torn jeans and dirty tennis shoes, and might not have appeared out of place at Heinrich Rogol's table. Novak searched his memory: had this man been eating with Rogol? Novak thought not, but he couldn't be sure. He rose and got ready for trouble.

The man halted a few yards away. Novak watched his hands. They remained in plain sight, still at his sides. The man smiled. "Hi," he said. "I understand you've got a nice dive boat."

The man's tone was friendly, his pronunciation educated, belying his appearance. If he was a creature from Heinrich's world, he must have occupied the top of the tree. "What about it?" Novak said.

The man showed no signs of feeling the rebuff. "I'd like to charter it," he said. "For a dive trip in the Exumas."

"The Exumas?"

"Yeah," said the man. "Norman's Cay, specifically."

Now Novak was certain that Lehder was trying to lure him back to Norman's for purposes unclear; unclear but menacing. "I'm not interested," Novak said, not taking his eyes off the man for a second. The man was slightly taller than he was, not as muscular, but ten years younger. Rapidly, Novak performed the calculus of impending violence.

"I need someone familiar with the waters down there," the man continued as though he hadn't heard. "Someone who's spent time on the island would be ideal. I'm told you qualify on both counts."

"Forget it," Novak said.

The man looked at him closely. Novak balled his fists

and got ready to fight. The man surprised him. He started
to laugh, a hearty unguarded laugh that expressed genuine amusement, although Novak didn't get the joke. "You
are a hard case, aren't you, Novak?" the man said. He
held out his hand. "I'm Bobby Eliot. It's about time we
got together."

Novak hesitated. "Why is that?" he asked.

"Because I think we can help each other. You can certainly help me."

"That depends whose side you're on," Novak said.

"I'm not on Lehder's side, if that's what you're asking,"
Eliot said. "I'm looking to take him down for good."

Novak shook Bobby Eliot's hand.

Novak and Eliot walked along the beach to a little palm
grove, where they sat down, out of sight. "I don't blame
you for being suspicious," Eliot said. "We've made some
mistakes."

"Like the dead man in the pine thicket," Novak said.

Eliot looked grim. "Holleran set us up."

"Holleran?"

"He's playing both sides. That's not unusual in this
business. Ferguson's doing it too. Didn't you realize that?"

"No," said Novak. "I did not. And how do I know you're
not doing the same thing?"

"I can give you a number to call at the embassy in
Nassau," Eliot said. "You can check me out."

"I intend to," Novak said, shaken by the revelations
about Holleran and Ferguson.

"Good," Eliot said. "Knowing who you can count on is
half the battle in an investigation like this."

"What do you mean?" Novak asked.

Eliot glanced around. There was no one in sight. The
wind blew harder now, stinging them with grains of sand.
"We're in a tricky position, Dick. This isn't Florida. It's a
foreign country. There are international implications to
what we do. The State Department's involved, and so is

the CIA. But their interests aren't exactly the same as ours."

"I don't understand."

"Here's an example. The Navy's got a submarine base on Andros. Direct access to the Tongue of the Ocean. One hundred and thirty miles or so from Cuba. And our lease with Pindling comes up soon. Do you see what I'm talking about?"

Novak wasn't sure he did. He made a leap that he considered a little wild. "Are you saying the Prime Minister of the Bahamas is involved with Carlos Lehder?"

It didn't seem to strike Eliot as wild. "There's nothing we can prove," he said. "But we've got reports that he's flown to Norman's in his helicopter. And Lehder's got a direct line into Nassau police headquarters. He knew that raid was coming before I did. Hell, he probably helped draw up the plans."

Novak couldn't keep the bitterness out of his voice. "So our own State Department is protecting Lehder so we can make Fidel say uncle, is that it?"

Eliot shook his head. "No. They want me to get him. It's just not their first priority, that's all. Their first priority is protecting our relationship with the government of the Bahamas. And the government of the Bahamas is Linden O. Pindling, now and for the foreseeable future. So when we move against Lehder it has to be surgical. In and out with no mess and no hurt bystanders."

"When?" said Novak.

Eliot laughed. "We've got a lot of work to do first. After the fiasco down on Norman's, Hanna's investigation is on hold. We've got to make the kind of case for starting it up again that he can't ignore."

"Meaning what?"

"Meaning we've got to produce hard proof that Lehder's doing what you and I know goddamn well he's doing."

"Smuggling cocaine."

"It's much more than that, Dick. I don't think you

appreciate the scale of what's going on. Did you see those guys in the restaurant?"

"Who are they?"

"Colombians. From Medellín. If our sources are right, that little group having lunch controls almost all the world's cocaine production. That makes them worth billions—and they're going to be worth a lot more if Lehder's plans work out."

"How so?"

"There are four parts to the cocaine business. Production, refining, smuggling, money laundering. Those guys have mastered three of them. They've rationalized the production, modernized the refining, hired the brains to do the laundering. But in terms of smuggling, they're still in the nineteenth century. A suitcase-full here, a girdle-full there, coke stashed up the asses of scared peasants trying to make it through customs in Miami or L.A. It's putting a cap on their profits and they've known about it for a long time. If I'm right, Lehder's the first one to show them the solution."

"And what's that?"

"What he's half-done already. Set up a little semi-independent state down on Norman's, with its nice harbor and convenient location between Colombia and the U.S. Buy protection from the Bahamians, equip himself with enough weaponry and electronics to stock a NATO base in case his partners ever turn on him, and then start bringing in coke by the shipload, unloading and repackaging at his leisure and flying the goods up north. In fleets. He's already doing it, but soon the scale will be so vast there'll be nothing we can do. Then the price of coke's going to start falling, and it'll roll over our cities like you can't imagine. And make Carlos Lehder rich beyond belief in the process."

"But Norman's is beautiful," Novak said. It was the first thought that had entered his head, and he had just blurted it out.

Eliot looked at him quizzically. "I guess so," he said.

"If you know all this about Lehder, why is he still at large?"

"What we know and what we can prove are two different things. This is a delicate operation. We need evidence—hard, incontrovertible, and in such quantity that ignoring it would lead to the kind of scandal politicians can't live with."

"What do you want me to do?" Novak asked.

"Like I said," Eliot told him. "I need someone who knows the waters and knows the island. Someone who has an excuse to be there."

"I seem to fit the profile, don't I?"

"You're probably the only man in the world who does," Eliot said with a smile. It faded slowly. "So are you in or out?"

"In," said Richard Novak.

26

The *Reef Witch*, lightly loaded, rode high on the water. Under a starry sky, Novak steered her safely from Nassau to Norman's Cay, rounded the island and approached from the south. He spotted the outermost of the Pieces of Eight, a low shadow straight ahead; his destination. Novak cut the engine and glided silently into a cove that was shaped like an arch on the foot of the little cay. As soon as the bow touched the sand, Bobby Eliot jumped out and pulled the boat up as far as he could. Then he and Novak chopped some brush and a few tree branches and lay them over the *Reef Witch*, rough camouflage but effective from aerial view.

On the heel of the cay, sheltered by low trees, stood a crude stone hut built long ago by fishermen. Novak and Eliot went inside. Through its open doorway, they had a good view of the marina, hotel, and airstrip on the other side of South Harbor. No lights shone, and the only sound was the sea, snuffling and hissing all around them. They unrolled their sleeping bags and went to sleep.

When Novak awoke in the morning, Eliot was already up. Novak found him prone behind a rock on the westernmost tip of the cay, peering through a long-lensed camera at Norman's. A pair of powerful binoculars lay beside him. Novak picked them up and looked across South Harbor.

Norman's Cay appeared in close-up, every detail clear

in the still air. The island had changed. A satellite communication center now stood beside the hotel, complete with dish antennae. Novak followed the thick cables trailing away to the back of the hotel, and up to the roof. Mounted on it was a fortified observation post, higher than any palm on the island. "A goddamn NATO base," Eliot said. Novak heard the click of his shutter.

After a few minutes, the sound of barking dogs floated across the water. Armed men in khaki uniforms emerged from the trees near the marina, walking a pack of leashed hounds. They moved purposefully down the beach. It was a patrol, well organized and official looking: the kind of sight a tourist might view with momentary dismay in some unstable state.

Not long after, the hotel Mini-Moke shuttles began driving back and forth along the main road. Eliot took out a notebook and began jotting in it. "Ten-minute intervals," he said.

"What do you mean?"

"Keep your voice down—sound carries," Eliot said. "The shuttles are patrolling too. They swing past the strip every ten minutes."

Novak trained the binoculars on the shuttle drivers. They too wore khaki. He was thinking how quickly the island seemed to have degenerated from a paradise to a neo-fascist Brigadoon, when a third group of men in khaki walked onto the marina pier, boarded a speedboat, and cast off. "Quick," said Eliot. He and Novak scrambled back inside the hut. Through the open doorway, Novak saw the speedboat skim out of the marina, bear straight toward them, and then veer off, around Battery Point to the western side of the island.

Novak blew an involuntary sigh. He glanced at Eliot, wondering if he had heard it. Eliot, writing in his notebook, gave no sign. "I thought they'd seen a glare off the lenses," Novak said.

"They're not that good," Eliot said. But he didn't sound sure.

On the other side of South Harbor, Norman's Cay continued to come alive. A jeep pulled up in the marina parking lot. Victor Forbes got out, walked to the flagpole, and raised a red, yellow, and purple banded flag.

"What's that?" Novak asked.

"The Colombian national colors," Eliot said. Novak wondered what Prime Minister Pindling would think of that.

Children neatly dressed in T-shirts and shorts and carrying books came into view on the main road. "Were there kids here before?" Eliot asked.

"No."

"He's working fast. Schoolkids. That means teachers and whole families. Christ."

"Why would he make things so complicated?" Novak asked.

"Don't you see? It's the smartest thing he's done. Those kids are better protection than a hundred goons on the beach. They make him look like a benefactor. This is all PR, Dick. that's why when we move it has to be surgical."

Novak thought there was more to it, just as Carlos Lehder was more than an ordinary drug smuggler. In his twisted way, he was trying to build some sort of island nation, and what was a nation without children? But Eliot had a point—Novak visualized the island going up in flames and children being hurt. He forced the image from his mind. If it came to that, or anything like it, he wouldn't care what happened to Norman's Cay, or if he ever got it back.

Construction workers lined up outside the hotel for breakfast. Later came mechanics in grease-stained overalls, and finally pilots in jackets and designer sunglasses. Whenever Novak saw someone he recognized, he pointed him out to Eliot. Eliot made notes.

Novak grew restless. Watching Eliot at work, writing in the notebook and taking pictures, he decided that there wasn't anything glamorous, or even intellectually challenging, about being a DEA agent. He was opening some of the food packages they had brought when he felt Eliot tense. Novak grabbed the binoculars.

A red antique sports car rolled up to the hotel. "An Excalibur," Eliot said. "Worth a hundred grand, maybe more." Carlos Lehder climbed out. Novak adjusted the focus. Lehder's face came sharply into view. He looked fit and relaxed, and wore his hair in a stylish new cut, parted in the middle. Heinrich Rogol and Jack Reed also stepped out of the car, carrying briefcases. They all went into the hotel.

"It looks like a business meeting," Novak said. "An ordinary business meeting."

"Exactly," said Eliot.

But perhaps this was a little different. Suddenly a helicopter rose into the sky behind the hotel and swept toward them. Novak barely had time to duck into the shadows of the hut, when the helicopter roared overhead, banked, and flew away toward the north. Eliot, Novak saw, had shown more presence of mind: in his notebook he had recorded the helicopter's identification numbers.

"What's going on?" Novak asked.

"Wait," Eliot told him, reloading his camera.

In less than an hour, the helicopter returned. Novak noticed that it carried a passenger. So did Eliot. He ducked outside the hut and snapped off a dozen pictures. The helicopter descended behind the hotel, out of sight. "Wasn't that a little risky?" Novak asked.

Eliot didn't reply. He remained quiet the rest of the day. Novak lay down on his sleeping bag and fell asleep. When he awoke, Eliot was still sitting in the doorway, watching Norman's Cay, the notebook in his lap, open at a blank page.

"Well," said Novak, "how are we doing?"

Eliot looked at him. "In what sense?"

"In the evidence-gathering sense," Novak said. "Hard evidence."

"Not bad," said Eliot. "You've got to be patient in this line of work."

Novak, who wasn't at all patient, said, "I bet I could find out more in one night over there than you could in a month in this miserable hut."

"Yeah?" said Eliot.

"Yeah."

"And how would you get over there so no one would notice? Crawl along the bottom?"

"Something like that," Novak said. "With scuba, in fact."

Eliot shook his head. "I can't let you do that," he said.

"Why not?"

Eliot recited some not very convincing reasons; and there was little conviction in his tone. Novak wondered whether Eliot had foreseen this moment from the beginning, had even planned it this way. Novak rose and went to the *Reef Witch* for his equipment.

That night, as Novak donned his gear inside the hut, Eliot said, "I can't take any responsibility for you. Whatever happens. Officially, you're on your own."

Novak, flipping on his backpack, grunted. He was learning to expect no more from officials of any kind. Carrying his fins, he made his way outside, down to the beach. "Wait," said Eliot, following. "Don't you even want to hear what you're supposed to be looking for?"

Novak paused, his feet in the water. "Hard evidence, right?"

"Right." Eliot seemed pleased with himself; the smile on his face didn't strike Novak as appropriate to the circumstances. He was still wearing it when Novak slipped underwater and out of sight.

Hard evidence, Novak thought, switching on his torch and illuminating a little half-circle of underwater night. Wasn't it reasonable that Lehder had cocaine cached secretly on the island? There could be no harder evidence than that.

The channel was shallow, no more than fifteen feet at its deepest. Novak swam close to the grassy bottom to lessen the chances of his light betraying him. Images streamed by: a bivalve in the deathgrip of an orange starfish, an octopus watching from behind a purple sea fan, a spotted moray on a nocturnal foray. Novak was only partially conscious of the life around him. His eyes were on his compass; he was trying to hold a course slightly south of due west. At first, it was easy. His heart beat a little too rapidly, but whose would not, alone at night and underwater? Then, about halfway across—Novak estimated the entire distance at just under half a mile—he began to feel the strong current that ran parallel to Norman's shore. It forced him to exert himself, slightly for a little while, but soon he was kicking as hard as he could, breathing in gasps and using far too much air. For a moment he feared that the current would overpower him and sweep him out to open sea; then, all at once, the tide slackened. He took a deep breath to collect himself, changed course slightly, and froze. A big shadow loomed just beyond the range of his torch. Novak knew what it was before it entered the circle of light: a hammerhead. But he wasn't prepared for its size. With a tremendous surge, it came flashing through the circle of light, shot past his head, and disappeared behind him. Novak jerked around, stabbed his light in the darkness. He saw nothing.

Novak turned slowly, probing the water with the torch. The hammerhead had been moving jerkily: a sign of agitation or hunger. Novak was without a bangstick, the only good weapon against a shark, or even his speargun, which was much chancier. All he had was his dive knife. Divers have a saying about the correct deployment of a knife in a shark attack: use it to cut your throat. Novak drew his knife.

Evolution has not programmed human beings to be alert for attacks from above. Novak had no warning. The hammerhead dove down at him from the surface, its open mouth passing before his eyes. Then it whipped around and came at him from the front, slowly, jerkily.

Novak pointed the dive knife at the shark and tried to

look aggressive. He puffed out his chest and gritted his
teeth around his regulator. The imitation led to the real
thing, as it had in similar circumstances before. Adrena-
line coursed through him and he no longer had to try: he
felt aggressive. He even advanced slightly on the shark. It
seemed to forget all about him at once. The hammerhead
backed away, out of the torch's light, and disappeared.
Novak swam on, feeling alert and even dangerous
himself.

He was still feeling that way when the bottom abruptly
sloped up and took him to the surface, a few feet from
the beach. He switched off his light and looked around.
The shadow of a hill rose not far away. He could distinguish the outlines of the hotel near its top; no lights
shone. He was somewhere between Battery Point and the
marina. Novak hid his gear, including the wet suit, in
bushes at the edge of the beach. Wearing only a bathing
suit, he made his way through the scrub and stepped out
onto the main road. He listened for sounds and, hearing
none, walked toward the hotel, his bare feet silent on the
warm pavement.

Novak circled the hotel, approaching from the patio
side. He was halfway up the steps when he saw something move on the patio, not ten feet away. He stopped
in his tracks, slowly backed down the stairs. A voice from
the patio said something in Spanish. Another voice
grunted in answer, from somewhere behind Novak. He
moved off the stairs and ducked behind a palm tree.

Two shadows came together in the darkness. More
words were exchanged. Novak heard liquid gurgling from
a bottle, then footsteps. They moved off, toward the road,
and out of range. Novak checked his watch: ten to one.
Would Lehder maintain twenty-four-hour patrols? He didn't
know. For the first time, he began to think in real terms
of what might happen to him if he were caught.

Novak crept around toward the business office and
peeked through the window. It no longer looked like a
business office. The room was crammed with radio and

radar equipment. There were four or five video screens, displaying glowing lines of data. A man was staring blankly at one of them. Its light turned his profile green. As Novak watched the man suddenly looked around. Novak ducked out of sight. No one yelled a warning, no one came running. He risked another peek. The man was still sitting before the screen, staring blankly.

Novak walked away from the hotel, down the road to the marina. There was no reason to look in the dive shop: it was hardly the sort of place Lehder would use for hiding cocaine. But he looked in it anyway: after all, wasn't it his?

He pushed the door open and shone his torch inside. Except for the single set of scuba gear that had been sent to him on the *Reef Witch*, everything was exactly as he had left it. He looked a little more closely and saw that the shop had been freshly painted. Had Dougie Hollins taken over his operation? Novak didn't care for that thought at all. Moving to the counter, he found his dive notebook open to the entry of his last dive. Hollins wouldn't have done that. Novak was struck by the eerie notion that Lehder had prepared everything for his return.

Novak switched off his torch, left the shop, crossed the road and stepped onto the airstrip. A dog barked, somewhere near the customs house. That set off more barking. The moon had risen and there was enough light for Novak to see low kennels that had been built near the customs house. He stepped back into the bushes. The barking ceased.

Novak tried to memorize all the changes he saw around the airstrip. There were two new hangars, a helicopter pad half-constructed, rolls of sheet metal, stacks of concrete blocks, coils of wire; and what looked like a squadron of light planes parked in neat rows. He wanted to count them, but he didn't dare, not with the dogs; that, and the sudden orange glow of a cigarette, in the shadow of the customs house.

Was it possible that the cigarette-smoking man's duty

was to take the dogs on nighttime patrols? How long would it take them to pick up his scent? It was time to go back.

But Novak didn't go back. Instead, he made a wide detour around the customs house and walked along the path to Kniskern's villas on Smuggler's Beach; and up to the door of the one he regarded as his own. Was it a likely hiding place for drugs? No. But Novak wanted to go inside anyway. For a moment, he felt like someone revisiting a childhood home.

Quietly, he tried the door. Unlocked. He pushed it open. No one snored inside, or turned restlessly in sleep. Novak flicked on his torch, quickly saw that the villa was unoccupied. Its only contents were his own things: his clothes, still on the chair by the bed, his books on the shelves, his papers on the desk, the picture of Chris still stuck into the frame of the mirror. It was like revisiting a childhood home, all right, and finding everything just as it had been, ready for his return. Again, Novak experienced the eerie feeling that he was expected on Norman's Cay, that Lehder expected him, was waiting for him to take his place in some scheme of things.

Well, Novak thought, why not?

Then, still feeling alert and a little dangerous, he returned to the beach near Battery Point, donned his gear, and sank back into the dark water.

27

Bobby Eliot didn't say, "I can't let you take the risk," or "It wouldn't be professional." He just said, "You're sure?" And Richard Novak said, "Yes." He became a secret DEA informant.

"This is what I need," Eliot told him: "Tail numbers of all the planes. Names of the pilots and everyone else involved. Outline of the day-to-day running of the operation. And the location of Lehder's stash, if there is one on Norman's or any of the cays nearby."

"Got it," said Novak.

"Elvis Welles on Highbourne Cay will be your contact."

"He works for you?" Novak said in surprise.

"Lots of people work for me," Eliot answered. "The trick is figuring out what other payrolls they're on at the same time."

"You don't have to worry about that with me," said Novak. It never occurred to him to ask for payment, and none was offered.

Eliot made no reply. Perhaps he'd learned it was unsafe to stop worrying about anything. Perhaps he didn't care what Novak's motives were. Novak didn't think much about his motives either. The only person who did was Chris. The day before Novak left on his mission, Chris said, "This isn't about your plans on Norman's anymore, is it? It's just about Lehder and all your frustrations."

"It's about doing the right thing," Novak had said, raising his voice.

Chris had paused a long time before responding: "You're letting him change you."

"Lehder? That's ridiculous."

Chris had started to argue, and reconsidered. "Just don't get hurt," he'd said. They said good-bye soon after.

On March 21, 1980, Novak cruised around the long arm of Norman's Cay, found the blue water channel off Battery Point, and swung around toward the marina. This was no furtive nighttime expedition; he came in broad daylight with the *Reef Witch* flying the Stars and Stripes in the stern.

A black cigarette boat roared out from the dock to meet him. Eliot had prepared him for that. Novak cut the *Reef Witch's* engine and waited, bobbing on the water. The cigarette tore around him in a tight circle, raising a rooster tail that splashed across Novak's deck. He read the name on its stern: *Eliminator*. The *Eliminator* glided to a stop, ten feet from his bow, its powerful engine idling at a low rumble. The fit-looking driver with a gold chain around his neck was new to Novak. Despite their proximity, he used a bullhorn to communicate.

"This is a private island," he said. He had a German accent, as thick as Heinrich's. He also had a gun on his hip. "You will leave at once."

Novak kept his tone pleasant, again according to plan; although perhaps not quite as pleasant as planned: the reality of the man in the *Eliminator*, with his bullhorn and gun, made it hard for someone like Novak even to feign politeness. "Tell Mr. Lehder that Novak has returned," he said.

The man's eyes narrowed. He drew his gun. "This is a private island," he repeated through the bullhorn, as though it were a mantra that had always worked in the past.

"I know that," Novak said. "I've got a house here myself. And Mr. Lehder will want to know I'm back."

The man put down the bullhorn and reached for his

radio. "Manfred here," he said. "I've intercepted an intruder in the lagoon. He says he knows Mr. Lehder."

Heinrich's voice came over the speaker. "What is his name?"

"Novak," said Manfred.

"Stand by," Heinrich told him. The radio went silent. The *Reef Witch* and the *Eliminator* floated together on the water. Manfred never took his eyes off Novak, and held the gun at his side.

The radio crackled. "This is Heinrich. Escort Mr. Novak to the dock. He is free to come ashore."

Manfred looked surprised, but he said, "Ja," and motioned Novak to the dock. The *Eliminator* followed the *Reef Witch* across the lagoon. Novak tied up and disembarked. Manfred made no move to come ashore. He stood at the wheel of the *Eliminator*, gun still in hand. Novak realized that Manfred was probably going to search the *Reef Witch* as soon as he was out of sight. Novak hoped he would. There was nothing incriminating on board. The pistol, box of ammunition, and two-way radio that Eliot had given him were already tucked inside his shirt.

Novak walked across the marina parking lot and onto a path that led around the airstrip to Kniskern's villas on Smuggler's Beach. He fought the urge to run. Look calm, he told himself, but he knew he wouldn't feel calm until the gun, ammo, and radio were hidden.

Novak reached his villa. A man in a khaki uniform stood by the door. The man wore sunglasses, making his expression impossible to read. Novak calculated the time it would take to wrestle Eliot's gun from under his shirt: longer than the time the guard needed to draw his own gun from the holster on his belt. Sound calm, he thought. He said: "This is my house. I'm going inside." The guard stepped aside to let him pass. The door was unlocked. Novak went inside and closed it.

No one was in the villa and nothing had changed. Novak hurried into the kitchen and opened the cupboard under the sink. He remembered that the floorboards had been loose. He pried two of them off and quickly dug a hole in the sand underneath. Then he packed the gun, ammo, and radio in separate sandwich bags, placed them in the hole, filled it in, and smoothed the sand. He was replacing the boards when he heard the front door open.

Novak closed the cupboard and quickly left the kitchen. He found Steve Francis glowering in the front hall. Through the open doorway, he saw the Excalibur parked outside, with Heinrich leaning against it and Lehder sitting at the wheel. "No one ever taught you to knock, Steve?" Novak said, and went past Francis and out the door.

Heinrich was glowering too, but Lehder smiled when Novak appeared. Novak walked to the car. Lehder stuck his hand through the window. Novak shook it.

"You're back," Lehder said.

"Yup."

Lehder was still smiling. At first glance, he looked as sleek as he had through Eliot's binoculars, but now Novak observed a tightness around his eyes and mouth, and swollen red veins in his eyes.

"Why?" asked Lehder.

"I like it here," Novak said. It was true. "There's no place like it for the work I want to do."

Lehder's smile broadened. "There's no place like it, period," he said. A faraway expression came into his eyes and the smile slowly faded. When he turned again toward Novak, his face didn't seem as friendly.

Novak returned to his script. "The hammerhead migration can't be too far off. It's my chance to really get some work done."

Lehder's expression relaxed a little. "Do you think other scientists would be interested in it?"

"The migration? I'm sure of it."

Lehder nodded. "One day Norman's will be home to scholars from all over the world," he said. "Artists, too."

Novak glanced at Heinrich and Francis, to see how they reacted to this delusion. What artist or scholar would come to a place overrun by uniformed goons and armed drug runners? The faces of Heinrich and Francis were blank. Novak turned back to find that Lehder was watching him. "Don't you agree?" he asked. "I thought you shared the dream of Norman's Cay."

"I do," said Novak. "That's why I want to make a thorough study of the entire marine ecosystem."

That brought back the smile again. It occurred to Novak that Lehder, surrounded by people like Ward, Heinrich, and Reed, might be starved for intelligent conversation. What truly big dreams would have roles for actors like them? He began to understand where he could fit into Lehder's plans. "Marine ecosystem" had done the trick. Novak readied a fancy little scientific speech in his mind, but he never got to use it.

Lehder's smile faded, quickly this time. Novak didn't remember these mood swings from before. He regarded Lehder closely.

"What are you looking at?" Lehder said.

"Nothing."

"Nothing?" His face twitched. "Why would anyone look at nothing?"

Novak had no answer to that. "I was just thinking about the hammerheads, that's all."

Lehder grunted. "The hammerheads. They always come back to Norman's, right?"

"Right."

"Just like you," Lehder said, his voice full of accusation.

You and me both, Novak thought, but he said nothing.

Lehder gave him a long look. "You can stay, Herr Professor. Just concentrate on your studies, that's all." He turned to Heinrich. "Give him a warm welcome, Heinrich." Heinrich smiled; on the steps of the villa, Francis snickered. Lehder switched on the engine and sped away.

"Let's go, Herr Professor," said Heinrich, motioning to a jeep.

"Where?" asked Novak.

"For a welcoming party," Heinrich said. "You heard the man."

They got into the jeep, Francis in front, Heinrich in back with Novak, both his guns visible. Francis drove past the airport, north toward Ed Ward's house. Was some party in progress at Ward's, Novak wondered? But the jeep turned off the road before Ward's house, and came to a stop in a clearing. In the clearing stood a wooden hut, big enough to shelter a generator. Or a man.

"Out," said Heinrich.

Novak got out. Heinrich motioned him toward the hut. Novak didn't move. Heinrich drew one of his guns and prodded Novak in the back, the way they do it in the movies. Novak found it wasn't easy to be as cool as a movie hero with a real gun in your back. He walked toward the hut.

Heinrich went inside. The hut was empty, except for a can of gasoline. Heinrich emptied it over the floor. At that moment, Novak turned to run. Francis was ready. He tripped Novak up, and fell on him on the threshold of the hut. Novak struggled, but Francis was younger and stronger. Heinrich stepped out of the hut, a book of matches in his hand. "We don't like nosy people on Norman's," he said. "Some people have to learn the hard way."

Heinrich lit a match, tossed it into the hut, and backed away. Francis still held Novak down, but now he used him as a shield. The hut went up in flames. They billowed to the treetops. The heat seared Novak's face. He tried to twist away, but Francis held him in place.

"They learn the hard way, but they learn," Heinrich said. He waited a little longer for the lesson to sink in before he told Francis to let Novak go.

Novak rolled away from the heat. By the time he got to his feet, the jeep was gone. He found that his whole body was shaking. Some time passed before the shaking stopped. Then Novak dusted himself off and started walking back to the villa on Smuggler's Beach: the villa to which he had legal title, the villa that made him a resident of Norman's Cay, a resident with rights and duties.

28

Novak knew at once that the villa had been searched. It wasn't that the searchers had been messy or destructive; it was just that they hadn't bothered to keep it secret. Drawers and closets were open and books and papers were out of place. With anxiety building inside him, Novak went into the kitchen and looked under the sink. One of the floorboards wasn't flush with the others. Novak threw it aside. Underneath, the sand seemed undisturbed. He quickly dug through it with his bare hands, and found the three plastic packages untouched. He reburied them carefully. What had Bobby Eliot said? *They're not that good.* Novak rubbed his shoulder, sore from his struggles with Steve Francis, and wondered.

Working undercover meant being sociable in a way Novak wasn't comfortable with even in normal life. He knew he would have a hard time being sociable with a few of Lehder's men, starting with Victor Forbes. That evening, he had a big rum-and-lime-juice in his kitchen, then went to the hotel for dinner.

The dining room was crowded. Pilots, mechanics, bodyguards, all waited their turn at an enormous buffet. Workers in the drug business ate well: steak, spiny lobster, a variety of fresh fruits and vegetables. Novak was helping himself when an American in the line turned and said: "Hi, I'm Tracy, hotel manager."

Hotel managers seemed to come and go with rapidity on Norman's. "I'm Novak," Novak said.

"I know who you are," Tracy said, and Novak steeled himself for trouble. But none ensued. "Welcome back to Norman's. Drinks are available at the bar. Just sign. Same for supplies—you'll find a good stock at the Emlin house. It's all taken out of the paychecks at the end of the month. In your case, we'll make some other arrangement. If you've got any questions, let me know."

"Thanks," said Novak, sitting down to eat. If Lehder was trying to keep him off-balance, he thought, it's working. Eliot had prepared him for a hostile reception or a friendly one, but not both at once.

He listened to the conversation of the men around him, and quickly realized he wouldn't learn much that way. The men seemed to be grouped by aircraft—pilot, copilot, assistants—and there was little mixing between groups. Was that part of Lehder's plan? It made sense in terms of security. The talk Novak overheard was of aviation, weather, equipment. Drugs were not mentioned. Was that part of the plan too? Or was it only because of his presence?

Novak polished off a steak and returned to the villa. He poured himself another drink and sat on the porch. As the sky began to darken, men appeared on the landing strip. Not long after, Novak heard the sound of an approaching plane. More men came onto the strip. From where he sat, Novak had a good view of them. But, despite the trees growing around the villa, they might have a good view of him too. He got up, went inside, and peered through the blinds.

Night fell. Searchlights flashed on from the nearby look-out towers. Seconds later parallel strings of landing lights illuminated the length of the strip. Ed Ward's bonfires were now obsolete.

Novak heard sounds: dogs barking on the beach; the plane in the sky; trucks on the road; the opening of the hangar doors. He stayed where he was, as Eliot had instructed. He was prepared to be a prisoner at night. That wouldn't stop him from observing what happened outside his cell.

The plane touched down and taxied to the head of the strip. The pilot jumped out and walked into the customs house with Manfred. Mechanics began servicing and refueling the plane immediately. Then they pushed it into the one of the hangars. As it passed under the light over the door, Novak read the number on its tail. He guessed that before the night was over there would be too many numbers to remember. He got his dive log from the desk and wrote down the number. It was an easy matter to conceal it among the figures used to record the dates, depths, and elapsed times of various dives. No one examining the book would make the connection.

The plane remained in the hangar for about ten minutes. Novak assumed that Lehder's men were loading it with cocaine, but he couldn't be sure until he'd been inside the hangar, and he saw how difficult getting in would be. He also saw, as the mechanics rolled the plane back out, that new numbers had been painted onto the tail. He recorded them in the log book.

Heinrich emerged from the hangar. He spoke to the pilot. The pilot boarded the plane. It rolled off down the strip, and was soon airborne, disappearing into the night sky. The sound of its engine had barely faded away before Novak heard another one. Two or three minutes later, the next plane touched down, rolled up to the hangar. The procedure was repeated with the same efficiency as before. There were no raised voices, no wasted motions. Heinrich and Manfred ran the show, and everyone—the pilots, mechanics, and armed guards posted here and there along the strip—obeyed them without question. Nineteen planes landed and took off in two hours that night. Novak timed the whole operation and wrote all the tail numbers, before and after, in his dive log.

When the last plane had taken off, the shore patrols returned and kenneled the dogs. Manfred's guards dispersed. Heinrich supervised the locking of the hangars, then led the mechanics away. Novak stopped peering through the blinds and went out to the porch.

The night was warm and quiet. The air smelled like paradise. Novak could almost have convinced himself that he had imagined everything. Then the Excalibur pulled onto the runway, its motor purring so softly that Novak hardly heard it. The car stopped. Carlos Lehder, alone, leaned back in the front seat and stared up at the night sky. Novak could see him clearly in the moonlight. Without making a sound, he rose from his chair and backed up until he touched the sliding glass door. He remained there, deep in shadow.

Lehder stopped gazing at the sky. Slowly he turned his head until his gaze fixed on Novak's villa. The moon shone in his eyes. He seemed to be looking directly at Novak. Novak stayed where he was, not moving a muscle. Was it possible that Lehder could see him? Surely not, thought Novak. He remained in Lehder's moonlit stare for what seemed like a long time. Lehder finally started the car and drove away. Novak wiped the sweat off his forehead and went inside.

The next day, following Eliot's suggestion, Novak began establishing his cover story, going about a routine designed to allay suspicion. This play-acting life was in fact the real life he had dreamed of leading on Norman's, diving the reef in the morning and spending the afternoons in the shop, writing his notes and readying gear for the next day's dive. The problem was that under the circumstances he didn't enjoy it.

Was his cover story believed? Novak wasn't sure. Although no one interfered with him on the *Reef Witch* or in the shop, he soon learned that his freedom was limited. Whenever he tried to go for walks on the island, he was stopped at the first roadblock, not far north of his villa. That meant he was restricted to the southern foot of the island, which included the airport, marina, and hotel, but almost none of the housing. He was a prisoner by day as well as by night; the size of the prison changed, that was all.

Novak's cautious efforts to elicit more information, usually through conversation at dinner, were fruitless. He never advanced beyond small talk; he never even learned the full names of the men he ate with. They called each other by first names or nicknames: Rocky, King Kong. Tracy, the hotel manager, was called Trace or Dick Tracy. Were any of these names real? Novak never knew. What little he gleaned came from his chambermaid. From talking to her, he gathered that by means of roadblocks and chain link, Lehder had divided the island into three sectors. Sector one was the southern bulge, where Novak lived. Sector two ran to the northern tip. The houses in sector two were occupied by the pilots, except for one that was used as the school. Sector three was the fishhook. It included Volcano, Lehder's house, and the houses of Heinrich and Reed. The houses here came with cooks, drivers, hot tubs, and private phones. Access was restricted to Lehder and his inner circle.

"Be patient," Eliot had said.

Novak tried to be patient. He dove the reef, he wrote his notes, he maintained the *Reef Witch* and his gear. He tried to lose himself in the rhythm of daily life, to become part of the scenery, like the cook cleaning grouper on the dock. The nights he spent quietly in his villa. He learned to stop listening anxiously for the sound of planes. It wasn't necessary. Every shipment was preceded by a man in khaki, who walked up Novak's path and posted himself outside the door. That didn't stop Novak from peering through the bedroom blinds at the arriving and departing planes, and writing their tail numbers in his dive log.

Being patient, Eliot had explained, meant not taking chances. Taking chances risked blowing his cover, and Novak didn't have to be told the danger of that. He lived unobtrusively in his circumscribed existence, until one morning in the middle of April.

Novak was in the shower when he thought he heard noises. He quickly shut off the water and listened. He heard a plane. That wasn't unusual. He was about to turn the water on again when a gun fired, not far away. It fired again. And again. Novak hurried out of the bathroom, pulling on his clothes.

He ran out onto the porch. A small plane was circling over the southern tip of the island, trailing black smoke. On the concrete-block look-out tower beside the customs house stood one of Manfred's khaki-uniformed men, holding up a rifle. Novak was about to step off the porch when a jeep came bumping across the grass and Heinrich leaned out, gun in hand. "Get back in your goddamned house," he said.

Novak went inside. The jeep sped off. He stepped back out.

Armed men came running onto the airstrip. Others were parking jeeps and trucks on the strip, blocking it. Overhead, the smoking plane was approaching from the south. If the pilot saw that the strip was blocked he gave no sign. He came in low; much too low. The plane never reached the runway. It dipped out of sight west of Battery Point. There was an instant of silence, then a tremendous crashing sound, followed by the boom of an explosion.

None of Lehder's men moved. It suddenly struck Novak that the plane must belong to the DEA. Why else would they be shooting at it? Perhaps Eliot himself was on board. The next moment, without further reflection, Novak was on his motorcycle, racing down the runway. Someone raised a hand to stop him. He went right by.

At the end of the runway, Novak jumped off the motorcycle and ran onto the shore. The plane, split in two, lay partly on the sand and partly on the rocks. Flames spurted out of the nose. Novak approached cautiously, doubtful that anyone could have survived. Then he thought he saw a movement inside the cabin. He ran to the plane. Fingers scratched at the blackened glass. Novak tried the door handle. Locked. He kicked in the glass. Heat and flames poured out. Novak knotted his shirt around one hand, reached in, and pulled the door open.

A man fell out and rolled moaning on the sand. Novak saw a woman in the back seat. She was silent and still, but her hair was on fire. Novak leaned into the burning cabin, grabbed her, yanked her out. Then he went after the pilot, strapped into his seat. Novak freed him, dragged his limp body out of the plane. Working feverishly, he rolled the three of them in the sand and tore off their smoldering clothes. It was some time before he noticed Heinrich and Manfred and a few others standing behind him, guns drawn.

"Help, for God's sake," Novak said. By now the two passengers were sitting up. They had suffered moderate burns, as far as Novak could tell, burns that required immediate attention but were not life-threatening. And one glance told him that these were not DEA agents but middle-aged tourists out on an island-hopping jaunt.

Lehder's men hadn't moved. Novak raised his voice. "What is wrong with you? These people need a doctor."

There was a long pause, as though Lehder's men were creatures from some other planet who didn't know how to behave on earth. Then Heinrich nodded to the uniformed men. Not very gently, not very quickly, they helped the couple into the back of a jeep. Novak turned his attention to the pilot.

"Leave him," Manfred said. "He had no business landing here."

Novak stared at him. Rage and contempt bubbled up inside him. He picked up the pilot and carried him past Manfred, toward the jeep. Heinrich stood in his way. Novak walked around him and laid the pilot in the back seat. Then he got in the front, pushed the driver aside, and drove to the hotel.

Heinrich and Manfred parked right behind him. Trace came out on the hotel steps.

"Call Air-Sea Rescue," Novak shouted to him.

"Stay where you are, Trace," said Heinrich. Trace stayed where he was.

Novak wheeled on Heinrich. "These people need a doctor. Can't you see that?"

"You don't give orders around here," Heinrich said.

"Then I'll go see Lehder myself," Novak said, getting back in the jeep.

Heinrich drew his gun and raised it. "You're going nowhere." Novak glanced in the rear-view mirror. Manfred blocked the way. He was pointing a gun too.

"Trace," Novak called to the island manager, still standing on the steps. "These people could die. The pilot will die for sure, if he doesn't get medical attention. Are you going to let that happen?"

Trace said nothing.

Novak got out of the jeep. He took a step toward Heinrich. Heinrich pointed the gun at him. Novak was so angry he might have taken another step, but at that moment the Excalibur, like a fragment from a much more elegant dream than the one that now pervaded on Norman's, drove into the parking lot. Heinrich walked quickly toward it. Manfred stayed behind, watching Novak.

Heinrich talked. Lehder listened. Then Lehder talked and Heinrich listened. Lehder drove off. Heinrich returned. "You have exactly one hour of phone time at the hotel to reach Rescue," he said.

Novak climbed the stairs to the hotel, feeling the eyes of Heinrich and Manfred on his back. He was lucky. He reached Rescue almost immediately. A plane arrived within an hour. The medics treated the two passengers and carried them on stretchers into the plane. They treated the pilot and loaded him on a stretcher too, but they covered him completely with a sheet when they took him away. Novak watched the plane until it vanished from sight. When it was gone he felt more alone than he ever had in his life.

29

The next morning, Novak boarded the *Reef Witch* and set out on the twenty-minute crossing to High-bourne Cay. He had made several trips to Highbourne for supplies since his return to Norman's and no one had objected; just the same, he kept looking back, watching for the rooster tail of the *Fire Fall* or *Eliminator* in pursuit. But no one followed him.

When he was still about a mile offshore, he shifted into neutral and radioed ahead to Elvis Welles. People from Norman's Cay might be on Highbourne at any time and he didn't want to be seen having an intimate conversation with Elvis Welles. Novak sat in his boat, bobbing gently on a glassy sea.

Elvis Welles had many interests. He rented out a few cottages on Highbourne; he operated a big charter boat called *Miz Clawdy*; he was a DEA informant. Now Novak saw *Miz Clawdy* cutting quickly toward him. He dropped bumpers over the rail as Welles came alongside; Welles tossed him a line and Novak tied the boats together. He boarded *Miz Clawdy*.

Welles stood barefoot in the shade of his tuna tower, pouring rum into two paper cups. He wore frayed shorts, a T-shirt so faded that its beer company logo was no longer legible, and a cap with an oversized bill: the image of a Bahamian boat captain with years at sea.

"Did any of Lehder's men see you go out?" Novak asked.

"Don't worry," replied Welles, "no one suspects me."

"But they might suspect me," Novak said.

"If they did, you wouldn't be allowed on Norman's," Welles said, handing him a paper cup. "Drink up." They drank rum and rode the gentle swells. Drink settled Novak's nerves; perhaps it had something to do with Welles's phlegmatic behavior, too. The sun shone down from a cloudless sky. The world might have been at perfect peace.

Novak knew it was an illusion. He put down his cup and took out the dive log. "What's that?" Welles asked.

"The tail numbers." Novak read them out. Welles copied them in a notebook of his own.

"Not bad," Welles said. Then Novak told him about the shooting down of the airplane. Welles's face hardened. He didn't like Carlos Lehder, not since the day one of Manfred's shore patrols had taken potshots at *Miz Clawdy*. "His time is almost up," Welles said. "You won't have to hang on much longer."

"How do you know?"

"Because Eliot won't need much more than this," Welles said. He paused for a moment. "They're planning the raid right now, in fact—Hanna's choosing the team this week."

"Hanna's had one raid already," Novak said.

"This will be different," Welles told him. He paused again. "One more thing—Eliot wants to know where Lehder stashes the coke before they move. A bust with no big seizure might not do any good, not with all the PR Lehder's got going for him."

Novak put down his drink. "Are you telling me there won't be a raid unless I find the drugs?"

Welles looked down. "I don't honestly know."

"But I haven't got a clue where it is," Novak said, making no attempt to conceal his exasperation.

"Eliot knows that. He wants you to have a look-see."

"A look-see? Tell Eliot they don't exactly let me wander around over there."

Welles took a big gulp from his cup. "You could sneak a peek inside the hangars, couldn't you?"

"With difficulty," Novak said. "And what if it's not there?"

Welles squinted at him for a moment. "What if, what if," he said, with a meaning unclear to Novak. Then he spat over the side and started refilling their cups.

"None for me," Novak said. Welles shrugged.

Novak climbed back on the *Reef Witch* and cast off. "Oh, another thing," Welles called to him.

"Another thing?"

"Keep an eye out for Hotel Kilo."

"What are you talking about?"

Welles shrugged again. "Eliot keeps hearing about Hotel Kilo. The word's out on the street in Miami."

Novak switched on the engine and sped away, insofar as the *Reed Witch* was capable of speed, in a bitter mood. There wasn't any doubt in anyone's mind that Lehder was a dangerous international criminal, yet he, an amateur, seemed to be the only one doing anything about it. Certainly he was the only one risking his life.

That night Novak heard the guard come up the path and stop outside the door of his villa. He went into the bedroom and looked through the blinds. The lights on the airstrip were shining again; and a string of fires blazed on the southern shore, from Battery Point to Taffia Point. Men crowded around the customs house and the hangars. The whole population of the island seemed to have turned out, including Lehder. Lehder stood by himself in the middle of the strip, staring up into the night sky. All at once, he held up a finger. Everyone stopped moving, listened. Novak went out onto the porch and listened too. He heard a distant hum from the sky. It grew louder and louder, until it was far louder than any plane Novak had heard over Norman's, and then louder than any plane he had heard anywhere. Everything shook with the sound: the customs house, Novak's villa, Novak himself. Seconds later, a massive twin-engine cargo plane, brown with white trim, landed on the little runway at Norman's Cay. Hotel Kilo.

Next morning, Novak awoke to find Hotel Kilo parked proudly at the head of the strip, and a gaggle of admirers standing around it. Novak opened the sliding glass doors and walked onto the runway. Manfred was there, but made no move to stop him. In fact, he seemed in a light-hearted mood. "What do you think, Herr Professor?" he asked.

"Quite an aircraft," said Novak, although the real question on his mind had to deal with the present location of the immense cargo the plane would be carrying. "Whose is it?"

"Ours, of course," said Manfred, a little miffed. "It's part of the Norman's Cay enterprise."

And what kind of enterprise is that, Manfred? thought Novak. He kept the thought to himself. "Very impressive," he said, and started for the marina.

On the *Reef Witch*, Novak got out his tools and began taking apart the engine. When he had seven or eight pieces strewn on the deck, he rose and walked to the airstrip, a screwdriver in his hand. The hangars were open. Novak approached one of them, almost close enough to see within. Then Heinrich stepped out.

"What are you doing here?" he said.

"I'm having engine trouble," Novak replied. "I'd like to talk to one of the mechanics."

Heinrich thought for a moment. While he was thinking, Novak peered over his shoulder into the hangar. He saw tire tracks in the front, a small paint shop in the back, and no sign of Lehder's cocaine. Heinrich moved closer to him, blocking his view. "What's so interesting?"

"Huh?" said Novak, looking at him in puzzlement.

Heinrich studied him suspiciously, then said, "I can't spare anyone right now."

"Maybe later?"

"Maybe," said Heinrich. "Meanwhile, this area is off-limits."

"I didn't know," Novak said.

"Ignorance of the law is no excuse," Heinrich told him. Was he trying to be funny? There was no sign of it on his face.

Novak returned to the *Reef Witch* and reassembled the engine. If Lehder's cache of cocaine existed, it was either in a house somewhere on the island, in which case his chances of finding it were nil, or it was buried somewhere in the bush. Of the two possibilities, that struck him as the more likely: a cocaine house would require a conspicuous guard detail and there was no evidence of one. But having thought through the problem, Novak was no farther ahead; he was not allowed to roam the island. He turned the problem over in his mind for several days, in vain. Then a pig came to his rescue.

Wild pigs roamed Norman's Cay, descendants perhaps of animals left there by the buccaneers. One of the pigs, a three-hundred-and-fifty-pounder called Judy, had become a pet of Lehder's men. The others weren't so fortunate, and were liable to be shot if they came within range. The pig that ambled into the gunsight of one of Manfred's khaki-uniformed men about a week after Novak's visit to the hangars looked particularly succulent. Lehder invited everyone on the island to a cookout on the hotel beach.

Novak, not normally a party-goer, arrived early. "Glad you could make it," Lehder said. "Enjoy yourself." He climbed into the Excalibur and drove off.

Novak recalled their conversation about the virtues of team play. He helped dig a pit in the sand, helped carry cases of beer down to the beach, helped the band Lehder had flown in from Nassau set up their equipment. The guests began arriving. They broke out the stimulants—beer, liquor, marijuana. The pig appeared, impaled on a spit. Not long after, a truck drove up from the airstrip. Francis opened the rear doors. Prostitutes, also flown in from Nassau, piled out. The noise level mounted. The sun dipped to the horizon, painting the already gaudy faces of the prostitutes a little gaudier. Any ice that existed was quickly broken. The pig rotated over a blazing driftwood fire. As shadows fell, Novak slipped away.

He made his way quickly past the marina and ducked into the scrub near the first roadblock. Here the island narrowed, squeezing the beach, the scrub, and the road into a thin corridor. Novak knelt behind a tree and studied the roadblock. It was unmanned.

He hurried past, keeping to the trees and scrub that bordered the road. His goal was sector three: Lehder had taken pains to make it the most inaccessible part of the island, he thought, and there must have been a reason.

The trees blocked the light of the setting sun, darkening Novak's way, but to his right the lagoon still held a fading glow. Novak was cresting Fish Tail Hill, the highest point on the island, when he saw the *Eliminator* motoring slowly into the lagoon, in the channel between the end of the fishhook and the first of the Pieces of Eight. In the *Eliminator's* wake sailed a big cabin cruiser he had not seen before. Both boats tied up at the island's secondary pier, not far from Lehder's house.

Crouching in the shadows on the opposite side of the lagoon, Novak saw a group of men disembark from the cabin cruiser and climb into one of the hotel shuttles. The shuttle turned and followed a jeep up the road, toward the northern tip of the island. Novak walked to within a few yards of the road, stood behind a big tree, and waited.

After a few minutes he heard the sound of approaching vehicles as they curved around Galleon Point and headed south. First came the jeep, with Manfred driving and khaki-uniformed men in the passenger seats. Then came the shuttle, with Heinrich driving and seven or eight men seated behind him. Novak had only a few seconds to observe them, and the light was almost gone, but he knew at once who they were: the men from Medellín. Last came Carlos Ledher, alone in his red Excalibur. The convoy rounded a bend and disappeared.

Novak forgot about the cocaine cache. The appearance of the drug producers on Norman's Cay was something that Eliot would want to know about. Novak stepped out onto the road and started running down the hill, back in the direction of the strip. He saw the distant twinkle of Lehder's taillights.

Novak soon lost sight of the taillights, but he assumed that Lehder was taking the Medellín men to the cookout, and kept running. He had almost reached the first roadblock, where the island widened into its southern bulge, when he again caught sight of red lights, blinking through the trees to his left. He halted.

A few steps away was a path through pines and scrub that Novak had noticed before but never explored. Novak looked around. Just enough light remained to illuminate the blackened branches of the trees, where the path had been widened, and the deep ruts made by the repeated passage of heavy trucks. Still breathing heavily from his run, Novak left the road and started up the path.

It led south along a narrow but densely vegetated spit that divided the lagoon on the east from a narrow cove on the west. Novak kept the red lights in view. Overhead the sky grew fully black and immense. Novak reached the edge of a clearing and stopped behind a clump of sea grapes.

The Excalibur, the jeep, and the shuttle were parked about twenty or thirty yards away. Headlights shone on a pit in the ground. It wasn't big or deep, just the right size to contain four garbage cans. Their plastic tops lay on a mound of earth, beside the Medellín men and Carlos Lehder, who were gazing down into the open cans. Lehder gestured. Someone laughed. The sound carried across the clearing to Novak, hidden in the darkness. Suddenly Heinrich, standing by the jeep, turned in Novak's direction. Novak dropped to the ground.

When he looked up again, the uniformed men were placing the tops on the garbage cans and covering the cans with sheets of plastic. Then they took shovels from the jeep and filled in the pit. When they were finished, Manfred raked the ground smooth. Everyone—Lehder, the Medellín men, Heinrich, Manfred, the guards—drove off.

Richard Novak came out of the shadows. He crossed the clearing and stood on the ground where Manfred had raked. He smelled freshly dug earth. He felt triumphant.

Not long after, Novak entered his villa. The noise of the cookout carried through the night. That was fine with him. He went into the kitchen, closed the doors and windows, shut off the light. In the darkness, he dug his radio up from under the sink and called Elvis Welles. "We've got him," he said.

30

Novak waited. He resumed his routine, surveying the reef, compiling his notes, looking busy. Sometimes he gazed out to sea, hoping for gunboats on the horizon. He waited.

On the third morning after his discovery of the drug cache, Novak awoke to the sounds of activity from the airstrip. He hurried out of bed and peered through the blinds. The strip was busier than he had ever seen it, busier than on any of the drug-running nights. Small planes were lined up at the head of the runway. As Novak watched, they took off, one after the other, and dispersed in the sky. A truck pulled Hotel Kilo into position. With a sinking feeling, Novak realized that he might be watching Lehder's entire supply of drugs leaving the island. He had to be sure. Novak pulled on his clothes and went outside, headed for the spot where the garbage cans were buried.

He hadn't gone more than a few steps when a guard stepped out of the neighboring villa and pointed an automatic rifle at him. "Get back inside," said the guard.

"I'm just going for breakfast," Novak told him. The guard moved closer. Novak heard the click of the safety. He backed toward his door. "What's going on?" he asked.

"Shut your mouth," said the guard.

Novak went inside and closed the screen door. The guard remained where he was. Novak heard him murmuring into a walkie-talkie. Five minutes later, Heinrich arrived. He strode up the path, .45 in hand, banged the door open and came inside.

"Didn't your mother teach you to knock?" Novak said.

Heinrich raised his gun, as though to strike Novak in the face. He held back. Novak noticed the circles under Heinrich's eyes, and the dark stubble on his face. Was he trembling slightly as well? For the first time, Novak knew how dangerous he was. "What do you want?" he asked.

Heinrich started to reply. His words were overwhelmed by a tremendous roar: Hotel Kilo was taking off. Heinrich jumped at the sound; the gun shook in his hand. Why was he so nervous? Was he in some paranoid stage of cocaine addiction? It occurred to Novak that the entire population of Norman's Cay might be in some stage of cocaine addiction. The thought scared him. He fought the urge to back away.

Heinrich was watching him. As the roar of Hotel Kilo diminished to distant thunder, Heinrich spoke again. "You're gone, Herr Professor," he said.

"What do you mean?"

"Gone," said Heinrich. "Off the island. For good."

"That doesn't make sense," Novak began. "My understanding with Mr. Lehder is—"

"Those are his orders, you tricky bastard," Heinrich said, his voice rising to a shout. "Move."

"Right now?"

"Immediately," Heinrich replied, now at full volume.

"All right," Novak said. In his present state, Heinrich wouldn't require much motivation to pull the trigger. "I'll just pack."

"You have one minute."

Novak went into the bedroom and opened his suitcase. Heinrich watched him through the doorway. Novak threw in some clothes, some books, the photograph of Chris, and, most important, his dive log. He tried to think of a way to retrieve the pistol and radio from under the kitchen sink without Heinrich noticing, and could not. Heinrich marched him down to the marina.

Novak boarded the *Reef Witch* and cast off. Heinrich watched him go without another word. Novak saw that he was not the only one putting to sea. Several boats were in the channel ahead of him, and the *Eliminator* was zipping back and forth along the southern edge of the lagoon like a sentry on speed. As Novak rounded Taffia Point he saw the boats ahead of him separate and motor off in different directions. He watched them in growing puzzlement. He took out his binoculars. Far to the south, he spotted the red hull of the *Fire Fall* slicing through the water. What was going on? He swept the binoculars through three hundred and sixty degrees. Dots appeared on the northern horizon. They grew larger, assumed the appearance of patrol boats and planes. This, he realized with bitterness, was the promised raid: too late. He could see that it had already failed. He spun the wheel, opened the throttle all the way and started after the *Fire Fall*.

With the binoculars, Novak was able to keep the *Fire Fall* in sight for awhile. He saw it alter course to the east, make a wide circle, and then head north, well out of the path of the oncoming fleet. Novak, too, changed course and tried to cut it off, but the *Reef Witch*, groaning with the effort, was just too slow. He estimated the *Fire Fall's* probable course and followed it himself. It took him to Nassau, where he docked that night.

Novak checked into a hotel and called the number he had for Bobby Eliot in Nassau. He was told that Eliot was in Miami. He called Miami and left a message. Then he went for a walk by the harbor. He found the *Fire Fall* docked in a private slip. Novak spent the next few hours roaming the beach hotels on Nassau and Paradise Island, looking for Carlos Lehder without success. He returned to his hotel room. Eliot hadn't called back. Novak went to bed and spent a restless night.

The morning papers didn't print a word about the raid. There was an article about Lehder, however, written by a credulous reporter and featuring an uncritical interview in which Lehder complained at length about harassment and threatened again to sell his Bahamian investments. Novak read it three times. Then he crumpled the paper into a ball and hurled it at the wall.

The phone rang. It was Eliot. "Get on a plane to Miami right away," he said.

"But why?" asked Novak. "Lehder's here, in Nassau."

"Then you're in danger. Go to the airport and get on a plane. Now." Eliot hung up.

Noval flew to Miami that morning. Eliot met him at the airport. "Want to go somewhere for a drink?" he said. His voice was subdued.

"I don't want a drink. I want to know what's going on."

Eliot put his hand on Novak's shoulder. "You've done a great job. We couldn't have asked for more."

Novak shook himself free of Eliot's hand. "What are you talking about? Lehder's waltzing around Nassau someplace and there's nothing about the raid in the papers."

"We're keeping a low profile, that's all."

"Why?"

Eliot paused. When he spoke, he was unable to look Novak in the eye. "No one got busted on Norman's, Dick. No one important, anyway. And we didn't find any blow. Not a gram. We leaked. Leaked like a goddamn sieve."

From what Novak had seen, he should have been prepared for that, but fury rose up in him anyway. "You're all a bunch of clowns," he shouted. "You, Hanna, everybody." People passing in the terminal turned to look.

Eliot's voice rose too. "Don't blame Hanna. His hands are tied." He continued more quietly: "And so are mine. It's up to the fucking politicians now."

"What does that mean?" Novak asked, although a premonition was forming in his mind.

"It means I'm off the case," Eliot replied. "I've been reassigned."

"Then what's gong to happen to Lehder?"

Eliot shrugged. "I told you—it's up to the politicians."

"I heard you. What does it mean?"

Eliot glanced around. No one was in hearing range. Still, when he spoke, Novak could barely make out his words. "Remember the helicopter we saw from that fishing hut?"

"Yes." Novak found himself whispering too.

"It brought back a passenger."

"I remember," Novak said. He also remembered the risk Eliot had taken to snap a photograph of it.

"Think about who that passenger might have been," Eliot said.

"I don't have a—" But Novak did have a clue. Eliot had just given it to him: *fucking politicians*. "My God," Novak said. "That sounds like valuable evidence." He grew excited at the thought. "It makes everything clear, doesn't it? It could break this case wide open."

Eliot laughed bitterly. "It's dynamite, all right. And they don't want it to explode."

"Why not?"

"Because he's our boy, Dick. I told you about the sub base on Andros. There are Bahamians who don't want us there, or who might drive a harder bargain."

"You mean this is all about fighting Russians?" said Novak.

"You could put it that way," Eliot told him.

"That's ludicrous. Are you telling me that Carlos Lehder's going to get away with what he's doing because of some superannuated cold warriors in Washington?"

"He's not going to get away with it," Eliot said. "He's been hurt already, thanks in a big way to you. Hanna's got some cops down there now on a permanent basis and they're cancelling Lehder's resident status."

"Meaning?"

"Meaning he can't remain on Norman's."

Novak brightened. "You mean he's been chased off?"

"That's the information I'm getting."

"Then there's no reason I can't go back, is there?"

Eliot frowned. "That's not a good idea. What if there's a leak about your involvement?"

"That won't make any difference if Lehder's gone."

"He may be gone," said Eliot, "but some of his goons are still there."

"Maybe," Novak replied. "But if I don't go back, then they'll figure out that I was the informer and I'll never be safe."

"That's pretty farfetched," Eliot said, but nothing in his tone backed up his words.

Novak didn't think. The words came by themselves. "I'm going back," he said.

Eliot looked at him closely. "Why?" he asked. Novak made no reply. "It's personal, isn't it?" Eliot continued. "You've got some kind of macho feud going on with Carlos Lehder. You've lost your perspective."

Novak remained silent.

His silence angered Eliot. "Go ahead then, I can't stop you," he said. "But that personal stuff is the sign of an amateur."

"So what?" Novak replied. "Are you happy with the job you professionals have done so far?" It was a good line, and Novak could see that it hurt Bobby Eliot. Nevertheless, for a second or two, the thought rose somewhere in his mind that there was truth in what Eliot had said about his motivation. For only a second or two: then he buried it. He was a legal resident of Norman's Cay, with rights and duties.

31

On February 26, 1981, three months after his meeting in Miami with Bobby Eliot, Richard Novak guided the *Reef Witch* back into the lagoon at Norman's Cay. No one watched him from the look-out towers, no patrol waited menacingly on the beach, no speedboat raced out to turn him away. Novak anchored in the marina, boarded his dingy, and started paddling toward shore. On his way he passed a big airplane, a C-46, half-sunk in the shallow water and crudely daubed here and there with swastikas. A wild hope awoke within him: had the island been abandoned?

If not abandoned, it had clearly changed. As Novak walked across the airstrip on his way to the villa, he saw that Norman the Knight, Lehder's armored good-luck charm, had been shot full of holes. One of his steel arms lay rusting in the dirt, like a gruesome relic of Agincourt. Novak was staring at it, lost in thought, when a jeep skidded to a stop beside him and a tall man dressed in the uniform of the Bahamian police jumped out, drawing his gun. "Hands on top of your head," he ordered.

"You're making a mistake," Novak said, but he did as he was told.

"You've made the mistake," the cop said. "This is a private island. No one comes here without permission."

"I'm aware of that," Novak said. "I've got a house on Smuggler's Beach." The policeman's eyes narrowed. "I've got papers in my pocket that prove it," Novak added. The man held out his hand, flicked his fingers. Novak reached into his pocket and handed over his contract with Kniskern.

The policeman scanned the contract. "Not good enough."

"What do you mean?"

"This says nothing about permission to come ashore. And this man Kniskern has no authority here. Authorization to land can only be granted by the owner."

"The owner?"

"Of Norman's Cay," the cop said.

"And who is that?"

"Mr. Lehder."

For a moment, Novak felt dizzy, as his body moved toward understanding faster than his mind. How could Lehder still be on Norman's Cay at all? Hadn't Hanna revoked his residence permit? And, it sickened him merely to pose the question, didn't it appear that this man, dressed not in some quasi-official getup, but in the uniform of the national police, was doing Lehder's dirty work? Were the police, who had been sent to rid the island of Lehder, now protecting him?

The policeman went back to the jeep, spoke into his radio. A few minutes later, another jeep rolled up, bringing four more Bahamian police. After it came the Excalibur, polished and gleaming. The doors of the car opened and Manfred and Lehder got out. Novak's questions were answered before a word was spoken.

Lehder looked him in the eye. "You seem to have a homing instinct for this island," he said. "Just like the sharks."

"I told you," replied Novak, remembering that it was Lehder who had seemed to him like a hammerhead at their first meeting at the hotel; an obvious image, perhaps, but disturbing to find it now applied to himself. "I like it here."

Lehder smiled, but fleetingly, and with only a suggestion of his old charm. He looked older, distracted, even dissolute. "I believe you," Lehder said. "But you have no permission to be here."

"No one told me it was required. I came here to do a job and I mean to finish it."

"And what job is that?" Lehder asked.

"Why, my research, of course," Novak answered, feigning puzzlement. He wasn't a good liar, and the reply sounded forced in his ears.

Lehder paused, but not for long. Maybe he was no longer thinking clearly; maybe Novak, a man of learning and science, personified his grandiose dream of an island nation; maybe Novak still seemed harmless to him. With more than a little hauteur, as though he were a latter-day prince of the Lorenzo de Medici type, he said: "You may stay." Manfred shot Lehder a surprised glance. "With the understanding," Lehder added, "that you keep to the shop and your villa while ashore."

"Agreed," said Novak.

Lehder nodded and got back in his car. "And Manfred will search you, of course." He drove off, leaving Novak with Manfred and the police.

Manfred perked up. He approached Novak. "Spread your legs, Herr Professor. Raise your arms."

The commands kindled rage in Novak. But he knew he must forbear, and did. Manfred patted him down, more roughly than necessary and at the same time in an exaggerated, buffoonish way: it was almost a parody. And why not? Manfred was a criminal cast in the role of a keeper of order. The performance amused the policemen, who grinned and nodded to each other. All except one, noticed Novak, struggling with his temper. That one policeman, standing a little behind the others, was watching with distaste.

In the days that followed, Novak, resuming his island routine, observed the changes that had taken place on Norman's. The schoolchildren were gone and so were the teachers. Tracy, the hotel manager, was gone too, and the job seemed to be unfilled. The hotel no longer served regular meals. Now there were cookouts on the beach instead, which often ended in bacchanals. Prostitutes occupied the hotel every night. It occurred to Novak that a bunker mentality now prevailed on the island. He recalled Eliot telling him that early in his career, Lehder had been nicknamed Little Hitler. The two thoughts now came together in Novak's mind, preparing him, perhaps, for the future.

A bunker mentality may have prevailed, but it didn't interfere with the island's commerce. Almost every second night, a guard stood at Novak's door. Lights were turned on at the airstrip, and planes landed, had their tail numbers repainted, took off. The only change was that now some of the helpers on the strip and in the hangars were being paid by the government of the Bahamas to enforce the law. One night there was so much traffic that the sky was filled with the drone of circling planes; a stack-up over Norman's Cay. Novak no longer bothered with his dive log. Now he took his radio out from under the kitchen sink, raised Elvis Welles on Highbourne, and quietly recited the tail numbers to him. He knew that Welles was relaying the numbers to Bobby Eliot in Miami. He had no idea what, if anything, Eliot was doing with them. He tried not to think about that.

About a month after his arrival, another plane went down. Novak heard no shots this time, just the scream of the engine as the plane came streaking in, much too fast, and slammed into the trees behind the hangars. Once again, Novak was unable to stop himself from getting involved. He pushed open the sliding glass door and started toward the strip. Manfred, standing near the customs house, saw him almost at once and angrily waved him back with his pistol. At that moment, an orange fireball shot up from behind the hangars. Novak knew there were no survivors; he went back inside.

That night the airstrip lay idle. Novak heard partying sounds, from the pond, the beach, the hotel. A few minutes after midnight, he dressed in dark clothes, took his flashlight, and went outside. Leaving his light off, he made a wide circle around the strip and came to a clearing behind the hangars; a clearing that hadn't been there before. It smelled of ashes. Novak flicked on his light, saw a circle of burnt trees and scrub, and in the center the remains of the plane, buried nose first in the earth.

He walked to the plane and looked through the wreckage. The remains of the pilot were still strapped to the remains of his seat. A few plastic-wrapped packages, sealed with duct tape, were scattered on the ground. Novak picked one up and opened it. White powder spilled into his hands. This was what it was all about, he thought: white powder. Worth corrupting people for, worth killing for, worth dying for. He washed his hands of it.

Novak shone his torch on what was left of the pilot's face. This was not an innocent man. Still, none of his fellows had even bothered to move him. Nor had they bothered to search for his cargo. What did that imply about the amount of drugs stored on the island?

A voice spoke from the darkness. "Just part of the cost of doing business."

Novak, his heart beating fast, stabbed his light wildly around him, picked out a man standing on the edge of the clearing. Novak didn't recognize him at first: the man wore jeans and a T-shirt, and an amused expression on his face. He came forward, examined the wreckage. "Looks to me like engine trouble," he said. "Occupational hazard." He smiled. At that moment, Novak knew who he was: the cop who had watched with distaste while he was being searched.

"You don't seem too upset about it," Novak said.

"Oh, it's terrible," said the man. "I just hate to think of anything interfering with Mr. Lehder's plans, don't you?"

Novak shone the light in the man's face, looked at him closely. The man shielded his eyes, but he kept smiling. "Better turn that off, Mr. Novak. We wouldn't want the

Germans to come prowling. I've had enough of them for one day."

Novak switched off the light. "You did this, didn't you?" he asked.

"Did what, Mr. Novak?"

"Sabotaged the plane."

The man chuckled. "Constable Paul Clarke," he said. "I'm afraid I had nothing to do with this one."

"But with others?"

Constable Paul Clarke chuckled again and ducked the question. "Pleased to meet you," he said. They shook hands in the darkness.

32

Constable Paul Clarke had a gift for sabotage and he enjoyed his work. Novak quickly learned to enjoy it too. They poured sand in the gasoline tanks at the marina, stole engine parts and dumped them in the pond, cut telephone and mooring lines, slipped the belts off the hotel generator, punched holes in the natural gas pipes behind the kitchen. They tried arson, igniting small fires in the machine shop and behind the customs house. One night—they always worked at night: by day Novak stayed rigorously within the lines Lehder had drawn, and Clarke faded into the corrupt ranks of the police—Novak realized that Lehder had used similar techniques to drive out the original residents. He turned the connection over in his mind. It added to his satisfaction until it collided with his memory of Chris at the airport: *This is changing you.*

But even if Chris was right, it was too late to stop. Lehder would soon know that he had enemies on Norman's, if he didn't know already. Novak didn't think that through to a conclusion: there were too many variables. He simply knew instinctively that they had to increase the pressure. Richard Novak was now committed to an all-out war against Lehder. He had been doing it for so long that it had begun to feel like his purpose in life. For the first time he had an equally committed ally, unaffected by the State Department, diplomacy, cold war complexities.

How to increase the pressure on Carlos Lehder? Late at night, on the dark porch of the villa, Novak and Clarke studied this question. They thought of sinking one of the drug-laden freighters in the channel, or blowing up the landing strip, or locating Lehder's stockpile of arms and dropping it in the sea. Then they had a better idea: why not steal the cocaine supply itself?

The night after this inspiration, Novak, carrying a shovel, took Clarke to the clearing in the scrub near Doubloon Bay. At the site, Clarke held a flashlight while Novak dug. The earth, dug many times already, hardly resisted the blade. It wasn't long before they were staring down into an empty hole: the sheets of plastic, the garbage cans, the cocaine—all gone. Lehder had moved them to a different location.

Clarke didn't seem discouraged: "There can't be many likely spots on an island this size. Let's eliminate them one by one."

"But that means roaming all over the island, maybe for weeks," Novak said. "Our luck won't hold that long."

"Not unless we invent a good cover story," Clarke said, smiling. Standing in the dark scrub, with the sound of a dog barking in the distance, Clarke seemed to be having fun. It was infectious. Novak found himself smiling.

"Like what," he said.

They developed a culinary interest in land crabs. Early every night, laden with crab-collecting gear, Novak and Clarke strolled along the beach, rambled through scrub and woods. It was all very public and noisy, with much shining of flashlights and loud pursuit. After, Clarke would invite his fellow cops to a crab bake on the beach. Soon Manfred's men began to turn up, and even Manfred himself.

They grew expert at catching crabs, so good that one of them could gather all they needed while the other searched for Lehder's stash. Gradually they worked their way north, past the first roadblock, up Fish Tail Hill, into the woods behind the pilot's houses. They looked for tire tracks, signs of burning and chopping, rake marks in the earth. Progress was slow, but they were learning to know the land as only hunters do.

After more than a dozen forays, they had worked their way to the Emlin house. It was Clarke's turn to gather crabs. Novak followed some tire tracks that led near the Emlin house before merging with a path that veered toward the beach. Novak heard voices, somewhere ahead. He switched off his light and advanced slowly.

He had gone a few hundred feet when the stars came out, no longer blocked by the trees. He was at the edge of a clearing. Novak ducked behind a tree. From there, he could make out three men, sitting on the ground, smoking cigarettes. He smelled coffee. The men had the air of workers waiting out a shift. They were guards, Novak realized. But guarding what? He looked around for signs of excavation.

A twig cracked, somewhere behind him. Novak turned quickly: fast enough to see the flash of a steel pipe coming out of the darkness, not fast enough to avoid it. The pipe caught him in the ribs. Novak felt a stabbing pain, as though he'd been speared. He fell breathless on the ground.

His attacker emerged from the trees, steel pipe held high. It was Steve Francis. Novak struggled to his feet. Francis came forward and swung the pipe. Novak's Marine Corps training took over. He stepped inside the arc of the swing and threw a right hand at Francis's head, striking a glancing blow. It was enough to make Francis cry out it pain and anger, rousing the guards. Novak heard raised voices, movement, confusion. He lined up Francis and threw another punch. This one landed squarely. Francis went down. Novak bolted into the woods and ran as fast as he could. For a few seconds there was nothing to hear but the sound of his own running. Then guns cracked behind him. He tried to run faster, although every breath dug points of pain into his chest. *Run*, he told himself. They could kill him with impunity, and he knew it.

Perhaps, had Novak been thinking clearly, he would have made for the *Reef Witch* and tried to escape by sea. But he wasn't thinking clearly. He ran straight to the villa on Smuggler's Beach, the villa he thought of as his own. Manfred and a few of his men were waiting on the porch. They grabbed him as he came up the steps, and threw him down on the deck.

Headlights shone on the walls of the villa, above Novak's head. He heard a car door slam, quick footsteps. Then Lehder was standing over him. His hair was wild, his teeth bared with rage; he was almost unrecognizable.

Lehder screamed, "Who's the fucking asshole that's supposed to watch him?"

For the first time, Novak felt the full malignant force of the man. At the same moment, he realized with astonishment that Lehder's fury wasn't directed at him. A German voice, Manfred or Heinz, said, "Him." Then came the sickening thwack of a rifle butt striking a human head. The man responsible for watching Novak fell on the porch and lay still beside him.

Novak struggled to rise. No one stopped him. The points of pain dug into his side no matter how shallowly he breathed. He put a hand on the rail to steady himself.

"Start talking," Lehder said.

Novak opened his mouth to begin the complicated recital of the land crabs and the cookouts. Instead he felt an urge to cough. A strong urge. He tried to fight it off, knowing how it would hurt, but he couldn't. Novak coughed. He coughed hard. The pain was excruciating. He coughed up blood.

"Answer the man, you little prick." It was Heinrich. He stepped forward and slapped Novak across the face. The land-crab story scrambled itself in Novak's brain. He had only one clear thought: he was going to die on the porch of his villa. They were going to beat him to death. He could feel the momentum of the event growing. Soon it would be irresistible.

"This is your fucking traitor, Mr. Lehder," Heinrich said. Novak looked at Lehder. Lehder's eyes were probing his own. "He's been trouble from the beginning," Heinrich said. He raised his hand to strike again.

"Just a second," came a calm, quiet voice. Paul Clarke. He stepped out from a group of men standing at the back of the porch. It was an act of real courage. "I don't know anything about this traitor business, Mr. Lehder," he said, "but Novak was just hunting land crabs. Manfred can tell you."

Lehder took a long hard look at Clarke. Then he turned to Manfred. Somewhat reluctantly, perhaps because it meant resisting the killing momentum, Manfred nodded. Heinrich lowered his hand. The tension began to dissipate.

There was a long pause. Then Lehder spoke. "All right," he said. "But he's off the island. Tonight. Is that clear?" He turned to go.

"Clear," said Heinrich. Novak started to cough.

"Something caught in your throat?" Heinrich asked. He whacked Novak on the back. The resulting jolt of pain almost knocked Novak down again. He clung to the railing, coughing blood. Lehder got into his fancy car and drove off.

Manfred and a few policemen marched Novak down to the marina. The *Reef Witch* was anchored a few hundred feet out in the lagoon. "Someone row him out," Manfred said. Paul Clarke stepped forward. Manfred's eyes narrowed.

Clarke rowed Novak out to the *Reef Witch*. Manfred watched from the dock. They spoke in low voices.

"You O.K.?"

"Yeah."

"Can you make it?"

"Yeah."

"Talk to Hanna."

"I'll talk to him all right."

Clark helped Novak onto the boat, helped him pull the anchor, helped him start the engine.

"Can you make it?"

"Yeah."

Clarke started climbing over the side, back into the dinghy. Manfred was still watching from the shore. "Better come with me," Novak said.

Clarke shook his head. "I'll be all right. You just get things started in Nassau, that's all." He got in the dinghy and rowed away. Manfred melted into the shadows.

Novak steered the *Reef Witch* into the channel. There was a light chop, something he would have hardly noticed in normal circumstances. But now he steeled himself for every bump. It didn't help. Every little wave on the ocean sent a corresponding wave of pain through his body.

It was a long night. Novak spent it clinging to the wheel, coughing blood, thinking: get things started in Nassau. He remembered every blow and every slight he had suffered on Norman's Cay. He reviewed them over and over. Novak needed fuel to keep going, and that was all he had.

The lights of Nassau appeared just before dawn. Entering the harbor, tying up, disembarking: all passed in a fog of exhaustion and pain. Then he was being admitted to the intensive care unit of the Princess Margaret Hospital, and treated for three broken ribs and a punctured lung.

"How long do I have to be here?" Novak asked the doctors. "I feel fine."

33

Carlos Lehder liked to spend time in his laboratory, especially when he was upset. He was upset now. The incident with Novak had upset him. It had driven a wedge between him and his men. They thought Novak was a traitor, an informer, and should be killed. How could that be possible? The man was merely a curiosity: he acted unafraid, which made the men distrust him, but he had no money, no influence, no power base. Lehder had never met anyone like that. Novak interested him, as a psychological study. At the same time, the man was a professor and a scientist. One day he would bring other scientists to Norman's Cay. Maybe regular international conferences would be held, sponsored by a foundation funded by Carlos Lehder. Driving to the end of the eastern hook of the island, he considered possible names for the foundation-to-be. Later he would jot them in one of his spiral notebooks, alongside his plans to build a zoo, to commission a statue of John Lennon, to set up an 800 number for drug deals, to buy a newspaper in Colombia and use it as a springboard for a political career. There was no limit. He was where Hitler was, sometime in the twenties. He would have to look through his Nazi literature and see if he could establish the exact year.

Lehder entered the lab, one of four new concrete-block structures set in a clearing in the bush. As an experimenter, Lehder worked on a grand scale. He dumped a kilo of his purest cocaine into a spaghetti pot of water, producing a milky solution. To this he added two kilos of Arm and Hammer baking soda. Getting the proportions right had taken some time; in the end he had settled on a simple two-to-one ratio.

Lehder then boiled the contents of the pot until nothing was left but a hard crust on the bottom. After allowing it to cool, he broke it into pieces that looked like small rocks: rock cocaine. Perhaps "rock" would be a good word for the new product. He tried to imagine it taking hold on the streets of American cities.

Lehder put a little rock in the bowl of a pipe, lit it, inhaled. Almost at once, the drug took control of his body and mind. Smoking cocaine magnified its effect many times. If it worked so powerfully even on someone as intelligent and disciplined as himself, what would be its influence on the streets of American cities? Huge, of course, whether sold as "rock" or under some other name, American cities were ripe for such a product, overwhelmed as they were by decadence. Lehder hated them. Yes, he was much more than a mere drug smuggler, much more even than the powerful international businessman he had become. He was a revolutionary leader of the Latin people: United States imperialism was the enemy and cocaine was the best weapon against it.

He hated the Americans. They had indicted him, and were trying to hound him off his island. It was costing him a fortune in bribes to remain. A business expense, sure, but a source of constant worry. His costs were rising and his profits weren't keeping up. The street price of cocaine was falling, and falling fast. That was due to the increased supply, which was to a large degree his own doing. Still, a source of worries. He worried; and smoked some more. The worries shrank away. Time ceased to be a factor.

But time came back, and with it, more worries. The incompetence of his men, for example. They were idiots. He had told them so many times to remove the sand pile at the end of the runway. And now the C-46 had struck it and crashed into the lagoon. It wasn't the only plane he had lost. The Lear jet had gone down in Haiti, with 4.5 million dollars on board. Idiots. All of them. Lehder was in a foul mood when someone knocked on the door.

Manfred. "The boat's all fixed."

The boat: more worries. He had bought another Scarab racer, brand-new, but the engine was malfunctioning. A Chevy block engine, 454 cubic inches. It should have been capable of pushing the boat to sixty miles an hour, at least, but it hadn't come close. What's more, the engine had smoked and made terrible noises. A mechanic had been summoned from Palm Beach and had spent two days rebuilding it. "All fixed," said the mechanic as Lehder and Manfred arrived at the dock.

It better be, Lehder thought. Or did he say it aloud? It didn't matter.

He got in the boat. The mechanic came with him, started the engine. It sounded all right. Lehder steered out into the harbor, increased speed. Immediately he heard a funny sound, and jerked around to look at the mechanic. The mechanic had heard it too: a puzzled expression came over his stupid face. Lehder opened the throttle all the way. The engine made horrible sounds and started to smoke.

"I—I can't understand it, Mr. Lehder. Better back off—you could do some damage."

"Shut your fucking mouth." Did he scream it, or just think it? It didn't matter.

Lehder roared into the dock, slowed down, told the mechanic to get off. Then he strapped himself into his seat, drove the boat in a wide circle, and angled into the dock. He was almost unaware of the people watching, of the mechanic in urgent conversation with the men who worked on the boats. Lehder bore down on the dock and smashed the new Scarab against it. Then he backed and did it again and again, smash smash smashing the goddamn thing. When he had it good and smashed he put it in neutral and opened the throttle all the way. You want to make bad sounds? You want to smoke? Then go ahead, you fucker.

The mechanic was yelling something from the dock, but in the din of the howling engine, Lehder couldn't hear him. He waited till the engines caught fire, then jumped on the dock. The boat went up in flames. Lehder felt triumphant.

Someone was tugging on his arm. The mechanic. "Sir? I figured it out. Your men say they've been filling her up with aviation fuel."

"So?"

"It takes regular unleaded."

34

"I don't believe it," said Assistant Commissioner Dudley Hanna.

Richard Novak, subject to a temporary pain in his side and a lifelong struggle with his temper, jumped to his feet. "Are you calling me a liar?"

"Sit down, Mr. Novak." Hanna's voice was firm, but there was uncertainty in his eyes. "I'm not calling you a liar," he said. Novak sat back down in the chair facing Hanna's desk. "It's just that I've got police stationed all over the island and there's not a word about any of this in their reports."

"Of course not," Novak said. "That's because they're not working for you anymore—they're working for Lehder. Except for Paul Clarke, and maybe one or two others. But do you really expect any of the honest ones to commit themselves in writing?"

"Why wouldn't they?" asked Hanna.

"Are you joking?" Novak replied.

Hanna glared at him. "Certainly not."

"Because," Novak explained, "they know that word will get back to Lehder, as it always does. But there are more drugs flying out of Norman's Cay that ever before."

Hanna opened a file on his desk and took out a sheet of paper. "I have records here of all air traffic on Norman's in the past month. There's no evidence that any of it is illegal."

"That's your whole list, right there?" Novak asked.

"Yes," answered Hanna, regarding him with puzzlement.

"Well here's the real list," Novak said, reaching into his pocket and unfolding several pages of densely packed printout. Elvis Welles had brought it to the hospital. "Bobby Eliot's been busting every one that shows up on his radar."

Hanna took Novak's list, compared it to his own. He stared at them for a long time, and when he looked up, had trouble meeting Novak's eye. "Eliot knows about this?"

"Damn right he does," Novak said. He knew that Hanna was embarrassed, but he was not at all inclined to ease his path. "Now what are you going to do about it?"

"It's going to require consultation," Hanna said.

"Consultation? And what's Paul Clarke supposed to do while this consultation's going on? He risked his life to get me out of there." Hanna frowned. "When was the last time you heard from him?" Novak added.

Hanna rose. "Stay right here." He left the office. Novak got up and looked out the window. He saw tourists in the street, sunburned and laughing. Hanna returned, looking grim. "Clarke hasn't been seen or heard from since you left Norman's."

Novak repeated his question: "What are you going to do about it?"

The next morning, Novak stood beside Captain Leon Smith on the bridge of the *Inagua*, steaming southeast toward the Exumas. The *Inagua* was a sixty-foot patrol vessel with heavy machine guns mounted fore and aft, and its commander was a big, powerful-looking man. The ship was manned by an elite force, picked by Hanna during the night and sent aboard without knowing their destination. Hanna ordered that radio silence be observed for the duration of the voyage. Novak watched the first green cays of the Exumas come into view, felt the salt air on his face, and was exhilarated. It was a kind of D-Day, he knew, an irrevocable turning in the tide of battle. He glanced at the cannon and found himself hoping for resistance.

The *Inagua* moved slowly through the channel and into the lagoon. No one fired a shot, no one called out from a look-out tower; a man cleaning fish on the dock glanced at the boat and resumed his work. The *Inagua* tied up. The men checked their guns and prepared to get off. Novak joined them. "Just a minute, Mr. Novak," said Captain Smith. "My orders are that you stay on board."

Had Novak still been a boy, he might have jumped up and down with frustration. "But why?" he said.

"There's no time to argue. This is a military operation and I am in command."

Novak took a step back and said no more. It required all his self-control.

The men disembarked and went quickly toward the hotel. Novak, watching from the rail of the *Inagua*, saw Captain Smith raise a bullhorn to his lips, heard him speak, although he couldn't make out the words. His men drew their guns. Moments later, uniformed police came out of the hotel, followed by some of Lehder's men. They stood in a row, facing the newcomers. Novak found binoculars and panned their faces. He saw Heinrich and Manfred. He did not see Lehder. Or Paul Clarke.

The island policemen handed over their guns. After a discussion, Heinrich and Manfred did the same. Further discussion ensued. Captain Smith did most of the talking, Heinrich the rest. After a few minutes, Captain Smith turned to Novak and motioned.

"Me?" said Novak, although he couldn't be heard at that distance. Captain Smith motioned again. Novak jumped off the dock and hurried toward the hotel. He could barely stop himself from running.

The island policemen gave him unfriendly looks. The faces of Heinrich and Manfred were openly hostile. Everyone knew now that he was the informer. Novak didn't care; in fact, he was proud of it. He walked up to Heinrich and said, "Tell Lehder I'm back."

Heinrich lunged at him. A big policeman grabbed him and held him back. Captain Smith said, "There'll be none of that—either of you." The moral equation rankled Novak. He stifled a hot protest.

Captain Smith turned to him. "He says Lehder's not on the island."

"He's lying."

Captain Smith came closer and lowered his voice. "He says he knows nothing about Clarke."

Novak spoke in the big man's ear: "He's lying about that too."

Heinrich and Manfred glared at him in silence.

Captain Smith addressed his elite force: "We'll search the island from one end to the other." He divided his men. One detachment entered the hotel and the nearest lookout towers and confiscated all the weapons they could find. Another group guarded the landing strip. Captain Smith and the rest climbed into one of Lehder's big passenger trucks and headed north on the main road. Novak went with them.

They disarmed the man at the first roadblock and replaced him with one of their own. They stopped at every house, rousting the pilots and their women, seizing weapons. When they reached Volcano, Lehder's house, the captain went by himself to the door and knocked. Novak hadn't seen Volcano in a long time. When Kniskern had first shown it to him he had thought it the nicest house on the island, the one he would have wanted as his own. He still thought so.

Margit opened the door. Captain Smith went inside. He came out a few minutes later, shaking his head. He got into the truck.

"Where is he?" Novak asked.

"She says he's off the island."

"It's not true," Novak said.

The Captain looked at him. "What makes you so sure?"

Instinct; that was the honest answer, but Novak didn't use it. "We haven't seen his car. It's like something out of a gangster movie. Normally it would be parked by the hotel, the marina, the strip, or here. Since it's not, he must have taken it somewhere else."

There was only one part of the island they hadn't searched: the southern tip of sector three, the end of the hook of Norman's Cay. A roadblock barred the way. They smashed through it.

Novak hadn't been at this end of Norman's since his first days on Norman's. It had changed. A rectangular clearing had been cut in the bush and four concrete-block buildings had been erected within its borders. There was a cistern, a pumping station, kennels. Dogs barked. The captain and his men got out of the truck, guns drawn. "Stay in the truck," he told Novak. "There may be shooting."

Novak stayed in the truck. There was no shooting. The complex was unoccupied. No sign of Lehder, no sign of Paul. "What's inside?" Novak asked as Captain Smith returned to the truck.

"Lots of electronics. And a lab."

"What kind of lab?"

"I'm not sure."

"I'd like to see it," Novak said.

"Not now," the captain replied. "I've got a job to do." Novak knew he was referring to Clarke. He pressed the subject of the lab no further.

Captain Smith drove back to the hotel with the intention of questioning Heinrich and Manfred more thoroughly. Novak wanted to join him, but wasn't allowed. For the first time, he began to believe that Lehder had slipped off the island. He walked across the strip to his villa.

It had been trashed: screens sliced, furniture smashed, walls punctured with bullet holes, clothes and books scattered on the beach in front. Novak went around the side to look in the generator shed, where he had left his motorcycle. As he opened the door, he heard gunfire. He turned and saw the Excalibur speeding down the road to the airstrip. Lehder was at the wheel, his long hair streaming behind him. The sight transfixed Novak. He didn't hear the door of the generator shed opening behind him until it was too late.

Novak wheeled around. Steve Francis came lunging out of the shack with a savage expression on his face and a tire iron in his hand. He brought it down hard on Novak's head.

Novak awoke on the ground outside the villa he thought of as his own. He squinted up into the sun. Shadows stood around him. They assumed the forms of men, men he knew well: Francis, Manfred, Carlos Lehder. His head ached. His vision blurred. He heard Ledher's voice. It was full of hate, but the words were unintelligible. Then one shadow came closer. Manfred, his gold chain glittering in the bright sunshine. Manfred kicked him with all his might in the ribs. Novak rolled on the ground and started coughing. Blood dripped from his mouth, onto the sand.

Manfred withdrew. Another shadow loomed over him. Novak twisted his head around, looked up. It was Francis. Francis held something that glared in the sun. It looked beautiful for a moment. Then Novak realized it was just a broken rum bottle. He tried to crawl away, but couldn't move. Francis bent over and rammed the broken end of the bottle into the small of his back. And again. And again.

Novak was barely conscious of Lehder's helicopter rising off its pad, and the gunfire that came too late. Then he was conscious of nothing. He didn't see one of Captain Smith's elite men come running around the villa, didn't see Francis jump up and run into the woods, didn't see the helicopter fade to nothing in the empty sky.

35

Novak opened his eyes. He was on a hard bunk, somewhere inside a ship. He could feel its engines. A face looked down on him, a bloody face, but full of concern. It was Paul Clarke. The ship's engine sent vibrations through his body. They hurt. Novak felt a needle in his arm. His eyes closed. He wanted to open them, to make sure he had really seen Clarke, that the man was O.K. But he couldn't.

Novak lay in a hospital bed, wrapped in a fog of pain and painkillers. Doctors removed some of the glass shards from his back and stitched him up. Afraid of damaging his spinal column, they left the rest of the glass inside.

People came to see him. They asked him how he was. He said he was fine. They told him comforting things.

Hanna: "You did a great job. We'll never be able to thank you enough."

Novak didn't know what to say.

"The situation on Norman's is under control at last."

"Yeah?"

"The *Inagua's* staying there for the rest of the month. I've got my best men on the island. They've confiscated all the weapons on the island and made lots of arrests."

"Lehder?"

"No."

"Heinrich?"

"No."

"Manfred?"

"No."

"Francis?"

"No. They got away."

"Did we find Paul Clarke?"

"Don't you remember?"

"We did?"

"We did."

Hanna: "Lehder had a lab down at the tip of the island."

"I know."

"He was doing drug experiments—trying to find a more potent form of cocaine."

"Did he?"

"We don't know. But he was also getting interested in rockets."

"What for?"

"To rocket his new cocaine into the States."

"That's crazy."

"Maybe he was crazy."

"I don't think so," Novak said.

Eliot: "You did a great job. We'll never be able to thank you enough."

Novak didn't know what to say.

"I've got great news—Lehder's dead! Someone shot him down in Colombia. His partners must have turned on him. He lost a lot of his influence with them because of what happened on Norman's. They were losing a bit too much coke on the Florida end. Thanks to you."

"That's great. How did it happen?"

"I'll let you know."

Eliot: "It was a little premature."

"What was?"

"Reports of his death. He got shot all right. He and Heinrich ran into an ambush near his ranch. Heinrich's dead. That's certain. Lehder took a bullet in the chest, but he managed to run away into the jungle somehow."

"Oh."

"But we caught up with Ed Ward. In Haiti. They handed him over, together with his wife, the von Ebersteins and the rest of his outfit. They're all in jail, but they're not the kind that do well in jail. They'll sing like birds in return for any sort of deal. Their testimony will put Lehder in jail forever."

"But how will you get him out of Colombia?"

Chris: "How are you?"

"Fine."

"You don't look fine."

"I said I was fine and I am. How's your mother?"

"Worried about you."

"Tell her not to worry."

"When are you getting out of here?"

"Soon."

"What are you going to do?"

"I don't know."

"You're going back to Concordia, aren't you?"

"Maybe."

"Maybe? Dad. You're not still thinking about Norman's, are you?"

"Why not? Lehder's finished down there."

"Mom wants you to come home."

"I know."

"Home isn't on Norman's, Dad. You must have learned that by now."

"I still haven't seen the hammerhead migration," Novak said.

Chris sighed. "You've let this become a vendetta, Dad. You're obsessed with it. You've changed."

Novak was silent.

His wounds healed, leaving him with scars on his back and forehead, and memories that affected him in ways he didn't acknowledge, not even to himself. "Don't be surprised if some of that glass works its way to the surface," the doctors told him. "It may take years."

Novak checked into Smuggler's Rest, a small hotel on the western end of New Providence. The Bahamian police had brought the *Reef Witch* back to Nassau. Novak's work permit was still valid. He accepted a job at Smuggler's Rest, taking tourists out to the reef.

He kept in touch with Hanna. Things on Norman's were quiet. Manfred and Francis were still free, but warrants were out for their arrest. They had the *Eliminator*. It had been sighted several times in the Exumas. A charter boat captain also reported seeing the *Fire Fall* on Eleuthera.

"Was Lehder on it?" Novak asked.

"He'd be crazy to leave Colombia now," Hanna said. "It just means that some of Lehder's goons are still on the loose. But it's only a matter of time."

"Is it safe for me to go back?"

"Now?"

"Yes. Now."

"Why would you want to go back?" Hanna asked.

Novak liked Hanna. He respected him. Hanna had to cope with pressures that Novak never fully understood. The man deserved an answer. Novak tried to formulate one. He said, "I want to go back. That's all." It was the best he could do.

On June 27, 1982, Novak took the *Reef Witch* back into the lagoon at Norman's Cay. From the water, the island looked almost the way it had the first time he had seen it. The microwave dishes and antennae were gone and most of the look-out towers had been dismantled. Novak tied up beside a small police patrol boat—the *Inagua* had returned to Nassau—and went ashore.

Norman's was quiet too, the way it had been on his first visit. But, up close, he saw it was no longer the quiet of a paradise in the midday sun; now it was the quiet of a paradise gone to seed. Weeds choked the paths around the hotel and the villas at Smuggler's Beach, and sprouted through cracks in the pavement of the main road. Cars and trucks rusted in parking lots or by the roadside. Cisterns were cracked, walls covered with graffiti, obscene in three languages. The houses had been looted and vandalized. Norman the Knight lay in pieces on the ground.

Novak reported to the police, reoccupied his villa, and began making repairs. Several times he saw remnants of Lehder's khaki-uniformed security force, now dressed in tatters. They eyed him coldly. Novak complained to the police and learned that no charges had been filed against some of the lower-level people. Their presence contributed to a sense growing in Novak that the island was somehow soiled. He fought against this feeling, but it never quite went away, except when he was diving. There, in the pristine waters of the reef, he could still revel in the purity that had drawn him to Norman's in the first place.

Then, even the bond between himself and the sea was attacked. One morning when he awoke and went outside he found the mutilated carcass of a big hammerhead waiting on his doorstep. He knew at that moment, even if he didn't admit it to himself, that the problems of Norman's Cay were inescapable.

Novak called Hanna. "I think you'd better get off the island," Hanna told him.

"Why?" Novak responded. "Things would be all right here, if your men just rounded up some of the leftovers."

"We need something to charge them with first," Hanna said. "And it's not just that."

"What do you mean?"

There was a pause. "Lehder bombed Nassau yesterday."

"What?"

"With leaflets. During the Independence Day celebrations. They said. 'DEA go home.' That kind of thing—calculated to appeal to nationalist sentiment. And hundred-dollar bills were stapled to some of them."

"So?"

"So I can't guarantee your safety. Not down there."

"Is Lehder still pulling strings in Nassau?" Novak asked, getting angry. "Is that what this is all about? I thought he was out of the picture. Where is he?"

Hanna didn't answer his questions. He said, "You'd better come here, Dick. That's all I can tell you."

"The hell with that," Novak said, and slammed down the phone. He wasn't afraid of the ragtag remnants of Lehder's dopehead army.

36

On the morning of July 14, 1982, Richard Novak awoke feeling tired. He had slept restlessly, troubled by memories of the dead hammerhead. The air in his villa was hot and still. He went outside, but it was no cooler. The sun, not yet high in the sky, was already blazing, and Novak broke into a sweat almost immediately. He decided to cool himself with a little snorkling before breakfast.

Novak walked to the marina. No one appeared; the island was quiet. The lagoon came gradually into view. Novak saw the *Reef Witch* floating safely at anchor. A beautiful day, the finest water he had ever dived, his own boat riding gently on it. For a moment it was as though his dream had really come true. Then the dark side of life on Norman's Cay revealed itself. The first troubling thing Novak noticed was that the police patrol ship had gone. There might be several reasons for that, not necessarily sinister. But then he saw the two Scarab racers tied to the dock: the *Fire Fall* and the *Eliminator*. Novak knew at once that they had come to kill him. He turned and ran.

The police, formerly camped in tents pitched behind the customs house, had moved into Kniskern's villas. Novak tore through the marina parking lot and onto the landing strip. As he crossed it, he saw the Excalibur parked near the hangars. Steve Francis was sitting in it.

He looked up and saw Novak. Novak heard a shout, followed by the barking of dogs. He crashed into the scrub on the far side of the strip and kept going.

Novak hit the road and sprinted toward the villas. The barking grew louder, closer, more enraged. Novak saw his villa, just ahead. He ran as fast as he could, but it wasn't fast enough. Pointed teeth raked his lower leg as he flew up the steps. The next moment strong jaws clamped shut around his calf. Novak fell on the top step, kicking desperately with his free leg. The dog's grip relaxed slightly. Novak rolled, reached for the door, had it half-open when a second dog leaped on his back. Novak felt its hot breath on his neck. He jerked to one side and jabbed his thumb in the creature's eye. It howled in fury. Novak got his feet beneath him, lunged into the villa, and fell on the floor.

A shadow flew over him, landed on the hardwood with a scraping of claws. Novak looked up into the snarling face of a big Doberman. He scrambled through the doorway into the kitchen, dove at the cabinet beneath the sink. His fingers struggled with the loose floorboards. Sharp teeth sank deep into his thigh. Novak cried out. The Doberman growled and bit deeper. Novak clawed through the loose dirt, groped for the plastic bag, tore the gun loose. The dog growled again, a deep sound, and murderous. Novak twisted around and brought the butt of the gun down hard on the dog's head. That made the dog growl ferociously and bite harder. Outside Novak heard running men. He clicked off the safety, pointed the gun at the Doberman, and pulled the trigger. The shot sounded like an explosion.

The dog went limp. Novak pried its jaws open and started to get up. Outside someone said, "He's got a gun." Novak reached into his hiding place and removed the box of ammunition. Then he rose unsteadily, went into the bedroom, and peered through the blinds.

Manfred, Francis, and the members of the khaki army had backed away toward the hangars on the airstrip. They held pistols, rifles, shotguns. Novak looked through the side window at the other villas: surely the police had heard the shot, surely they saw what was happening outside. He was thinking of calling for help when policemen emerged from the villas. They emerged, but didn't even glance his way. Instead they walked in the opposite direction, down the beach and into the trees. At first, Novak didn't understand: it hit him slowly, and hard. By the time he did understand, the police were gone. He wanted to shoot them all.

Novak went into the bathroom and dressed his wound as well as he could. He thought quickly. One man with a pistol couldn't defend the whole villa from the gang outside. His best chance lay in blocking off one portion and holding that. He chose the bedroom because it had two windows and overlooked the landing strip. He didn't doubt for a moment that he was fighting for his life.

Novak collected his shells and his radio and went into the bedroom. He stood the mattress in the doorway, leaving a narrow opening into the kitchen. Then he piled the bed, the end tables, and the chairs against the mattress. He placed the dresser between himself and the window facing the strip. After that he hunkered down, switched on the radio, and called for help. He hoped to God that Elvis Welles was listening.

The day passed in stalemate. The khaki army, without a real leader and unbalanced by the knowledge that Novak was armed, lingered around the hangars. By afternoon, they had broken out a bottle of rum. They were within shooting range, but Novak didn't fire. He used the radio, he watched, he waited. He couldn't kill them all.

"Welles. This is Novak. Come in Welles."

But Welles didn't come in, and night began to fall. In the darkness, Novak wouldn't be able to see his attackers closing in. He realized that they had been waiting too. Maybe he should have tried to make a run for the *Reef Witch*. Too late. He sat behind the dresser, gun in hand, and waited.

The sky grew dark. Then, to Novak's surprise, the landing lights flashed on. A light plane touched down at the head of the strip and taxied to a stop. And another. And another. Was it a rescue force? This question was answered when a fourth plane, a big turboprop Aero-Commander, came in. It shot down out of the sky and landed flawlessly on the painted numbers on the strip, halting with a shriek of its engines. Novak knew who was piloting it even before the door opened and Carlos Lehder stepped out.

Cheering, shouting, firing in the air, his men rushed to his side. "Joe! Joe!" Novak heard them call; the name reserved for his friends: Novak himself had used it, in the days he had fooled himself into thinking they might be partners. Now it was clear: they were enemies, even natural enemies, like two hammerheads fighting over the same mate.

The men shook hands with Lehder, exchanged high-fives. Lehder's hair was even longer than the last time Novak had seen it, and he wore military camouflage instead of silk. The image of the international businessman had vanished, like a costume sent back to wardrobe. Lehder was now the guerilla fighter, the revolutionary leader, come to liberate his land.

Novak saw Manfred talking to Lehder. Lehder turned and looked at Novak's villa. He nodded. At that moment, Lehder, standing on the strip, stood about twenty-five yards from Novak's villa. Novak was a good shot and Lehder was well within his range. Novak raised his gun, sighted along that imaginary vector from the end of the barrel to Lehder's head. Everything had built to this moment: wasn't it almost as though it had to happen? The power to kill Carlos Lehder was his. He had only to squeeze the trigger.

Richard Novak didn't do it. Not because he feared the retribution of Lehder's men: that thought didn't occur to him. But he did remember Chris's words: "You've changed." That memory mixed with images of the hammerheads in all their brutality, images of Lehder, images of himself.

Maybe he and Lehder were both like hammerheads, but there was a difference between them, a difference expressed by Novak's reluctance to fire at that moment, regardless of consequences. Novak lowered the gun. Someone stepped in front of Lehder. The opportunity passed.

Lehder's men unloaded more weapons from the planes. They spread out along the strip and advanced on the villa. Novak heard a shouted command. A fusillade of shots rang out, smashing every window in the villa, ripping through the blinds, thudding into the walls. Novak dove behind the dresser and fired back.

"Welles. This is Novak. Come in Welles."

No response.

Novak heard men running around the villa, heard footsteps on the stairs, heard Lehder say, "Break it down." A smashing noise followed, and the front door fell inside the kitchen. At the same moment, the lights went out. Novak knelt behind his barricade and fired through the narrow opening, into the darkness. Someone cried out. Footsteps retreated, out of the kitchen, down the stairs. "Fuck," someone said. Then there was silence. Novak knelt behind the barricade, heart pounding, sweat dripping down his face. Had he driven them off? Yes. But it was only the first attack. How many more could he withstand? He picked up the radio.

"Welles. This is Novak. Come in Welles."

No response.

The second attack began with the sound of jeeps and trucks rumbling across the strip, toward the villa. For a moment, Novak thought they were going to bulldoze it to the ground, crushing him inside. Instead, they began circling, driving through the parking lot and cutting a path through the scrub between his villa and the next. Round and round they went, faster and faster. He heard the wild laughter of the men inside. They fired at the villa from all directions. Bullets tore into the mattress, the dresser, the walls. Someone hurled a bottle inside. It shattered on the floor at Novak's feet. They shouted insults at him in Spanish, English, German. They loved what they were doing, Novak thought. Or was it simply a cold-blooded attempt to terrorize him? Maybe they realized he couldn't hold out forever and were waiting for him to tire and let down his guard before exposing themselves. Novak was thinking about that when through the din he heard soft footsteps in the kitchen. He crouched behind the barricade and fired again into the darkened room. This time there was no cry of pain, but the same hasty retreat.

The trucks kept circling wildly, a carousel of death. Dust and fumes filled Novak's room. Lehder's men shouted, whooped, taunted; and fired round after round. Novak crouched in his little furniture fortress, bathed in sweat, firing back only when he heard someone trying to enter the kitchen. Help me, God, he said to himself. I've tried to do what's right. I didn't pull the trigger when I had the chance to murder my enemy. God, help me.

A bullet tore into the chair beside him. Novak fired back into the darkness. A barrage of automatic fire raked the walls in response. Novak huddled behind sticks of furniture. All at once, it struck him with certainty that he was about to die on Norman's Cay; far from home. *Help me, God.* But the gunfire didn't stop. If anything, it grew more intense. Was there another source of shooting, approaching from somewhere in the distance? Novak wasn't sure. Trucks roared, guns cracked, men shouted.

Then, all at once, came silence. Novak didn't even notice it at first: the din continued in his ears.

He rose. His bedroom was full of smoke, dust, and fumes. Still crouched, he moved to the glassless window, looked out. The landing lights had gone out, but dawn was breaking and there was enough light to see a sight Novak did not at first comprehend. Carlos Lehder, in his guerilla outfit, was running as fast as he could across the tarmac, running the other way. Some of his men were running after him, but Lehder did not wait for them. He scrambled into his turboprop and banged the door shut. Moments later the plane screamed down the runway and roared into the sky. Lehder's men, the men who called him Joe, scattered into the trees.

All around Novak's villa, cooling engines made popping sounds. Novak stepped outside, saw the jeeps and trucks, ringing the villa, now abandoned. The island had grown quiet. His attackers were gone.

Novak moved onto the strip. He walked the length of it, toward the southern tip of the island, pistol still in hand. The sun topped the horizon, bluing the sea. Rays of light shone on the white hulls of the *Inagua* and another gunboat, anchored offshore. And then Richard Novak was running onto the beach, waving his arms madly. He had won.

"Picked up your message," said Elvis Welles with a little smile. "I got right onto Hanna. He was pretty quick, all in all."

Pretty quick? Novak looked at Welles and laughed. Then he took his diving knife and cut the Colombian flag down from the pole at the marina. He understood the meaning of what he did: Lehder's twisted vision of an outlaw nation died at that instant.

"We came in shooting," Welles said. "It must have sounded sweet in your ears."

"I'm not sure I heard it," Novak said. Welles thought he was making a joke, and clapped him on the back.

Novak and Welles walked around the island. Hanna's force, under the command of Leon Smith, the captain of the *Inagua*, had arrested everyone on Norman's Cay and seized all the weapons. Lehder, along with Manfred and Francis, had escaped. "Don't worry," Welles said. "It's just a matter of time."

Looking around, Novak knew that Welles was right, and that Lehder probably knew it too. He had destroyed everything he could before leaving, an act that reminded Novak again of Lehder's "Little Hitler" nickname. The planes in the hangars, the houses, the lab, the hotel, shuttle buses, boats—all trashed, burned, scuttled. Columns of smoke rose all over the island. They found Lehder's dogs locked in cages at the bottom of the lagoon.

All Novak's equipment was destroyed too. The *Reef Witch* was gone. Novak spent several days searching the bottom for it, without success. It must have been sunk in deep water. When Novak realized that, his dream of life in paradise died completely, just as Lehder's had. But he didn't mourn for it. In his moment of triumph, Richard Novak no longer needed Norman's Cay.

In the end, Norman's Cay belonged to the hammerheads, as it had for millions, possibly tens of millions of years. Before he left, Richard Novak finally witnessed their mating. They appeared suddenly, by the thousand. One morning he found them massed in the lagoon, so densely that they blocked the sun. Novak, watching from the bottom, saw the sea darken, saw fins flashing above him, saw the rough courtship of the sharks. The males began by running their snouts along the flanks of the females, but were soon raking them with their teeth, biting their bellies. Novak watched as the males mounted from beneath, coiling around the females, clamping their teeth on the fins of their mates, clutching the lip of the female organ with one clasper while ramming in the other. Only then did the females respond, taking bites out of the males as each mating pair pumped across the lagoon. Blood spurted and dripped, and spiraled down on Novak. This was brutal, not a fairy-tale vision of nature but something much closer to Tennyson's image: "red in tooth and claw." Richard Novak, on the bed of the lagoon, was enthralled. He forgot the human side of Norman's Cay, with all its failings: political corruption, diplomatic chicanery, cowardice, drugs, Lehder. He would keep forever this image of the hammerheads in the pond at Norman's Cay. To Novak, it was an image of the unsullied nature of Norman's Cay, the nature he had come to protect. And he had protected it. Richard Novak left the island without regret.

EPILOGUE

A few days after leaving Norman's Cay, Richard Novak met his son Chris at the Pelican Point Restaurant in Melbourne, Florida, and told him everything. Chris looked at him in silence. Novak, thinking he still saw disapproval on Chris's face, did not want to argue: he wanted reconciliation. "Look, Chris, maybe I was wrong. Maybe I should have taken your advice. Maybe—"

Chris took his hand. "No, Dad. You were right." Those words made Novak very proud. Chris smiled at him. "Even more important, you're safe. And now you can go back whenever you like."

"I don't think I will," Novak said.

"No?"

"I'm going home."

"Mom'll be happy about that," Chris said.

Dorothy Novak was happy. She met her husband at the front door of their house, took in the new scars on his tanned forehead, said nothing. She hugged him. It was exactly what he needed. Dorothy only heard his story later, on a day when a jagged piece of glass from Steve Francis's bottle worked its bloody way out of his back, requiring a quick trip to the hospital. Novak was left with more scars, Dorothy with an understanding of how close she had come to losing him forever.

*   *   *

Carlos Lehder was arrested and is now in the federal penitentiary in Marion, Illinois, serving a sentence of life without parole, plus 135 years. Lynden O. Pindling is still Prime Minister of the Bahamas. Richard Novak resumed his former life, as a professor of German with a passion for the sea.

ACKNOWLEDGMENTS

Many private citizens and government officials, both here and abroad, have made significant contributions to this book, often times at considerable risk to their careers and lives. Those whom we are able to thank in print are listed below.

In the U.S.: Andrew Antippas, Charles Beckwith, Joe Broido, Glen Brown, Kathryn Currey, Douglas Driver, Allan Emlin, Greg Von Eberstein, Barbara Von Eberstein, Bob Feldcamp, Larry Ferguson, R.C. Gamble, Paula Goins, Jack Hook, Charles Kehm, Charles Kelly, Philip Kniskern, Robert Merkle, Ernest Mueller, Richard Novak, Chris Novak, Robert O'Leary, Michelle Reed, Jack Reed, Vickey Sanchez, Tim Seldes, Edward Shohat, William Simpson, Joseph Stahlin, Robert Starratt, Gray Thomas, Ron and Sissy Turner, Manuel De Dios Unanue, Stephen Weinbaum, Polly Whittell, John Winston, David Woodward, Harry Yourell, Bill Yout.

In the Bahamas: Harold Albury, Skip Allen, Paul Aranha, Ben Astrada, Eileen Carron, Paul Clarke, Roger and Cathy Crew, Ray Dillon, Charles Lightbourne, Patrick Erskine-Lindop, Peter Fletcher, Dudley T. Hanna, Joe Hocker, Penny Spenser, Marcus Mitchel, Roger Pyrfrom, Ken Rolle, Norman Solomon, Floyd Thayer, Penny Turtle.